Given In Evidence

Jonathan Davies

CORONET BOOKS
Hodder and Stoughton

First published in Great Britain in 1995 by Hodder and Stoughton
First published in paperback in 1995 by Hodder and Stoughton
A division of Hodder Headline PLC
A Coronet Paperback

10 9 8 7 6 5 4 3 2 1

A CIP catalogue record for this title is available
from the British Library

ISBN 0-340-63231 3

Typeset by Avon Dataset Ltd, Bidford-on-Avon

Printed and bound in Great Britain by
Cox & Wyman Ltd, Reading, Berks

Hodder and Stoughton
A division of Hodder Headline PLC
338 Euston Road
London NW1 3BH

za Cica

Part One

Chapter 1

What happened was this: John Howard was going from Jamaica to London, and he had two identical suitcases.

One he had bought in New York. It still had the sales receipt in one of the side pockets. He could prove where he was on the date of the receipt, not New York. In that suitcase he put two sets of clothing. Both sets were too small for him.

In the pocket of one of the jackets there was a letter written to a Mr John Lockhart at an address in New York. The letter contained an account with American Express, a bill incurred in Vancouver which had not been paid. American Express were complaining.

The Vancouver transaction was dated 12th August. On that day an English team had played cricket against a local West Indian side near Montego Bay. Howard had entertained part of the English team that evening at his swimming-pool, just near the ground. Later he sent photographs of the party to one or two of the players back in England.

He still had their addresses in his diary.

While he packed the suitcase he wore rubber gloves. He put in a pair of shoes, a little smaller than his own. Several other things. A hairbrush with hair trapped in it. Not his own hair.

A beard trimmer, he was clean-shaven. A novel in Spanish, along with a teach-yourself Spanish book and a notebook referring to underlinings in the novel.

Next to the novel, there were three talcum-powder containers.

In the other suitcase he packed his own things, as he did so a friend videoed him. He did not wear the gloves.

She included a message on the sound-track as she filmed, she told her friend that Howard was bringing the money she owed her and thanks for the holiday.

Howard waved the clip of money as he packed the suitcase, he grinned, then he shoved it into a shoe.

He sent a message on the videotape to Leon. He spoke in Spanish. John Howard's Spanish was perfect.

In his wallet, a folded receipt from the Bank of Jamaica recorded the purchase of £6000 in dollars in his name, and with it a receipt for $2000 in the name of the friend who was sending the money. Both transactions were obtained on his credit card. You can't argue with a receipt.

On the top of the suitcase there was a linen jacket, not a suit, of precisely the same colour as the jacket at the top of the other case.

Howard carried the video film separately.

He had obtained a builder's estimate for work to his house in England. He folded it into his wallet. It was his reason for flying to London.

He booked an Apex ticket in his own name, from Montego Bay, through Kingston, to Heathrow, London.

In New York, paying by credit card in the name John Lock, he had already booked a single ticket, full price no reductions, Kingston to London. This bill was paid by cash, using another account in Vancouver to fund the transfer.

He went to Montego Bay and booked his case containing his own clothes on to the plane.

A friend, using an American passport in the name John Lock Hart, boarded at Kingston, the plane's first stop.

While he waited for the plane to arrive, and while Howard was in the air from Montego Bay, the friend bought some small pieces of clothing at Kingston airport and placed them and the receipt in the suitcase.

The receipt was dated and timed automatically by the till computer.

Lock. Lock Hart. Lockhart. Anybody would be confused.

Seven hours later the plane landed at Heathrow and John Howard waited to pass through immigration control.

He was not in a hurry and hung back in the long and slow-moving queue. After about forty-five minutes he arrived at the luggage carousel. Both his bag and the identical bag carried by his friend had arrived at the luggage carousel before him.

John Howard picked up his partner's bag and went through to Customs.

He left his own bag, $2000 and all, going round and round.

On the ticket fob of the bag he was carrying, almost hidden in the small window designed to carry it, there was a visiting card in the name Lock.

His friend, who had not waited at the back of the immigration queue, had gone through Customs without a bag. He had gained nearly an hour on Howard and was already waiting for his flight to take off for Holland; as Howard approached Customs, he began the steep flight to Amsterdam.

At about the same time a call was made to British Airways in Heathrow for John Lock please to phone Kingston urgently, leaving a message, in case he could not phone, 'Leave London soonest opportunity'.

Howard went through Customs unquestioned with the bag he had picked up.

It was a bag that he could prove beyond doubt, had he been

asked, was not his. He had picked it up by mistake. In the talcum-powder were three and a half kilos of pure cocaine. It was a valuable mistake.

He did not think himself safe yet. The Customs could, if they knew about him, be letting him run, to see whom he met.

He went to the hire-car desk and entrusted his bag to a red cap, arranging to meet him at the car. The moment he passed the bag on to someone else then Customs, if they were following him, would arrest him. It was the first test. They did not.

He collected the bag half an hour later after a scrappy meal in one of the airport restaurants. Then he drove the hire car round the M25 and north into Croydon. He arrived there at 9.30 in the morning.

As usual there was, by this time, a queue outside the station multi-storey, and cars were being allowed in only one at a time after a wait.

He did not see anyone get out of a car behind him. He was waiting on the hill leading down to the car-park entrance, and anyone doing so would have been unable to avoid observation.

Eventually they allowed him in and he drove round and round up the spiral to park at the top level in one of the reserved empty sections. For a moment after he got out he leaned on the balcony watching the Crown Court and the railway line to Brighton below him.

Still there were no suspicious movements.

Then he took the lift downstairs. It would have been impossible to follow him once he had entered the car park, unless the watcher had stood waiting in the same areas as he. He had seen no one.

From the car park he went to the railway station and took a Newhaven train. He left the train at its unscheduled but regular stop at Lewes. From there he walked to the White Hart Hotel.

He had already handed the cocaine to a man who approached the train as it drew out of Haywards Heath. By that time Howard knew with absolute certainty that he had not been followed.

It only remained to return the bag he had picked up. He pointed out in his letter that he had had to force open the bag, but he thought if it were returned to Kingston it might be claimed by Mr Lockhart to whom it seemed to belong. It was flown to Kingston by DHL the next day.

He wrote a letter to the British Airports Authority describing his own bag. That bag never passed Customs and was eventually returned by British Airways to Montego Bay. British Airways apologised for the fact that it had been misdirected so that its owner was not able to find it at the Heathrow luggage pick-up point.

The only part of the transaction that was recorded was the return of an unclaimed bag to Jamaica, one of thousands of pieces of airline luggage that go astray every day.

Howard's journey netted him £95,000. He was paid by one of Scully's taxi-drivers in cash when he was picked up on his return to London.

Now he could do what he had come for, find out what had happened to Nadim Janjoa.

Chapter 2

A week earlier Emily Clarke, young, newly qualified and still learning, left the Cock and Feathers in Fleet Street just as the other lawyers who gathered there every night began to arrive.

She turned left and then left again, back into the Temple, where she had parked. As she made her way down Middle Temple Lane, a car, misjudging a little outcrop in the narrow medieval road, swerved slightly and splashed rain on to her shoes. It had not been a good day.

The morning had started with a letter rejecting her application for the second six months of her training. This was her fifth rejection.

Things were becoming desperate, and the day had not been made better by her growing realisation that her present pupil master, who had seemed so self-confident when she first met him, was in fact a figure of fun in the Temple, and because of that unable to help her. He had made it no easier by falling in love with her.

She could tell not only by the normal signs but by the fleeting looks of amusement on people's faces as they entered a group.

As an undergraduate she had been able to deal with the problem easily enough, and indeed had had to do so often.

Then she owed nothing to nobody. But here she was now with a good honours degree, presentable and begging for a place somewhere – beholden to this man – worse, to these men.

There were some who would still not even consider taking her, a woman, as a pupil. That was, she supposed, to be expected. But what she had not expected was the complicated nature of the rejection.

For there were those who would have taken her for training but didn't want to be seen to be helping someone so attractive and consequently so – well, dangerous to be seen with.

She noticed it in the way that some people, after looking at her directly the first time, would not look at her directly again. This she attempted to combat by dressing severely, even dowdily but, like the librarian in the film, she only became more attractive for it.

Her friends in the big, muddled flat where she lived were drifting away, either quickly moving up the pay scale or settling for marriage. The men she knew were becoming overworked, or if they were not, then they were invariably stupid.

She was becoming isolated and her isolation was transforming itself into other people's perception of her as aloof. Now she found herself more often sitting alone, and worse, she was beginning to prefer it.

She reached her car and climbed in. For a moment she sat there. Still and all, she thought – it was her mother's expression and she sometimes said it to herself, thinking of her mother so English, Canadian now, so far away, always so far away, as long as she could remember – still and all, there's always cocaine.

She turned her car into Dalston, along the high road and down one of the side turnings leading over to Hackney.

On her left there was a grey estate, terraced in balconies leading back and up from the road. The windows were spotted with light but as often as not they were broken and blocked with cardboard or with heavy wood.

Broken toys lay on the balconies. On one balcony, tethered to the window, there lay a heavy black dog. It leaped up and strained towards her as she stopped. She got out of the car and locked the door.

Past the end of the street a siren whined and a bus, a large parcel of warm light, turned into her road. She waited and then crossed behind it, beginning to run as she reached the other pavement, uncomfortably conscious that her neat court shoes were not finding Dalston's sodden pavements welcoming.

The wind whipped around her raincoat and she wished for a moment that she had waited to change into jeans before coming. But she was keen, unaccountably keen, to get hold of this.

On the other side of the road there was a row of modern houses, 'town houses' they would have been called in the local-government brochure. Outside one or two the gardens had been carefully tended, the dark shape of a jasmine trailed up a trellis around one door, but light from the uncurtained window next door showed the neighbouring garden ragged and unkempt. They were feeble attempts to create a private space in the face of overwhelming decay.

She walked past the houses and down the access road to the side. The road opened up into a parking space and then turned into another lane running down the back of the houses.

As she went past the car park a security light snapped on and illuminated the pitted surface of the road. She picked her way through the puddles, grateful for the light. A dog started barking.

A four-foot gate opened into a small garden at the back of the house. On her right there was a whirligig clothes-line flapping in the wind, empty crisp packets had blown up against its base, and rotting under a tarpaulin there was the

11

remains of a yellow car. How it had got into the garden was not clear.

On the back wall of the house behind her, concealed in a junction box, there was a video-camera. It followed her progress, past the car park and through the back gate. As she went into the garden it began to close up on her until she filled the screen.

The policemen watching in the local police station grinned at each other.

'What's this, then?' said one.

'Scully's piece of fluff?' said another.

A woman police constable tried to join in the male joking but was unsuccessful; the atmosphere became slightly strained as they sat watching the time slipping away in hours, minutes and seconds on the bottom left-hand corner of the video monitor.

Emily knocked on the door. Nothing. She knocked on the boarded window next to it. There was a movement and a shout, 'No business,' then there was silence.

She stood there, shocked to notice how disappointed she was.

There was a movement behind her and a man came into the garden. He walked to the window and knocked. 'No business now,' the voice, it was a woman's voice, repeated. The man turned on his heel and left. Emily didn't like to hang about but felt she had to, where else was she to go?

She knocked again and immediately called out, before the woman could reply, 'Scully sent me.'

'Hey, then, why did you not say so?' said the same voice. A curtain flicked at the window and she saw herself being inspected, then there was a scuffling at the door and after a while it was pushed open towards her.

Immediately inside there was a wrought-iron grill which covered the whole of the opening. It was still closed. On the other side there stood a large woman looking at her. 'You say you a friend of Scully's?'

'Yeah,' said Emily.

'Well, you better come in.' The woman turned and walked away. Emily watched her huge body sway across the kitchen, she picked up a key from a hook on the wall and returned to the grill.

'We keep ourselves locked in case of visitors,' she said, opening the grill.

Emily stepped into the bright, warm room. It smelt of soda. Along the wall to her left there was a stove, a sink, then a work surface. On the stove was a pot of boiling water. In the opposite corner there was a baby watching her carefully from a high chair.

As she stood for a moment in the doorway a brown cat took the opportunity to flash through the opening and out into the dark.

She disappeared into the house and the police filled in their log:

20.47 Blonde IC 1, girl ?25, 5'7" entered garden. Knocked. Man IC 3, 6'0", 30s, into garden, knocked. Nothing. Away.
Blonde girl above knocks again. Door opened by Target 2, girl enters.
Cat leaves.

They settled down to await further developments. They wouldn't have to wait long.

'You sit down, then, we are expecting Mr Scully. What do you want? Do you owe him money then, my dear? I do hope not.' The woman was Jamaican and her voice swooped and cracked. Her warm large face regarded Emily affectionately. She sat down in a cushioned chair near the baby and started spooning food from a small round glass jar. The baby did not take its eyes from Emily but opened its mouth automatically at the approach of the spoon.

Emily did owe Scully money. A lot of it, but she did not want to talk about it.

'No, I was looking.'

'Well, if you wait there, my love. We are expecting him now,' said the woman, and she pointed to the door of the kitchen. Emily went through and up the stairs. The woman did not follow, so she went into the first room she came to at the top – a bedroom.

On the wall facing her there was a poster of a green naked woman, apparently manacled to a stake, rising out of some ferns. Underneath the poster there was a brass bed. On the bed there were piles of clothes, some still in their bags. A leather jacket, a beaded short evening dress, a suede jacket and a steam iron. Lying amongst the clothes was a shiny, modern, brass carriage clock and a portable typewriter. There were nine pairs of boots against the wall.

She pulled back the lace at the window and looked out at the street below. She could see her car on the other side of the road and for a moment she wanted to be out of this place, then she saw a blue motor car, the colour flashing as the security light flicked on in the side street.

A few moments later she heard a shout. 'Hey, it's Scully.' She had never met Scully. No one ever had. Most people knew of him only through his mini-cab drivers and only then when they had bought a lot of times.

Emily had first come across Scully at a dinner party in Hans Crescent. The men round the table, though none was older than twenty-five, were wearing dinner jackets and the women full evening dress. They had drunk champagne and eaten lobster.

The meal had been served by two maids – who would have thought that the word meant anything still? – wearing black and white.

After they had eaten, the host had pulled out a phone and looking round had said, 'Who's for afters?' At least five people had put their hands up, as though answering matron at school. Then they had dug money out of their pockets.

He had phoned and, as he remarked at the time, quicker than Pizza Hut, there came a knock on the door. Some cocaine appeared.

Emily was shown how to draw a line; she left her body behind and her mind glowed. With cannabis she had felt the presence of an idea, but with cocaine she was the idea, clean and pure.

Then her host, still sitting at the head of the table, fell face forward into a cake.

Scully seemed to serve afters at most of the dinner parties she went to and then she realised he would deliver plain. There didn't have to be a dinner party. As she got the number. Now she owed him £2000.

Emily listened to the conversation downstairs. 'Well, then, Scully, we been expecting you lately.' There was a grunt and she heard the sound of someone sitting down. The baby made a noise. Then there was the sound of it being hushed to sleep by a man's voice.

The kettle was switched on and the man said, 'Well, an infusion will do right enough.'

Emily moved out to the hallway and stood at the top of the stairs. From there she could see part of the kitchen floor and a man's legs. He was wearing a pair of dark flecked trousers and a pair of woven plastic shoes, scuffed and torn.

By what she could see she judged he could be no taller than she was, perhaps rather shorter. He was bandy-legged in the way that someone pretending suddenly to be an old man might bend and shuffle. But this man was light on his feet and he had moved across the space into which she could see nimbly, like a dancer.

The kettle boiled and she could hear water being poured out. Then the remark, 'Here you are.' She sat down on the stairs.

'There's a lady here to see you,' said the woman, and the man grunted a question.

'Up there,' was the reply, and the legs turned towards the staircase.

Scully came out. If asked she would say he was a man of about sixty. But how to be sure? Maybe he was fifty, since he didn't look any age at all – save that he was no longer a young man.

He was short, much shorter than she was. He was dressed in a beige windcheater, zipped up, partially covering a white shirt and a tie, beige and brown with a diamond pattern, neatly knotted over the nylon shirt.

The cuffs of the windcheater were fastened at his wrists and on the back of his head was a brown trilby. He had a rim of short hair round his bald head, a pencil moustache and his eyebrows curled up, giving his face an enquiring look.

He was wearing a signet ring but nothing else, no studs, no jewels. In his hands, huge hands, he held the baby against his shoulder. It slept peacefully, totally abandoned to him. He walked towards Emily and looked up at her, and she saw his eyes shining. He stood there.

'Well, mistress, what can I do for you?' he said politely.

'My name is Emily Clarke.'

He stood there looking at her, his hand softly caressing the back of the baby's head. The baby moved its face into a more comfortable position, opened its lips and a small drop of saliva fell on to his shoulder.

Then he stepped forward and offered his hand. For some reason this surprised Emily who expected – she did not know what – something else.

'Mistress, I had expected that you would call.'

Listening to him speak she realised how Jamaican English is still eighteenth century in tone, he had just used a vocative and made it sound like one.

'Now that you are here we must arrange to talk. But it would be better that we left now, I am expecting some people. I have come only to leave some things.'

'I want a score,' Emily said. She needed to say this and once she had said it she felt relieved, despite her surprise at herself for being so insistent.

Scully turned and looked at the woman, who went to a cup and took a little piece of silver paper from it. 'And again,' said Scully. He handed Emily the two balls of silver and she paused for a moment then put them in her mouth, under her tongue.

Again she felt absurd, behaving in this way, but unaccountably better when she had hidden the drug.

She started opening her bag. 'Another time,' said Scully. To the woman he said, 'Does Squiddley know?'

'Yes. He'll be here later when they've gone. The money is on the table.'

Emily followed the woman's glance and on the table, under a bottle of baby dessert yoghurt, there lay a bundle of notes thick enough to raise the bottle an inch and a half from the surface. The top note was fifty pounds. She could not see what was underneath, but if they were all fifties then there must be two thousand there at least.

'Come now, mistress,' said Scully, and he elaborately shepherded her out of the kitchen door into the night. 'You had best sit here,' he said, opening the door to his car which was parked outside the garden.

'But my car?'

'Please, mistress, sit here.' Now she noticed a note of urgency in his voice. She looked at him again, she had never seen anyone so ordinary. She got in. At that moment the alleyway crashed into light and sound.

Two police vans came round the corner where she had walked, spraying gravel and water. The garden gate was smashed open and police swept up the path.

The small car seemed to be engulfed. But Scully was quite calm, he found his keys after much searching through his trousers, started the engine, got into gear with difficulty and drove carefully around the corner. After pausing for an age at the road, peering to his left and right, he dragged the car into the street with the engine whining.

He steered the car with his hands straight out in front of him, ineptly and mostly in the middle of the road.

Before long he had gathered a queue of honking impatient drivers behind him, cursing him for being an old incompetent who shouldn't be allowed out.

Chapter 3

On 7th November, the same night that Emily met Scully, the Karachi plane landed on time at London airport, disgorging three hundred and twenty-five passengers into terminal 3 Heathrow.

As the plane emptied, the cold, damp London air began to scour the sweet-smelling overheated cabins.

The majority of the passengers were Pakistani and they moved as a group down the twisting passages that led to immigration control. On the way this tide of people met another jumbo-load of travellers just arrived from Maryland. The two groups began to mix.

Eventually the advancing crowd piled up against the barriers of immigration control and slowly began to drip one by one on to the immigration officers' desks.

The Americans jostled uneasily with the Asians, unaccustomed to being just as foreign as those that they felt really were foreign, watching the unusual sight of others peeling away to be treated more favourably than they under the UK and EEC passport notices.

As disorientated people do, they began to talk a little more loudly, becoming more aware as time went by of their size

19

and vitality in comparison with the other queue of travellers.

From the Karachi plane prodigious amounts of luggage began to block the passages. Children began to run about; the smell of spices grew stronger. In each bag there were herbs and vegetables. In one wicker basket there was a dead lamb carried by a Bulgarian who had joined the flight at Frankfurt.

Ahead of the queue there was a row of desks, some five-feet high, each with a tall stool. An applicant for entry stood at each desk, like a schoolboy at a master's desk.

Syed Ali Zaidi Muazzam was standing about four passengers away from the head of the queue. He was alone. He was a tailor. A passport and a ticket had been obtained for him by Choudhary Janjoa, who ran a travel agency in Karachi. With the ticket he had been given £300 and the address of a hotel in Earl's Court.

He was coming, he was told, to this country to meet up with an employer who needed him in London to price and estimate the cost of making clothes to sell in the English market.

His calculations would help his employer to offer prices immediately 'rather than be on the phone to Delhi all the time' – he was told to say that to the immigration officers.

Before he left Pakistan he had been taken by car to a villa a little north of Karachi, where he had met two others just like him. They had slept in the same room. This he had found odd, and unsettling, since he had never slept anywhere other than his own house. Nor had he slept well, being constantly woken by the grunting of his companions. When he did sleep he had dreamt wild dreams.

In the morning he had eaten nothing save some milk and eggs, and then, encouraged by two other men, well-dressed men who had arrived at the gate of the house in a huge Toyota jeep with Nadim Janjoa – he had seen him from a window – he had swallowed twenty-three small black balls. It was eighty per cent pure heroin.

He was hungry now as he stood in the queue. He had not eaten for twenty-four hours. He had been too frightened even to drink, for fear of what it might do to his stomach, and he had sat hardly moving in his seat all the way from Karachi. He could not read and he had stared in front of him fixedly. He was terrified.

His stomach felt distended and he was beginning to feel the pains returning. The cold London air, even here inside the terminal, was picking at his legs.

The immigration officer looked at him with contempt and signalled to another man, clearly a Pakistani, to come over to translate. Muazzam told his story, showed his visa, obtained after an equally unpleasant experience in the consulate at Karachi, and there was silence.

The English official sat writing on the back of the card which Muazzam gave him. The translator spoke into a black package he had with him and at the same time thumbed through a thick book containing a long list of names.

The room was vast. There were no windows and as far as Muazzam could see there were passages. It may even have been that they were under the ground already. He had been told that large parts of London were underground. But most overwhelming was the light. It reflected off every surface. All around, it seemed to Muazzam, there was a sound of screaming.

A loud voice announced something. Muazzam jumped and felt his stomach heave. He could still taste the rubbery flavour of the pills he had swallowed. He longed for a nut. As he did so another spasm gripped his belly.

The Englishman spoke quietly, turning away. Muazzam understood that he had been dismissed. He followed the direction that the immigration officer had indicated and set off down some more passages. He moved slowly and uncertainly. He had seen crowds before, had been amongst them on his visits to town, but not such a crowd as this. Most of the people surrounding him were huge, wearing thick quantities of clothes and moving very fast.

At one point the ground itself started moving and he stood still, as did those around him, swept along by the earth itself. He had no control over his actions, he had no intentions, he divorced himself entirely from what was around him and reflected again upon the promise that had been made to him.

He had been promised more money than he thought it possible any person could in fact give another. Yet the impossible was the common tale of those who went to the West, so at the same time he did not find it strange. He only reflected upon his family's good fortune of being in this year, the year in which his child was to be born, the chosen ones.

His wife had cried at his departure. Over the short time they had been together, they had grown to love each other in much the way that love grows for familiar surroundings, only more powerfully since here the object of love was a person.

She had not understood his explanation that his skills were needed to assist a man in London, even though she knew he was the best tailor in his area.

It was she who had recognised Janjoa when he came the first time, recollecting him from a wedding she had attended once. But she had not really understood the idea of flying so far until he found a photograph of a plane in a weekly magazine; although she had understood that he would have to take eggs and milk to prevent his stomach from rejecting the pills that he, who had, after all, never travelled before, had to take.

He intended to be home again within three weeks, in time for the festival.

The moving walkway dumped him into a large room, crammed with people. Ahead of him, amazingly, he saw his bag tied with string, moving round on a great revolving circle. He stepped forward, quite swiftly for one who moments ago had seemed utterly distant, snatched it up and again found himself in a crowd flowing this time towards the Customs hall.

In the hall there was a small gesticulating crowd, and he could see the lamb being poked about.

He tried to buy a ticket from the uniformed guard for the train to London, but one of the other men standing next to him wearing the same uniform leant over and said to him in his own language that this was not the place.

He was told that if he followed the red sign of a circle with a line through it he would get there. It was a very effective piece of advice and he soon found himself at the railway. He did not know that he was being followed.

In the crowd behind him was Nadim Janjoa, who had been watching him since the plane left Karachi. Also watching was Paul Gregory of the Heathrow Customs Investigation Unit. He had picked Muazzam out at immigration after being alerted by Customs intelligence on the subcontinent. All three of them boarded the tube to London.

Just after Muazzam had gone through immigration, Gregory was told the name of the hotel where Muazzam was heading. He had not been surprised at the choice, it had only confirmed what he knew already. Everything was working out precisely as had been forecast at the briefing.

It had already been decided that Muazzam, and the other two couriers if they were seen, would be allowed to run. Now that the information on their destination was confirmed, it was all the safer.

Still, he was taking a risk, he didn't want to lose £600,000 in class-A drugs on the streets somewhere off the Piccadilly line.

Muazzam got out of the tube at Earl's Court – he had been counting the stops. He climbed the stairs to the street nervously.

He had already been astonished by the sheer size of the town. From the tube window he had seen below him row upon row of substantial houses, each with a solid roof, its own front door and outside each door there had been a car. Sometimes there were cars outside areas of grass, cars that had no clear owner. He had seen eight buses parked in a street. All the shops had glass fronts. Some of the lights were on in the streets in the daytime.

Although he recognised some of the products advertised in the great posters he could not read one word of the writing – save on one occasion when he saw an Indian film advertised. He had seen the film some time before in the village square.

As he reached the top of the stairs he stopped, taken aback by the traffic noise. On the pavement outside there was a man sitting on the ground. He was crying, or so it appeared at first. Then Muazzam realised he was not crying but singing. Another man came along and reaching down his hand pulled him up. Both of them clung together for a moment then staggered backwards, pushing up against a passer-by.

Each of the two was carrying gold cans in his hand. The man who had been barged into took no notice and walked quickly away. The other two men started shouting after him but did not follow. No one else reacted to these events at all.

Muazzam and the two men stood on the pavement. After a moment Muazzam approached the men and held out the piece of paper in his hand. 'Argyle,' he said. It was the name of the hotel and it had been going round and round in his head since he had been told it a day and a half before.

The more drunk of the two men took the piece of paper from Muazzam's hand and ate it.

For a moment Muazzam could scarcely conceive of what had happened and what it meant. Other than the passport he kept in his underwear, he had no papers. He had nothing to show him where he was going or what he should do in this horrifying place. Both the men facing him were a head taller than he, both looked incredibly strong. One was being sick at his feet. For the first time the shadow of events began to loom over him.

'Argyle,' he repeated. One of the men, the one not being sick, stepped forward, preparing to hit him.

Paul Gregory saw what was about to happen, he saw the whole operation about to disappear in a moment. He tapped Muazzam on the shoulder and turned him slightly away from the punch.

The drunk overbalanced and Paul Gregory moved Muazzam further down the road.

No one took any notice at all of these events as the traffic roared around them, save Nadim Janjoa, who stood a little way off, watching.

Gregory said to Muazzam, 'The Argyle?' And pointed to Earl's Court Square, giving him a slight shove. Muazzam, by now used to being pushed, shoved and guided, continued on his interrupted way.

Gregory set off in the opposite direction watched by Janjoa, who, after a few moments, seemed satisfied and turned to follow Muazzam.

Chapter 4

Muazzam arrived at the Argyle to find himself expected. He was greeted by a man who spoke his language and who signed him into room number 8. He didn't touch the register since he could neither read nor write his name. The desk clerk led him upstairs, showed him the room, pointed out the lavatory and bath and left him there. He was also handed a package of herbs and shown how to use the electric kettle.

Muazzam poured on the boiling water, smelt it, realised what it was. Then he drank it and went to the lavatory.

At that moment Customs officers invaded the hotel. They came assisted by eight policemen in uniform.

Nadim Janjoa was standing on the steps as the group swept past. He was shoved out of the way by one of the officers, slipped, fell and found himself in the gutter. He heard the shout 'Customs' and realised what had happened.

In his hand he had his passport ready to check in to the hotel.

For a moment he lay on the drain in the gutter, feeling the world turn upside down, then he let his passport, and with it his plane ticket and his wallet drop into the water below. He became nobody.

Carefully he got to his feet. Another Customs man passed him.

'Just watch it,' said Janjoa. The Customs officer looked at him blankly, not seeing him. Janjoa's eyes flickered over the man's face and he covered his fear with a gesture of annoyance. 'Look what you've done.'

It was a mistake to have said anything. The Customs officer stopped momentarily, attracted by a quaver in the voice, but he saw only a well-dressed Indian dusting his trousers down at the knee. For a moment an apology began to form on his lips, then he took Janjoa by the arm and forced him up the stairs. They had said detain everyone, so that's what he did.

Paul Gregory had run into the hotel past Janjoa as he fell. The front door opened into a passage. There was a plastic pay phone and just beside it a glass panel which could be slid back to let the receptionist speak. In the clerk's room, not much bigger than a broom cupboard, there were three Customs officers. Beside them stood the desk clerk, frozen in an attitude, stupefied by the noise and movement.

Two of the officers were stuffing papers into plastic bags. The third had the hotel register. 'Try room eight!' he shouted to Gregory.

An officer just at the door of the room shouted, 'Bagging Jefferson A, bagging B, bagging C.'

Beside him stood an elderly woman, stock-still, staring at Gregory, one arm raised above her forehead, shading her eyes or expecting to be struck – it wasn't clear.

From the end of the passage there was a splintering noise; suddenly the woman was lifted straight up as an arm went round her waist and she was carried forward, her arm still raised, past him. A voice shouted 'Bastard!' with astonishing violence, and Gregory took the staircase steps three at a time.

He went past the first landing. In the passage to his right a police-officer pushed himself forward from the wall, hit the door opposite and rebounded as if he had tried to crack open a marble plinth. He crumpled back holding his shoulder. Then the door opened tentatively. The police-officer, still holding his shoulder, raised a boot and kicked it. There was a gasp of breath and the slim hand that had showed for an instant in the opening crack disappeared from the door's edge, the door bounced back from what it had hit and very gently clicked tight shut again. Wearily the officer prepared himself for another shoulder charge.

Gregory reached the top floor. He paused, gazed around and saw room eight. The door opened immediately at his touch. The window was open. A suitcase lay on the bed with some clothing spilling out of it. There was a pair of sandals on the floor.

He felt the kettle on the sideboard. It was hot, and there was a pool of water on the Formica surface.

He turned, puzzled for a moment. Then four steps took him down the passage outside. There was a door beneath a glass overlight. He kicked the door open and it smashed back against the wall. On the lavatory in front of him, his knees bare, sat Muazzam clasping a mug. He looked up at Gregory in wonder.

'I think you'll find that that lavatory doesn't work,' said Gregory, 'we've come to fix it.'

A police-officer appeared at Gregory's shoulder. Gregory indicated Muazzam, 'That's one of the ones we've come for. He's a swallower. Help take him to Fetter Lane, caution him.' The police-officer stepped forward and indicated that Muazzam should come with him. Muazzam did so.

As the police-officer took him to the stairs, he told him that he need say nothing. Gregory could just distinguish the words as the officer slurred them, 'anything you may say', then he heard the officer ask a question, and again heard it repeated at the top of the stairs, 'How much are you carrying?'

The two of them disappeared round the corner.

Muazzam had been sitting on the lavatory when he heard the crash of the Customs entry. He heard a shout then the sound of running steps that stopped outside the door.

There was quiet for a moment, then the whole of the door facing him seemed to disintegrate. A man was standing there, he said something. Muazzam remained, not moving at all.

A policeman, Muazzam understood the uniform, appeared and pulled him from the room; he followed, had to follow, pulling at his trousers and shirt. As he went down the stairs the man spoke to him, and Muazzam turned towards him lifting his arm in a gesture of incomprehension. The policeman responded to this by twisting his arm; Muazzam fell and rolled six steps down the stairs.

'He tried to run,' shouted the policeman, who dragged him to his feet, and took him down the stairs, where he was put in a white van and driven through the streets.

At Fetter Lane, Customs headquarters, Muazzam was signed in by the custody officer. He was given two rooms with a special lavatory and watched every moment by a series of bored officers.

'Our record was a Dutchman,' one said to him, 'fourteen days and still he produced nothing. We knew he had something inside him because the drug test was positive. At the end his stomach was like a washboard, you could tap on it like a drum.'

The officer rocked back in his chair, watching the silent man before him. Surely no one could be so meek as this man? Not without intending it anyway.

'Oh, I forgot you're not speaking, are you?'

Muazzam said nothing. He stared down at his legs. Occasionally he would trace a thread through his clothes, straightening it and then tying the end expertly. Otherwise his busy hands lay useless in his lap. Any movement he made was watched carefully.

After some hours, men suddenly appeared and took his clothes from him, leaving him with a paper suit. He shivered in the damp cold.

But over the next twenty-eight hours he produced the little balls of heroin. They were washed off, signed into a drugs store, then taken for forensic analysis. At each stage a statement was taken setting out the details of the amounts.

Muazzam was offered a solicitor. He was offered an interpreter. A pale man in a brown suit came and spoke to him in his own language, translating at the same time to another Customs officer. They asked if he had been travelling alone. He did not reply.

Everyone agreed that Muazzam was refusing to speak, they weren't even sure in what language he was refusing. So at that stage only the arresting officer, PC Williams, claimed to have heard him speaking – in perfectly good English.

Then in a bewildering change of approach these officers told him, on a number of occasions, that he need say nothing. He had nothing to say. He said nothing.

After two days the custody officer arrived at the cell door to decide whether an application could be made to keep him in Customs custody any longer. He even asked Muazzam through an interpreter whether he wanted to be consulted. It seemed clear to Muazzam that these people, who it seemed were not policemen but working with them, were not going to let him go.

He said nothing.

The custody officer, the man in charge of Muazzam's detention, then reviewed the evidence with Paul Gregory.

'That policeman, what's his name? Williams, the one Muazzam tried to get away from, was right. He's not going to say anything. It's about time he was charged. Our time for holding him without an application to the court will run out tonight. He's produced the evidence, so why wait any more?'

'I want an admission,' said Gregory. 'I want to hear him say that he knows it's illegal to import drugs, and I want to hear him admit that he knew it was drugs he was carrying, and not diamonds or emeralds or some such bullshit. Without that I don't feel properly prepared.'

'Look, of course he knows it's illegal to import drugs, do you think anyone's going to believe he thought it was legal? Why'd he swallow the stuff then? If he thought heroin was legal he would have carried it in his pocket. That's what pockets are for. You don't need an admission.'

The custody officer paused. 'Anyway, Williams, the officer who arrested him, he's covered it. He said that the man admitted he knew what he had in his stomach just before he tried to run away. There's your admission for you. Why run if he was doing something legal?'

'I wouldn't put it past Williams to invent that to justify hitting him,' said Gregory, 'just invent it.'

Gregory watched the custody officer to see his reaction. The custody officer looked at him blankly – this Gregory was a little too keen for his taste.

It was a stand-off Gregory couldn't win. He had no reason for going to the magistrates for an order allowing him to detain Muazzam longer, besides, even if he did, Muazzam wasn't going to say anything anyway. He had made that clear.

'OK,' he said, 'we'll charge him tonight.'

Chapter 5

Jeremy Scott, Barrister, of 6 Tasker Walk in the Temple, looked at his opponent wearily.

The man's name was Plunkett. He was a newly elected Tory MP, and the son of a Tory MP. He was wearing, Scott was amazed to see, black lace-up boots. His hair was cut short and his ears stuck out aggressively. But most of all there was the unfocused look in his eyes that comes from continually addressing people in groups.

'But you must agree that criminal work by comparison with civil work is a doddle,' Plunkett said. His conversation was studded with prep-school language. He was offering companionship – do you want to declare yourself 'one of us'?

It was an offer Scott refused. He had always refused it.

Plunkett went on, and as he did so, his glasses flashed. They were metal and hooked violently around his ears. He held up a set of papers. 'Look at this then, I'm making a Brodie list in response to a Mackintosh Hardie set of interrogatories sprung on us at the last moment. Now, that's what I call work. Building contracts,' he muttered, and threw the papers back into his bag, 'but this stuff,' he pulled the case he was doing against Scott out of the bag, 'this is just social work. I only do it so that the Attorney knows that I am still in the business.'

What on earth is a Mackintosh Hardie interrogatory? thought Scott, but instead he asked, 'Why should the Attorney want to know you're still in business?'

Plunkett flashed his glasses dangerously. 'Prosecuting drug dealers is what needs to be done, less understanding and more convicting, that's what we need,' he said. 'Your client is a shit. Look, can't you get him to see sense and plead guilty now and then we can all go home.'

'He won't,' said Scott, 'he never has.'

Plunkett ploughed on, 'The police caught him fair and square. He was running away and trying to get rid of the evidence, enough stuff for twenty or thirty deals.'

Privately, Scott thought much the same but he wasn't going to give Plunkett the pleasure of agreeing with him.

'He says he isn't guilty, what can I do?'

'You can tell him what anybody of any sense would do in his situation' – Plunkett turned and began to pull his gown, wig and bands from his bag – 'plead guilty now and stop wasting our time.'

'You and the lady who runs the prosecution service,' said Scott. 'The trouble is that people don't organise their lives to fit in with your idea of common sense. Anyway, perhaps he's innocent.'

'Some hope,' snapped Plunkett. He was not used to exchanges of opinion that extended over such a lengthy period and he was growing tired. 'See you upstairs.'

'Why is it all right for prosecutors to believe their case, but if defence counsel believes his client then it's naïve?' said Scott. But Plunkett clumped out of the room without replying.

Scott put on his gown and bands, and hooking his wig over his finger he twirled it around like a frisbee.

'That's because it is naïve,' he answered his own question, and went in search of Courteney Masida.

* * *

Courteney Masida was charged with possessing cocaine with intent to supply. He was looking at five years.

He was also going to lose his Triumph Stag, his wad of money and his record collection if the police had their way.

Scott knew Masida well, though oddly he could never remember what he looked like. He could remember only his fingernails. They were lacquered hard, mahogany brown, like a Chinese emperor's, and sharpened to save him the bother of having to carry a knife.

Scott went to the main hall at the entrance of the court. He had been coming to this court for years and was well known there. He said 'Hi!' to a court usher, who grinned at him, then hello to the telephone operator.

The operator, George, used to have a cosy little room where he couldn't be got at unless you knew where it was. It had had pictures of cats on the wall, potted plants and an easy chair. Scott used to go in to chat, but now George had been placed right out in the open behind a circular counter and had been told to wear a little name-tag.

Scott had tried to sympathise with him about it all, but had discovered to his surprise that George rather preferred it.

'Have you seen my Mr Masida, George?' he asked.

But he was interrupted. 'Are you in Masida?' said a voice next to Scott.

Scott turned and saw a girl. She was blonde with startling violet eyes, wearing a wig and gown that were obviously both new.

For a moment the dirt and despair of the court were emphasised by her freshness.

'Yes,' said Scott.

'I'm looking for Mr Plunkett,' she said, 'I was sent down to help him.'

Scott smiled. 'Poor you, trying to help the Plonker,' he said.

And then realising he was being unfair since the girl was clearly nervous, he said, 'Well, the last I saw of him he was going for a coffee in the Bar mess.'

She looked at him blankly.

'That's upstairs,' he said, pointing towards the lift. 'Just go on in, you'll recognise him, short hair and round glasses. Don't be surprised when he barks at you.'

The girl looked at him for a moment. Scott felt the cool glance of her violet eyes and was sorry he had teased her, but she turned before he could say anything to put it right and walked away.

She was wearing a severe suit, rather plainly dressed.

He remembered how once he had been told that women barristers try to dress down to avoid drawing attention. Odd how the effect was almost always completely the opposite.

The girl stopped at the lift and turned as she waited for it to come. She caught him looking at her and he dropped his eyes.

'When you've a moment,' said George at the desk behind him, 'when you can drag yourself away from the scenery.'

Scott laughed. 'Well, it's an improvement over fag-ash Gertie,' he said.

'Your Mr Masida,' said George, 'he's over there. I told him you were here.'

Scott looked and then remembered Masida. He was sitting on one of the long wooden benches. He was leaning forward with his elbows on his knees, holding a woolly hat in his hands.

'Why do defendants turn up at court?' Scott said to George. 'He must know what's going to happen.' George shrugged and picked up the phone.

Scott never ceased to be amazed by people's meek willingness to come to court to be locked up, even though he knew it was stupid to be surprised. Masida had nowhere else to go, and nowhere to run.

Masida was very black and very English. He had grown up

in Brixton. He had never known his father. His mother had left for the Caribbean some time ago, giving him her flat. Courteney Masida didn't know where she was, nor did he care.

He had never travelled out of London. He once told Scott, in one of the few complete sentences Scott had heard him utter, that he had never seen a cow. Scott couldn't remember why on earth the subject should have come up, but he knew that Masida thought Oxford was in America.

The boundaries of his life were the police, mainly Detective Sergeant Dunn of the Brixton Drug Squad, the need to deal drugs to make money, and music.

What is one to say? thought Scott – Sad really? No, not sad at all, the Plonker was right, the man is a complete shit.

'Hello, Mr Masida.' Scott stuck his hand out.

'Oh hello, Mr Scott.' Courteney Masida stood up and shook Scott's hand limply. It was a surprising touch from such a big, violent man.

'Well, we had better have a talk. Is the solicitor here?' Scott looked around.

This was Scott's life.

He dealt in medium to serious crime, though medium, serious or trivial it didn't make much difference to him. To the clients it was all the same, because though they didn't always show it, they were all equally anxious about the result.

Not much difference in pay either, but from the point of view of status he hadn't done very well. He sometimes thought about that. But it was important not to let that get in the way, or you might start thinking that the case you are doing doesn't matter very much – then you get bored and that way disaster lies.

Scott was over thirty now, and single again. His wife had left him at a set of traffic-lights in Victoria Street, just before the turning into Vauxhall Bridge Road. She got out of the car, that was the last time he saw her. He tried, unsuccessfully, not to think of her.

What he didn't know for sure, though he thought it was happening, was that he was hardening and becoming nasty.

His mother, a nurse, had once had to attend to a little baby. 'It wasn't clean,' she said – she had had to lift a complete scull-cap of hardened skin from its head – 'but underneath the cap, the baby's head was soft and the skin smelt quite, quite pure.'

But Scott always remembered the shell being cracked from the child's head, not the softness underneath. The same thing was happening to him. He could feel the callous growing over him.

'Now, Mr Masida.' Scott opened out the folded brief of papers, setting out Masida's defence. 'The police say you did it. You say you didn't. That's it really, isn't it?'

'Well, yeah,' said Masida, sucking his teeth.

More and more, Scott's two lives, his professional and his private lives, were bleeding into each other.

When he cross-examined he did not need to summon any energy at all. It was there waiting, venomous, just beneath the surface.

And out of court he could hardly trust himself to talk at length unless he was totally relaxed, in case he found the anger and strength of his job – after all he practised arguing the way a weight-lifter practises lifting – sweeping through the conversation. People don't like being cross-examined at the dinner table. They prefer to talk to the person sitting on the other side.

He dealt with this the way he had always dealt with loneliness – by bearing it.

'What I need to know is the exact layout of where this all happened. It's just outside Brodrick's in Railton Road, isn't it?'

Courteney Masida nodded.

'You say you were there buying some drink out of hours?'

Masida nodded again. He never spoke unless he had to.

'I thought there weren't any licensing hours any more but there you are. You were there in Railton Road buying drink out of hours, and Mr Dunn turned up in his car. Not his car,' Scott knew that in fact Mr Dunn owned a 1932 Austin which he kept in the car pound in Croydon, 'not in his car, in his unmarked police car.'

Detective Sergeant Dunn was one of the nicest men Scott knew, always ready for a chat and a coffee if possible, but he wasn't a witness in the case this time so Scott wouldn't have anyone to talk to.

Another nod.

'And two policemen in plain clothes get out. You recognised them.'

Scott paused for effect.

'Shall we tell the jury that?' he asked. 'But they might think if you go round recognising policemen that you've got a record. And they would be right. So we had better not tell them that. They walked towards you. The car drove off and as it did so they grabbed you. You were standing by your car. Which is a . . . yes' – Scott turned the page, pretending to be surprised – 'yes, a convertible Triumph Stag, bright yellow.'

He paused and leaned back, looking at Masida over imaginary spectacles. 'Why do you like to be so conspicuous, Mr Masida? I wouldn't have thought it helped you. You should be anonymous like me.'

Courteney Masida laughed but still said nothing. He wasn't going to join in, he was happy just watching this man who had a way with words.

'They say you threw a matchbox away which had drugs in. They say you ran for thirty yards before you threw it. They say they grabbed you at the junction of Railton Road and Kellett

Road, which is thirty yards from Brodrick's. You say you didn't throw anything at all, that all that is rubbish and that's that.'

Courteney Masida watched Scott and then he spoke. 'You just cut up them officers for me, Mr Scott.'

'OK, Mr Masida, I'll do that for you,' said Scott, wondering what Plunkett would have said to that.

Chapter 6

The time for holding the men arrested at the hotel uncharged ran out and the custody officer took Muazzam from his cell to the charge room, where he was lined up with the four others.

Next to him was the clerk who had signed him into the hotel, the man who had shown him his room and the two other travellers.

'You are each charged that on the 7th November you were with others knowingly concerned in the importation of two kilograms of diamorphine contrary to the Customs and Excise Management Act 1952. You need say nothing, but what you say will be taken down and given in evidence.'

Each of the men was charged with importing the total amount of drugs that had been found.

The custody officer paused in front of Muazzam. Muazzam said nothing for a moment, and then said, in Punjabi, 'Who are you?'

'So you'll speak now?' said the custody officer. 'Given up pretending, now that you're being charged? Come on, sunshine, you know precisely what's going on.'

As Muazzam was returned to his cell, Nadim Janjoa was taken past him to be released. There was no evidence to hold him, no evidence he was involved, they did not even know his name.

As they passed each other, Gregory watched. He wanted to see if there was any sign of recognition. Muazzam made none at all – there was nothing to be said. And Janjoa, who had expected just such an encounter, did not allow a flicker to cross his face when he saw Muazzam.

Nadim Janjoa collected his belongings from the desk officer. When he was asked to sign, he did so with his left hand. No clear name had appeared on the custody record, he had refused to say anything at all. He had not even asked for a solicitor.

Gregory watched from the door of the room opening off the hallway. He saw Janjoa pick up his jacket – there had been no identifying mark in it – watched him settle it on his shoulders and press it smooth.

The officers had distinguished him from the others by calling him the 'smart one', as he was so much better dressed than they were.

Gregory saw him disdainfully refuse the scrap of paper in the plastic property bag, a hairdresser's hand-out, saw him turn on his heel and leave the building.

Gregory knew Janjoa had come from Karachi with the others, but he couldn't prove it. His clothes were Pakistani. His voice was Pakistani. He even moved like someone from Pakistan.

Gregory could smell it. Was it a smell? Maybe it was the smell of Pakistan. But to Gregory the real evidence was that Janjoa's eyes would not meet his, that his anger at his arrest was not quite real.

There was no evidence against him – yet. Until Gregory managed to get it the only evidence against him would be that Gregory knew he was involved, knew that his presence at the Argyle was not a coincidence, not enough for court, but enough to keep investigating.

As Janjoa walked down the steps into the night, two men who had been waiting by the door stepped forward. 'Excuse me, sir,' one spoke to Janjoa, 'I am an immigration officer. We have reason to believe you are in this country illegally. Could you please come with us.'

Janjoa smiled when he saw Gregory watching.

'Don't worry, I'll come and visit,' Gregory said. He turned and went up to the section canteen.

For an unexplained reason the coffee in the canteen was real. It didn't come in a plastic cup out of a vending machine. It was served from a pot and you could drink as much as you wished.

There was a story that the coffee was the gift of the man who had once owned the building, or sold the building, to HM Commissioners of Customs and Excise. Or perhaps the man had only tried to buy it or sell it – or something. The reason for there being good coffee could hardly be as exotic as the fact that it was there at all.

'OK, Merv?' said Gregory, sitting down.

Merv Stockwood grunted and continued eating his all-hours breakfast.

'Have you done those statements?'

'Give me time. I've only just finished the arrest paperwork. I've got trouble with the documents that Illingworth uplifted.'

Customs still had their own language and they clung to it tenaciously. Documents were 'uplifted' rather than just found, 'uncustomed goods' were still 'seized as forfeit to the Crown'. Senior officers were called surveyors, where the police had inspectors.

'I can't work out from the property sheets where the clothes came from, and I don't want to have to wait for Illingworth's statement before sealing it all up,' said Stockwood.

Gregory listened but hardly paid attention. How could he

prove that the smart dresser was involved? First, he needed his name.

'Look, let's review what we've got.' Gregory loved this time more than any other. It was better even than the excitement of following someone, or going through property to see what evidence would fall out of an arrested man's pockets.

This was the real investigation, turning the matter over and over in his mind, looking at the events from the point of view of each participant, seeing how two unconnected things might connect and finish the story.

'We've arrested six people. We've got the owner of the hotel and the desk clerk. The evidence against them is separate from the others. We still need to get their bank statements. We'll see if we can find the plumber who put that crazy lavatory in.

'We've got three couriers. Each of them carrying two-thirds of a kilo of heroin. Two have coughed. Both say they knew they had it and they knew it was heroin. Both say that they were forced to do it.

'Then there's the third courier, Muazzam. He's different from the others. He's said nothing in interview. He's said nothing at all, save to Williams, who took him downstairs.'

Gregory stopped and reflected on this. 'That's pretty odd if you ask me, why talk at that point and then say nothing later? But there you are. He admitted to Williams that he knew what he had swallowed, and then he tried to run. So there's a strong case against him.

'But the last one, the smart one, we don't even have a name for him. Immigration have got him now, but they won't keep him long. I reckon we've got about five days to get a case against him. We need a name.'

Then he remembered. 'Did Cash show his photograph to the couriers, like I asked him?'

Gregory had not been able to speak to Tom Cash since he

had asked him to slip past the custody officer with an interpreter and have the informal interview.

'Yes, he left a note,' said Stockwood. 'I haven't looked at it yet. Here it is.' He read it out. 'One said he recognised him but didn't know a name.'

'I knew it,' said Gregory. 'I knew he was involved. I'd better get to work. Fix those statements. Get Williams's statement, I'm going to have to get my report ready.'

He got up and stretched. He had been on duty now for seventy hours, and had had about seven hours' sleep. 'We're agreed, are we, that you are going to court tomorrow to look after our side of it?'

Then he sat down. 'You know, I bet Muazzam is the one to ask about Mr Nobody, the smart one. Off the record. Perhaps once we get him talking he'll talk sense. Why don't we contact Bill Squire? Why don't we do that?'

'The surveyor won't like it.'

'The surveyor won't have to know. As far as he's concerned Bill was the duty solicitor,' said Gregory. 'Why don't we ring Stanhope's now?'

Bill Squire's bleeper bleeped and he woke up immediately. He was used to waking up in the middle of the night and was well prepared. He got up quietly, careful not to disturb his wife. The bleeper meant that the phone would ring in about fifteen seconds, the delay while the call was rerouted.

The time enabled him to get out of the bedroom and into the spare room he kept as his study. He had a pad and paper there, a map of London and a chart of call-outs.

There were also all the necessary Legal Aid papers pre-typed, his business cards, the book of matches with the name of the firm on and the special packets of cigarettes again printed with the name of the firm.

The phone clicked, about to ring. Before it could do so he

picked it up. 'Bill Squire here. Stanhope and Partners.'

Bill Squire was a solicitor's clerk. He was in his sixties but still looked fit, save for the swell of his belly that showed under the dressing-gown cord. His face was full and friendly, the result of a hundred thousand sincere handshakes, and he still carried the tan of an expatriate. In the small bedroom in Thornton Heath he seemed faintly exotic.

'Customs here, Bill.' Bill Squire liked to be called Bill. He especially liked to be called Bill by Customs officers. He had had good relations with Customs officers over the years, and now they reminded him of his time in the south.

He had always entertained visiting Customs officers and policemen when they came to the official residence, downstairs in his part of the embassy, in what he jokingly called the 'sergeant's mess'. The ambassador's wife had had an unerring ability to identify those who should be entertained by Bill and those who shouldn't, that is those to whom she should herself offer sherry.

Of course Bill Squire knew that those whom he entertained were the chaps who really kept things going, and on a number of occasions he found himself remarking with a jerk of his thumb upwards that it was all very well for them upstairs, but without him and those around him in the sergeant's mess, matters would go downhill pretty rapidly.

He professed himself not impressed by qualifications, letters after your name and all that hoity-toity, remarking that without a dose of good common sense then mostly it all came to nothing.

The voice on the phone said, 'I've got a chap here who needs your help. A swallower. Heroin, about two-thirds of a kilo. One of six arrests. The others have gone duty solicitor. He speaks Punjabi and English. You won't need an interpreter, although he hasn't said much to us.'

'Where are you? Fetter Lane or Heathrow?'

'Oh,' the voice laughed, 'lucky you asked, otherwise you might have been off down the M4. No, we're at Fetter Lane.'

'No chance of me taking the wrong turn, laddie. I'm a little too canny for that, been caught before, but long before your time.' Squire chuckled. 'Be there in thirty-five minutes. What's his name?'

'Muazzam.'

The Customs had successfully sold Muazzam down the river.

It generally took Bill Squire about thirty-five minutes at night to get from Thornton Heath to central London. He charged an hour to the central Legal Aid fund. Tonight the road was wet and the lights shone on the cold tarmac.

He stopped at the all-night chemist in Streatham to buy a mouth spray and used it standing outside by the road.

He watched the customers in the shop. Even at this time, nearly three o'clock in the morning, it was very busy. He had noticed how the shop had expanded over the four years it had been there.

His firm's business had expanded also, although in their case it had not been merely the location that did it but his hard work.

He was available, like the chemist, twenty-four hours a day. This year he had brought in nearly £124,000 of chargeable work, though being a clerk and unqualified he didn't get a percentage, only a salary.

Other people were doing very well out of him. A phrase formed in his mind and he saw himself perched on his stool in the sergeant's mess, sighing, 'It was always thus.'

But he was doing well too. He reflected on the events of the last few years. When he had retired he had not expected to be able to replace his old green Triumph with this Audi. He became aware of the quiet, green-lit efficiency of his car. It was some car, and when it was parked at the flying club at Old London Airport the club looked, he thought, the better for it.

A police car came towards him, silently but with the blue light flashing, doing at least ninety along the dual carriageway from the top of Brixton Hill.

Bill glanced to his left as he reached the top of the rise where the road curves to the right. He had picked up an eight-handed murder just down the road here, outside the wine bar.

He carried on over the junction of the South Circular.

Tosswill & Co. had co-defended in that case. He drove on past their offices. They didn't advertise, didn't even have 'Solicitors' up on a plate outside the office, yet they were one of the most successful firms in South London. Mrs Tosswill, though gone now, was still a legend.

He drove under the bridge. Bon Marche was on his left. He could remember when he originally left London after the war, how Brixton was a place where artists and painters lived. You could see the blue plaques all over.

It was strange how sometimes he would go to an address to take a statement or find a witness, and there, on the wall, would be the name of a music-hall star that he remembered his mother talking about. He glanced to his right as he went down Brixton Road – there was a plaque for Dan Leno over there by Myatt's Fields.

But now, but now . . . he didn't pursue what he knew would be a depressing train of thought. Brixton was different.

He came to Elephant and Castle: leaving the dark mass of the Crown Court on his right he drove through and crossed Blackfriars Bridge, turned left after Ludgate Circus and parked outside the Customs building.

Ted Turner let him in. 'Hello, Bill. Late-night call?'

Bill Squire smiled. 'No rest for the wicked, Ted, you know that. And you better than most.'

Ted laughed, feeling pleased at the camaraderie of it. He

signed Bill Squire in and let him go down the passage alone. Squire headed for the third floor. He knew the building well.

He had been to the twice-yearly parties for three years now and savoured feeling at home, savoured being able to walk around without an escort. He stuck his ID badge to his lapel.

'Hello, Bill,' said Paul Gregory. 'We've got him in here, but let's sign you in to see him first.' They went to the custody officer and Bill Squire gave his firm's name.

Gregory said, 'He hasn't asked for a solicitor. To be frank, he hasn't said a word here, but when he was arrested he admitted he knew what he was carrying, so according to the Codes of Conduct we have to give him the chance of commenting on our record of what he said.'

Bill Squire didn't have any time for the parliamentary Codes of Conduct governing police and Customs investigations. Allowing people to refuse to answer questions, insisting that records of conversations be shown to arrested men as soon as possible – there was a whole stupid book of it.

Privately he thought that the fact that a man need not answer questions when arrested was absurd and when he got an opportunity in congenial company he would say so: 'If a man is innocent why can't he say so there and then?'

To most policemen it seemed a good question too, and Bill Squire found himself more and more in demand at police stations to sign the Legal Aid forms and to advise men who had been arrested whether to answer their questioning.

'What? That's new.' He laughed. 'What's happening? Didn't he say he'd been forced to carry the drugs? Forced to swallow them, or had been told nameless things would happen to his family if he didn't do it?'

Gregory laughed. 'You know them as well as we do, Bill. No. He only said that. And since then he's said nothing. Can we show him the notes first, then leave you with him?'

'Suits me,' said Squire.

'Look, there's another thing you can do for us,' said Gregory. Immediately he regretted that he had said 'for us'. He watched but there was no response to the error.

'We've got a photograph of another man. Could you show it to him? It would help him probably if he could give the face a name.'

Bill Squire seemed not to notice the oddity of the defence being asked to help the Customs investigate the crime.

'Sure,' he said. He knew it was the price he paid for the work he got.

They showed him into a cell, all of them crowding into the small space. Muazzam sat on the scrubbed pine seat looking up at the four men who had come in. He had not the slightest idea who they were.

'You probably won't answer,' said Gregory, 'but here goes. When you were arrested, PC Williams asked you if you knew what you were carrying, and you said, "Of course I bloody do, do you think I'm crazy?"

'The officer made a note of this in his pocket book, I now have to give you the opportunity to confirm or deny you said this. I must warn you that you need say nothing . . .' and his voice trailed off into a drone.

Muazzam looked at them blankly.

'I don't think he understands,' said Gregory. 'On the other hand, he spoke good English to PC Williams. Look, we can get you an interpreter, Bill, if you want. The duty solicitor has got an Urdu speaker on his staff, he's downstairs with one of the others we have arrested.'

Bill Squire saw his new case disappearing into the hands of the duty solicitor. The interpreter would just transfer the Legal Aid, he didn't owe anything to Bill Squire. He was probably a Pakistani and they all stuck together.

'No, no need, if he speaks English we'll get on. You know me with clients.'

'Don't forget the photo, Bill,' said Gregory as they left.

'First things first,' said Squire. He pulled out the Legal Aid forms. 'You need a lawyer.' Muazzam said nothing. 'Come on, laddie, I'm on your side.' Squire filled in the form, name Sigbhat Muazzam, it was on the Customs documentation, address – in custody, date – da-di-da, income – nil, capital – nil, rest not relevant, charge – importing, reasons for needing representation – likelihood of custodial sentence of great length. Bill gave him the form. 'Sign here, and here.' He gave Muazzam the pen, put the form down on the bench and waited. Muazzam didn't move. He had not a clue what this man was talking about.

'Come on, old son, I know you're upset, but let's get this over with.' Bill took the pen, put it in Muazzam's hand and guided it to the paper. Muazzam made a scratching motion and a scrawl appeared.

'That'll do,' said Bill. He folded the paper and put it away. 'We send that off to the Legal Aid people, I'll have someone in court tomorrow. You won't get bail on this, you know that. Now there is just one thing, do you recognise this photograph?'

He showed the photograph that Customs had taken of Janjoa. 'Janjoa,' said Muazzam automatically.

'Oh good, so you can talk. Look. Can't stay now. You can have these,' he left a packet of cigarettes with the firm's name on them.

This was his own idea, and of all the things he had done for the firm was the one he was most proud of. 'I'll see you tomorrow, probably at Elephant and Castle.'

He left the cell. There was no doubt he had got a good case. This was a good six-hander, six defendants. Cases like this usually fight, since the defendants get no benefit out of pleading guilty, they would get much the same sentence whichever they did so they might as well take the chance of an acquittal.

It could last three weeks, perhaps even longer if the solicitors briefed the right barristers, who would spin it out. It was a non-standard-fee case certainly, there would be extra fees and, frankly, it would involve very little work.

He saw Gregory waiting. 'How about one of your coffees?' said Squire. 'I've got what you want. You know you can rely on Stanhope's. The name of the man in the photo is John.'

Chapter 7

'Can I see the exhibit?' said Jeremy Scott.

PC Williams, uncomfortable in the witness-box, shuffled through the papers and handed the usher a polythene bag which contained the matchbox in which the drug was found. It was carried slowly round the court.

They were in court number one. Courteney Masida had drawn Judge Wrigley to try his case. He was unlucky, he could expect double the usual sentence if he was convicted.

His Honour Judge Wrigley was smouldering on the bench, and Jeremy Scott wasn't having much luck.

'Get on with it, Mr Scott,' growled the judge.

Scott got on with it. 'This is the matchbox containing the drug that you say he threw away when you caught up with him?'

'Yes,' said the officer.

Scott took the matchbox from the court usher. It was inside a sealed polythene bag, with a document. He had hoped it would be there. It was called a submission document and it. was what he was looking for.

He had not been able to look at it before the court sat, since any inspection of exhibits is always done in the presence of a police-officer, and Scott always applied the basic rule: never, never look at exhibits with a policeman looking over your shoulder. If you do that then they find what you find.

Everyone remembered the terrorist who might not have been convicted had not his counsel gone through the pockets of his clothing in the presence of a police-officer. That barrister had found a list in a pocket, previously unnoticed, with the names of half the Cabinet on it, plus addresses. So had the policeman.

'I am going to open the packet now, if I may, Your Honour,' he said, opening it before the judge had time to object. He got the submission document out.

A submission document is the official police summary for the use of the forensic laboratory which is asked to examine the exhibits. He read it: 'Form HO/FOR 01. Submission for examination for prohibited substances. Defendant was stopped at Lawrence Road. On approach by police, D threw down matchbox and ran off. Matchbox found to contain fourteen folds of white powder. Suspected to be cocaine.'

It was a different version of events. Scott made a show of examining the matchbox carefully, leaving the document apparently disregarded in the plastic bag.

The police-officer watched him sullenly from the witness-box.

'Do get on with it, Mr Scott,' said the judge again. This was going to be a trying morning.

Speaking slowly and deliberately so that everybody understood the times involved, Scott asked, 'Your evidence yesterday was that you wrote up your notebook half an hour after your arrival at the police station?'

'Yes.'

'And you wrote it with the other two officers who had been present at the arrest?'

'Yes.'

'Is that why their accounts are word for word the same as yours?'

'Yes.'

'The time at which the notebook entry was made was between nine fifty-five and ten forty p.m.?'

'Yes.'

'Another matter.' Pause. 'Am I right that it is you, the arresting officers, who provide the basic information for investigating the crime?'

'Yes.'

'And only you?' He realised he had made a mistake. The question was not accurate enough, and PC Williams was able to lift the pressure of the close questions with a long reply.

'No. Not only me. It could be any one of the officers at the scene, or one of the officers at the police station, who spoke to the defendant.'

'No,' said Scott, 'I meant by my question that only you, or one of the other two officers at the arrest, could describe precisely what happened at the time of the arrest. Only you could provide this essential information.'

'Yes.' As long as Scott asked tight enough questions to force the policeman to stick to one-word answers then the witness was no danger. He could take him wherever he wished.

'Another detective takes over the investigation, but his knowledge of what occurred can only come from you?'

'Yes.'

'And what you say happened during the arrest is in your notebook?'

'Yes, I've just said that. He swung his right fist at me and hit me in the face.'

The judge was not going to control the witness, instead he encouraged him, 'Did that cause you much pain, Officer?'

'Yes, I was off work for five days.'

Now was the time to attack the timing of the notebook. He

knew he had to show that the officer could not have written the notebook entry at the time he said he did. Then when he eventually produced the different version of events it would be much more effective.

'Going back to your notebook. You say you wrote it up in the canteen together with the two other officers – PC Denison and PC Weinberg.'

He was careful not to ask if they were together all the time. Anyone hearing him say 'together' would assume it meant all the time.

'Yes.'

'But let's look at the custody record.'

He turned to the jury, to tell them what the custody record was.

'The custody record is the official record, precisely timed, of what took place at the police station from the moment the defendant arrived – isn't that correct, Officer?'

He turned the speech into a question just before the judge intervened to regain control of the court.

'Yes,' said the policeman.

'Now, earlier in your evidence you said that my client Mr Masida was strip-searched?'

'Yes.'

'And you did that?'

'Yes.'

'And that strip-search took place at nine forty-five and ended at nine fifty-five. Look, it gives the times on the custody record. So you couldn't have been in the canteen at nine fifty-five writing down what had happened, could you? At nine fifty-five you were searching the prisoner?'

Both the judge and the police-officer saw how weak the question was. They were meant to. The officer got in first.

'The times on the custody record aren't accurate to a second,' said PC Williams, 'I would have brought him back

56

from being searched, given him to the officer in charge of the custody record and then gone off to make the notes. From my memory the custody record is about right.'

Then the judge stuck his oar in, 'This custody record can't just be produced from thin air, you know, Mr Scott. Have you asked for the police-officer who wrote the document to be called as a witness?'

The remark was designed to make it difficult for Scott to continue. But questions like that often help the defence. The judge wouldn't like the answer.

'But, Your Honour, how could I give notice that I needed the officer who made the record to come to court when I did not know in advance that PC Williams would be contradicted by the document?'

The judge didn't like that. The jury didn't entirely understand what was happening. But it was becoming interesting. They watched intently.

'Please be careful what you say,' said the judge, 'the document doesn't contradict the witness. PC Williams has just said that he accepts the times on it. He relies on it.'

The judge could no longer object to the use of the custody record in cross-examination without looking a bit silly. He had pointed out that the witness himself relied upon it. It couldn't be better.

The jury, only half understanding what was happening, thought this must be important or the judge would not be making a fuss. But they also thought the officer was right – there was no contradiction. He said he had finished searching the defendant at nine fifty-five, and then started writing up his notes at nine fifty-five, so where's the great mistake? The officer was obviously right to point out that the record supported him. But it was beginning to be fun.

'You say that the custody officer is right about his note of the times, then?' Scott pursued the point.

'Yes.'

'Well, I suggest that you could not have been making your notes along with the two other officers, since the record shows clearly that at nine fifty-five you were strip-searching the defendant?' He repeated the stupid question. There was no harm in looking a little dumb for a moment.

The policeman relaxed. If this was the best that this brief could do then no worries.

'I just said,' he allowed himself a note of exasperation, 'that the times may seem exact, but we would have started to make the notes immediately after we searched him.'

'You said – "would have started" – do you remember whether you did or not?'

'Yes, I remember it. I remember making the notes together with the other officers in the canteen.'

The officer had made the mistake. He was finished now, though he didn't know it.

'And you made the notes together?'

'Yes.'

Pause. Scott paused long enough for everybody to be uncomfortably aware of the silence.

'But that can't be right. Look. Look here on the same custody record. At ten ten p.m. it says the defendant was read his rights. The station officer read out to him that he was entitled to a lawyer, and that's timed there at the bottom, at ten ten p.m.' He waited for the officer to look at the copy and then continued.

'And you've just agreed that the time is put there as things happen, so it must be right. And it is countersigned by an officer who was also present, PC Weinberg, so he couldn't have been in the canteen making notes with you. He was busy countersigning the custody record.'

No reply from the officer.

'And look, he was obviously there for some time. He has

countersigned the list of the prisoner's property. That's noted on the same page at ten twenty – ten minutes later. Ladies and gentlemen,' Scott turned to the jury, 'you don't have this document now but you will have it. You will be able to look at it when you retire for your verdict.'

Nothing from the judge, nor from the prosecution.

Again Scott pursued the officer. 'He couldn't have been with you.'

Again there was silence.

'Could he?'

Scott watched what was happening, as though he were not involved in it. He was able to think quite detachedly during this kind of questioning, even carrying on two entirely different lines of thought at the same time.

There must be a time, he thought, when a conjuror in front of his audience has already done his trick, even though he is still shuffling the cards. The audience is still desperately concentrating on his hands to see what happens, but since the card has already moved, the conjuror can do what he likes. He can play any game he likes. It must be a good time to have fun in.

More silence.

'Could he?' Scott repeated. He kept his voice soft and quite steady.

He wouldn't let go now. Once, when he first started this job, it was embarrassing to stand looking at a hooked police-officer and he used to let up to break the tension. But not any more, now he just stood there.

The policeman, he reflected, was, no doubt, honest, and had been made to look perfectly dishonest – a policeman in full uniform in front of a jury, twelve people who now couldn't bring themselves to look away and yet who had difficulty in bringing themselves to look directly at the witness.

There must be a dozen explanations for the discrepancies

in the documentation, but because the witness had tried to take him on earlier over the weak question and said he was certain about it there was nothing now he could change or explain.

The policeman regretted the moment of pretended exasperation. So did the judge. Both were silent.

'Well, if you can't answer that,' Scott said, after about an hour and a half, 'how about this one? You wanted to get permission to search the defendant's home?'

'Yes.'

'To do that you have to persuade a senior officer to allow it?'

'Yes.'

The witness would not argue any more now. He was mesmerised by his situation. He might even accept every word said to him.

Once, a police-officer who got into this state after Scott's cross-examination agreed that his evidence was that the defendant's chin must have struck his fist by accident. The *Guardian* printed that without comment.

'One of the arresting officers had to give the inspector information in order to get authority to search Mr Masida's flat. That must have been done in the charge room so that the result would be filled in on the custody record?'

'Yes.' The officer could have said that the application might have been made in the canteen, or he could have said I don't remember, but by now all the fight had gone out of him.

'Then let's look at the custody record. Same document. That happened at ten thirty. The inspector has noted it on the sheet. So you couldn't have been in the canteen making notes. One of you was in the charge room speaking to the inspector.'

Silence again.

Plunkett broke the silence in an attempt to help his witness.

'But how can this officer account for a document that he didn't fill in, or even sign?'

It was the judge's objection over again. Of course it allowed Scott to comment.

'But My Learned Friend should remember that this part of the custody record has been filled in by the inspector and he is a witness in the case. If his statement is right it was this officer who came to him asking for permission to search at ten thirty. We have his statement. It's at page twelve of the depositions, Your Honour. So PC Williams couldn't have been drinking tea in the canteen writing his notes.'

The jury looked through their documents again, and Scott was able to talk to them directly while the judge and the Crown lawyer were looking at their own papers.

'You haven't got this document, ladies and gentlemen, but you will hear it read out. I'm sorry I have to take you on a paper chase where you don't have all the papers, but I'm afraid it is the only way I can help my client.'

Now the jury were more than just interested. This is what it was meant to be like at court.

'Mr Scott . . .' warned the judge.

'Someone, you, Officer, reported to the inspector at ten thirty. How could you have been elsewhere writing up the notes? Do you remember reporting to the inspector?' He would have to answer if only to relieve the tension.

'No.'

'But you remember sitting in the canteen writing the notes – even though it is now clear that it did not happen? You actually remember something that did not happen?'

'Oh, really, this is just comment!' said Scott's opponent. There was no answer from the police-officer. Everybody ignored the interruption.

'There's no answer, is there? I'll tell you what happened. You didn't write the notes up together. A story was agreed and it was written up later.'

'No. We did it as I said.' The officer stuck to his discredited evidence.

'How about this, then?' said Scott, he used the phrase as a challenge. 'The powder in the matchbox which you say the defendant threw away was sent off to the laboratory to be tested?'

'Yes.'

'You have it there in the bag. Take it out.' PC Williams took the box that Scott had earlier examined out of the polythene bag.

'It was sent off to the laboratory?'

'Yes, we sent it off.'

'Sent by the officer who took over the investigation of the case?'

'Yes.'

'But that officer wrote something. Take that piece of paper out of the bag, Officer. He wrote, you've got it there: "The Defendant threw the matchbox down and ran off." How could he have written that? That completely contradicts what you said in evidence. You said that you found the matchbox at the end of the chase when you caught him.'

The judge exploded, 'How can you ask that question? He can't account for what someone else has written.'

Scott had prepared his questioning with just that complaint in mind.

'But Your Honour will remember that we established only a few moments ago that information about what happened at the arrest could only have come from this officer. I am only enquiring why the information is so wrong – given its source.'

To the witness he said, 'You said in evidence just now that the defendant ran away and that when you caught up with him, about forty yards down the road, he struggled trying to get rid of the drug. Here it says he threw it away as you approached him. How can that be?'

'I don't know. It's not what happened.'

'We know you *say* that now. You *say* that what you wrote in the canteen with the officers is right.'

'I say that what I remember is right.'

'Your memory seems to be wrong. You can't all have been in the canteen writing it out together.'

'We did.'

'You say that the custody record which is designed to record where people are is wrong?'

Silence.

'A few minutes ago you were agreeing with it.'

Silence.

'But you must say that. You have to say that the policeman who kept the custody record is wrong. There he is sitting in the charge room with a clock on the wall in front of him. He's got nothing to do but drink tea and look at the clock. But you say he got the times wrong.'

No reply.

'Earlier this morning I suggested to you that the struggle had taken place by the car. You denied it then. Yet here is a document which says that the matchbox containing drugs was dropped at the start of the incident. That's by the car. Just where I suggested to you that the struggle took place. How do you account for that?'

'He can't,' said the judge, 'you know he can't.' The judge meant that the witness could not be expected to answer for the accuracy of something which someone else wrote.

But the jury thought that the judge had decided that the policeman could not answer the question.

Scott decided to emphasise this. 'But he said he must have been the source of what the detectives put on this document . . .'

'That's enough, Mr Scott, don't argue.'

It looked as though the judge was intervening on the officer's behalf. Which he was.

'Well, I'll sit down if that's enough.'

It was as good as television for the jury. Time for lunch.

'That's not the way it should be done,' said Plunkett.

'Well, it seemed all right to me,' said Emily.

Douglas Plunkett was annoyed. Scott had destroyed his case out of nothing, and now this, this pupil girl, was arguing with him. 'Well, it wasn't,' he said, letting his annoyance show for a moment. 'Take it from me, it just won't do to harass the witness like that. Many judges would have stopped him.'

Well, the judge tried to but Scott wouldn't let him, Emily thought but decided not to say out loud. She was beginning to learn her place.

'Wrigley should have stepped in sooner.'

Emily watched Plunkett's mouth moving. It seemed to have a life of its own.

Plunkett piled food on to his plate. They had gone up to the Bar mess. At the counter you could take as much food as you wished for a set price.

'It's wrong that these sharp defence lawyers . . .' Emily heard the word with disbelief. 'It's wrong that these sharp defence lawyers are allowed to browbeat the police, who after all are not allowed to answer back.'

Plunkett stopped for a moment and wondered whether he had got that right – it was civil servants who couldn't answer back, wasn't it? No matter.

He found room on his plate for some more food. 'They are not allowed to answer back, and anyway they are snowed under with paperwork. If policemen have to write everything they do down, how can they be expected to deal with questions based on what they wrote all the time?'

Again he hesitated faintly. Had he got that right? He felt so angry.

They found a place and he sat down opposite Emily. For a

moment his attention shifted to her. As she sat down she had to negotiate the long bench, rather easier to do if you were wearing trousers not a longish skirt. Even the furniture was designed for men. Plunkett watched her legs.

'Is that all you are going to eat, my dear?'

He felt protective of this chit of a girl. Not just protective, more, it was more than that. He couldn't identify the feeling, but a moment later it had gone, covered over by hunger as he surveyed the plate of food before him. He looked up.

'Only an apple? You'll waste away,' he said. He took a mouthful. 'Well, how are you getting on?' Another mouthful. 'I mean, in the job.' His whole face worked away at the food. 'I know that it's difficult for young barristers to get on now, but myself, I never thought this was a woman's job. I always say that advocacy is difficult for a woman's voice. They can get screechy.'

His voice trailed away as he ate and his attention returned to his plate.

Emily watched him, hoping that the feeling of distaste welling up in her didn't show.

Chapter 8

Downstairs, Scott was waiting at the door for the gaoler. Masida had been put in custody over lunch in case he sat next to a juror in the court restaurant.

'Hello, Mr Scott,' said the gaoler.

'Mr Masida, please.' And Scott went to an interview room to wait.

'It'll be a while,' shouted the gaoler, 'he's being fed at the moment. Will you wait?'

Scott said he would.

Sessions had a magistrates' court attached to it to cope with the amount of work, which meant that the cell area was much busier than usual, but Scott was still surprised when he saw a solicitor walk past with a pile of hamburgers.

It was Monty Bach. He sent work to some of Scott's colleagues in chambers and occasionally Scott saw his clerk drinking with Monty outside the Clachan Pub.

Monty went into the next cell. The tops of the walls between the cells had a pattern of gaps between them and it was possible to hear what the prisoners next door were saying. Scott had heard them talking. By their Welsh accents he had guessed that they were either Pakistani or Indian. But then Monty Bach spoke.

'What's he here for?'

'Importing drugs,' was the reply. 'He's got Bill Squire acting for him. He's signed the Legal Aid papers.'

'Will he change solicitors?'

'I'll ask him. He doesn't speak a word of English. He says he's just a tailor.'

There was conversation in a foreign language. 'He says he doesn't understand. He wants to go home to his wife. If you arrange that he would be grateful.'

Monty laughed. 'I'll arrange that. Does he want a hamburger?'

'No. He's strict. But he'll have the chips.'

There was a pause. 'Get him to sign these and this letter.'

Monty Bach was famous for the standard-form letter he carried around with him, requesting that Legal Aid be transferred to his company. It was how he got a lot of his work, snatching it from other solicitors. The hamburgers were well worth the clients they got.

Scott guessed he was overhearing the letter being produced. Again there was silence, then some more foreign conversation.

'He's happy to sign. He's asking when will he be able to leave and see his wife? I told him quite soon, but that you have to talk to various people.'

'Is he fighting his case? Does he say he is not guilty?' said Monty. There was more bird-like talking. Scott sat looking up from his paper smiling. This was the business area that he didn't have to get involved in.

'Yes.'

'Good,' said Monty.

'He says that he didn't know what he was swallowing. He was told it was necessary for air travel to take something to weigh the stomach down. They told him that all people on their first flight take it.'

Monty Bach laughed. 'What about the other two?'

Obviously, Scott thought, there were some others in the cell.

'They've got Farakian. He employs a clerk from the same area as they come from. They were telling me how good he was. They won't change solicitors.'

'Well, see if you can manage it. Now, about your case. I've got Tozer for you. It'll cost, but your father has agreed.'

Tozer was a member of the chambers where Scott used to be, and was doing well with Monty Bach's help. Scott was curious to hear what they would say, but at that moment he was interrupted by the arrival of Mr Masida. He was about to get another reminder that Courteney Masida was not a pleasant man.

'That fucking copper ought to be done over. Lying bastard. I weren't struggling with him by the car.'

Scott saw the whole case beginning to disappear down the pan. All the cross-examination had been on the basis that Masida had told him that the struggle with the policeman had been by the car and not further down the road. He had pretty well shown the jury that the police-officers had made it all up, and yet here was the client on the verge of ruining everything.

This was the danger of talking to clients too much – they kept changing their stories – no wonder the rule was get the story once and stick to it.

'But, Mr Masida, you told the police-officer who interviewed you that you were arrested just near the car. You told me outside the court not three hours ago that you were arrested by the car. You told the solicitors the same. You heard me put it to the officer in court that you were arrested there and you didn't object then.'

'Well,' Masida said.

'Mr Masida, as I understand it, you say that you were jumped on just by the car, that you only struggled because you were surprised, and that you didn't throw any matchbox away at all. And you say that you didn't run forty yards down the road.'

'Lying bastard,' said Masida.

'I hope you mean the policeman and not me, Mr Masida.'

Masida looked at him. Something began to stir behind the blank expression on his face.

'Mr Masida.' Scott leaned forward and looked him straight in his eyes. 'Look at me,' he said.

He had discovered that when you say that to a client they tend to recognise that what is being said is important. These things, he decided, operate on a fairly primitive level.

Courteney Masida's eyes eventually swivelled round and focused on Scott's face. Scott spoke slowly, 'Is what you told me this morning right, Mr Masida, or is it not right?'

'Well,' said Masida. In other circumstances he would have nutted anyone who spoke to him like that.

Out of the corner of his eye Scott could see Monty Bach go by, closing his briefcase. A voice shouted out, 'See you.' Scott thought he had better stop talking about what happened at Masida's arrest in case it changed again.

The defence had been surprisingly consistent until now and he was clearly better off not pressing his luck.

He went upstairs to the Bar mess for lunch.

The sessions Bar mess, in what used to be a big gloomy room serving brown soup and omelettes, was now busy and full of fettucini salad.

There was Tozer. Scott was amused to see him, having heard what he had downstairs. Appearing in the magistrates' court for Monty Bach was a little beneath Tozer's dignity.

'Hello, Tozer,' he said, 'how's Sally?' Scott hoped he had remembered the name of Tozer's latest correctly.

Tozer paused before replying, to make sure he wasn't being teased, either by word or gesture. He decided he wasn't.

'Oh, hello, Scott.' Tozer affected a bluff surname approach as if to emphasise that he was a member of a gentleman's

70

profession, redolent still of public school and the services. 'You here? What you doing?'

'Possession with intent, in front of Wrigley. What a day.'

Even in the short time it took Scott to reply, Tozer's eyes drifted away from him and over his shoulder to examine whether there was anyone else more important he should be talking to.

'Oh,' Tozer said. 'Hello, how're you?' He spoke to someone passing behind them.

'Tozer,' Scott said. Tozer hardly noticed he had spoken. Scott looked at him again, reflecting on the confident blond face. He said, 'Tozer' again and paused. After a moment, Tozer's eyes swivelled back. 'Tozer, speak to me, how are things?'

Tozer considered again then answered. 'I've got a day off, and Monty asked me to come down to look after one of his toe-rags. A thousand pounds on the brief, not going to refuse that.'

What kind of client pays a thousand pounds for counsel to represent him at the magistrates' court? thought Scott. Aloud he said, 'Coo, that's good. Nice money,' and he meant it.

The thing about Tozer was that despite his being in almost every way totally appalling, or maybe because of it, he was genuinely successful.

There was a movement beside them and a tall, dark woman, rather older than they, dangling a cigarette in her mouth, sat down. She was known as the Lady Bird and was Tozer's idea of success.

'Hello, Tozer,' she said, and nodded to Scott.

'Hello, Mary, you still here?' Tozer's voice contained a Welsh lilt which contrasted with his appearance.

Scott watched. He was aware as Tozer spoke that he was about to get a lesson in how to get on in life. What the probation reports called social skills.

'How are the policemen managing, Mary?' Tozer said.

In court two, Mary Bracken was prosecuting three policemen for beating up and then arresting a mini-cab driver who had refused to take them home because they were drunk.

'You know,' she said, 'those policemen organised their notebooks and got a complete lying version of what they said had happened within half an hour of dragging the cab driver back to the police station. It was a complete version,' she repeated, 'even though,' she paused and started counting on her fingers, 'it wasn't their police station; they weren't on duty; and one of them who was meant to have signed the book didn't even go with them to the police station.'

Tozer grunted non-committally.

She carried on, 'Let's imagine you had been briefed to defend that taxi-driver. It would have been impossible. You wouldn't even have been allowed to see the police notebooks till you got up to cross-examine during the hearing, let alone have a chance to get them examined by the forensic scientists. It's dishonesty on a scale that makes defending the people they pick on a hopeless joke. It was only because one of the policemen blew the whistle that he was acquitted.'

Scott hoped that a similar conversation was taking place in the jury canteen between her jury and his.

'Oh, I don't know,' said Tozer. It was one of his favourite expressions when he wasn't entirely sure what line to take in a conversation.

He was cautious because Mary Bracken was saying out loud what most of them knew but few would admit to for fear of complications – that if a group of policemen wanted to convict someone and they were even halfway efficient, then there was nothing anyone could do about it.

'Oh, I don't know, we've got better tests now,' said Tozer.

'Oh yes,' said Mary, 'it took the police forensic department two months to prove that the notebooks were untruthful, and even now they're backtracking a bit. How could a local solicitor have organised that on Legal Aid? Quick, efficient forensic evidence is only available to the prosecution. They can research the case at their leisure. If the defence wanted to do it they wouldn't even be able to get hold of the exhibits properly.

'What I think is odd,' she went on, 'given the police's knowledge of what forensic scientists can do, is how long it's taken the junior ranks to realise that they could be caught out by ESDA tests.

'That test has been around for years, they've been able to check on written confessions for years. Senior officers knew all about them. Look, if the police really were inventing false evidence against those six Irishmen, Farrell and the others, they must have known they would eventually be found out.'

Farrell and the five others had been released by a dismayed Court of Appeal only weeks before, after nine years in prison.

Scott thought what she was saying was strange. He repeated it to himself: 'If the police really were inventing false evidence.' He was surprised at her remarks. She was assuming that the police hadn't invented the evidence. What she was saying was that the evidence wasn't false. It was only the way it was recorded that was doubtful.

The papers had been full of little else save the Farrell appeal result for days, the television screen repeating pictures of their release from the court. Six men, some quiet, bewildered, others incoherent with joy and anger, being let out into an empty area of the street outside the Old Bailey, surrounded by police holding back a wildly cheering crowd.

Tozer said, 'But we know what Watney was like.' Watney was one of the officers in the Farrell investigation.

'And the judge,' laughed Mary Bracken.

Scott understood neither of these remarks.

'Are you saying that they were actually guilty?' Scott recognised the clumsiness of his question the moment it came out. Why couldn't he effect the same tone of chumminess that Tozer was so good at? Or rather, why was it, if he did try to effect it that it sounded so false?

Mary Bracken turned and laid her hand on his arm. 'Well, we know three of them were involved, don't we?'

'That's all right then,' Scott said, and again regretted speaking.

Tozer was on to what he had said instantly. His ability to spot dissent had been honed as a consequence of years of being an outsider, years of having to put up with rebuffs, real or imagined. 'Oh, oh,' the sound was a sing-song, almost a hunting cry, 'what do you think then, Jeremy, I suppose you think they are all innocent?'

'Oh, Tozer,' Scott said, and smiled. He had found that if the prey does not run then pursuit is unlikely, better to stay absolutely still and say nothing.

Then he said, 'I have to go and look after my dreadful Mr Masida. Good luck with your policemen, Mary.'

He set off for court one; it was coming up to two o'clock and being on time was important with Judge Wrigley. The judge had been known in the past to go into court despite his usher's protests that there was no one there except an outside clerk eating an apple and reading the *Sun*. When he was in the judge would keep up a running commentary on the late-comers like a master of ceremonies in a music-hall.

But today as Scott came down the passage to the court and pushed back the last of the five sets of swing doors, he was interrupted by Murphy sticking his head out of counsel's entrance. Murphy was Judge Wrigley's usher; some said he had been with him in the navy. 'No hurry, Mr Scott,' Murphy's Irish accent came out like sunshine when he was happy, 'His Honour's gone. He was taken over all ill at luncheon and has gone.'

'What tosh, Murphy. He's just gone home, you know he

likes to go home early on Fridays.'

'That's just not true, Mr Scott. What would you be saying such a thing for? He called me to his room himself. He was not feeling so good and he asked me to tell the list office.'

By now, no doubt, Wrigley was on a train to Kent. He was capable of leaving the court like lightning if his list of cases ended more quickly than the court staff expected, before he could be given more work, though it wasn't often he abandoned a case in mid-trial.

Well, that was that.

Scott went into court to find the clerk addressing the jury, who were putting on their coats and organising their handbags and umbrellas. 'That's it, I'm sorry, ladies and gentlemen, we'll see you on Monday. Ten thirty.'

Scott waited until he had finished and then went to the clerk's desk to make sure that he had been marked down for a full day's work. He didn't see why he should lose money to pay for the judge's afternoon in the garden.

'He's remanded your man in custody,' the clerk said.

'What! Why?'

'I don't think he liked his eyes.' This was the Crown Court at its most tyrannical.

'He can't do that, he was only in custody for lunch. He's on bail.'

'Why not?'

'The judge didn't even hear me argue it.'

'His Honour would have done it anyway.'

'But how am I going to explain it to Masida? He'll kill me. He already thinks we are all part of a big conspiracy to do him down.'

'Let me tell you something,' confided the clerk, leaning over from his high desk until his head was directly above Scott's, 'we are.'

'Well, I am going to complain to the Perfect English

Gentleman. Wrigley can't do that. It's grossly unfair – even if it is Mr Masida who is getting locked up.'

As Scott said it he regretted it. Regretting things he had said seemed to be something he was doing that day.

The Perfect English Gentleman, the second senior judge in the building, sat in court three and his court wouldn't rise till four o'clock. To speak to him Scott would have to hang around. But he was stuck with it now, he couldn't back down.

He went on, 'I'll tell the prosecution so they can come if they want. You had better let court three have the papers in this case.'

'Do what you like, lovey,' said the clerk. He pulled out a huge pair of marmalade-rimmed spectacles and stumbled up the steps through the curtain behind the judge's chair. All the lights in the court went out.

Scott went downstairs to the cells and gave Masida a highly edited version of why he was probably going to spend the weekend in Brixton prison.

Chapter 9

'This is the booking-sheet print-out. From the third column you can establish where the ticket booking was made, Thailand, Karachi, Frankfurt or London. It only gives one name for the passenger not the full name, so you cannot be sure that it will tally exactly with the aircraft boarding-list print-out.

'The boarding list is made up straight from information given at check-in, but we don't include the ticket origin on that list, you have to use both together for the full story.

'Trouble is, name variations occur between the two lists, because a particular ticket may have restrictions on who can use it and people use middle names or they share names so that either one of them can turn up and use the ticket.

'Different people fly out and back on a shared ticket. The ticket you're searching for may be an open ticket, I see the others were, and then anyone can arrive at the airport, there may be completely different names referring to the ticket depending on which list you're using.'

The morning after Janjoa was taken by immigration, Paul Gregory had gone to see the support services of the international flight ticket agency. The computer in front of him was interrogating the computers at the places where the Karachi

77

flight had stopped, and the connections.

Perhaps he could establish whether anyone travelled with Muazzam and the other couriers by checking the original aircraft flight-lists. He might find a trace of the smart man.

'Of course if the chap you're looking for was really skilful he could have joined the flight at Frankfurt with a ticket that did not originate in Karachi at all.'

Gregory knew this, but he was not going to interrupt the helpful flow of the director of computer operations. It was difficult enough to get this information normally, and he was lucky to have got the director on a good day.

'Hello, what's happening here?' said the director as the screen in front of him suddenly started moving. The whole group of names started scrolling down the page. Then they stopped and went into reverse. From the top appeared another name going in the opposite direction, until it stopped. Then Gregory realised it was his own.

'Well, how did that happen?' said the director. 'You didn't fly on this flight, did you?' The director was never surprised at what Customs officers were doing.

'No,' said Gregory.

The director typed in 'origin please' on the screen, then Gregory's name. The machine – was it a machine? that seemed a ridiculous word for something you had to say please to – paused, then said 'Sigbhat'.

'Sigbhat? Where's Sigbhat?' said Gregory.

'Sigbhat,' shouted the director, 'what are you up to?'

A smiling face, obviously belonging to Sigbhat, appeared from round a dividing screen in the room. 'Mr Gregory, you've just arrived on a steerage-class ticket from Angkor Wat.'

'Do you mean that this list can be changed?'

'Oh yes, everything can always be changed. Which parallel reality do you want?' said the director. 'How did you get into the system, Sigbhat?' he shouted.

'I used the secondary route that we talked about,' came the reply. 'It works.'

'I want the parallel reality which shows me who got on the plane in Pakistan and where they sat,' said Gregory.

'That's what you're getting,' said the director. 'As the song said, "you always get what you want, but do you get what you need?" '

'We'll see,' said Gregory. 'Could you write out a witness statement for me so we can prove the print-outs in court if we have to?'

'Already done,' said the director, opening a drawer on the desk. 'All you have to do is fill in the dates. I've already signed fifty of them in case people come round when I'm not here.'

A witness statement is not something you can sign in advance any more than you would sign your cheque-book right through when you got it. Gregory showed his dismay at the director's comment, just as he thought he was expected to.

'You don't think these statements mean anything, do you?' the director said. 'Look. The court asks me to make a statement saying that the computer is working properly. That's a dumb question, it's like asking me if the transport system is working properly. Which bit? What's working properly mean? It's working properly even if it's only including every fifth letter in every word, if that's what someone's told it to do.

'I went to court once to give evidence. But I found I couldn't answer the questions. It wasn't because they were difficult to answer but because they didn't qualify as questions.'

Gregory didn't get involved in the philosophy, he took the print-outs, a plan of the inside of a Boeing 747 and went.

When he got home his wife wasn't in, probably collecting the kids, so he was able to go straight upstairs to his attic room. He had bought this house because of the room. None of the others on the same estate – how his wife objected when he spoke of their living on an estate! – had a room like this. It stretched the whole length of the house, had roof windows on three sides. The previous owner had been a builder and had put it in himself.

The builder was one of those people, Paul thought, who didn't have the letters after his name that bring status but who in fact are the people who make things work.

In the big room when he moved in there was a drawing-board, huge, a good six feet by four, almost the size of a double bed. It could not have been brought up the narrow stairs. It must have been brought in when the roof was off. It was perfect for the kind of work Gregory had to do.

He spread the lists on the table. Each contained three hundred names, in different orders, although the divisions were all set out alphabetically. Unfortunately he discovered this was less than useful, since the alphabetic choice merely reflected the first name given.

Names vary in the way they are used. He remembered how when he started with Customs he had had to unlearn the idea of Christian names and ask people instead what was their first name. They weren't all Christians.

Even to say first name was not much use with people who did not necessarily keep their names in any set order, or people whose names depended upon who was addressing them.

Strange that, some cultures put names in a different order if you are talking to a subordinate. But then he thought that's not so strange. At school when you became senior you could put your initials first, so it had been P. J. Gregory, instead of Gregory P. J.

He started on the sheets. After a few moments he found Muazzam, booking in at Karachi and then on the equivalent entry boarding at Karachi. The ticket number printed on the computer sheet coincided with the ticket stub that they had found on Muazzam, and the print-out confirmed again what his ticket said, one bag in the baggage hold. Beyond that nothing.

The names sitting near his seat number G4 meant nothing to him. He found the names of the other two couriers, sitting next to each other, about six rows in front of Muazzam.

Gregory looked for a John. He thought it an unusual name for an Asian, then he remembered where he'd got it, Bill Squire. Bill Squire was so dishonest that what he said meant very little. Still, might as well try. There were four Johns getting on at Karachi, but none of them had an Asian name, they were Robertses and McCleans. He cross-checked. None of them had bought their ticket in Karachi.

There were one hundred and eighty-five men who got on at Delhi, of those about a third were not Pakistani, so he had about one hundred and twenty.

As he checked he realised that there was a large party clearly flying together, their ticket numbers were consecutive and had a different structure from most of the others. He might as well take risks, so he put them aside. It's OK to take risks as long as you know you are doing so. It's assumptions of which you are unaware that should make you nervous.

As he thought this he saw Janjoa's name. Janjoa – John? He had been told John, could this be him? He was sitting behind Muazzam. He had boarded, Gregory checked, alone, certainly there were no consecutive ticket numbers. He had had no luggage. He had an open ticket. He had no special reductions on it. He had boarded, he checked down the other list again, in Karachi. Janjoa, Nadim Janjoa – the second list gave the full name – was a name to watch.

He found five other names that fitted that pattern, boarding alone at Delhi, no luggage checked in to the hold. That was the real eliminator – after all, the man arrested on the hotel steps had no bag with him, and he was male and an adult. But none of these others had the name John anywhere concealed about them. He highlighted the names and packed the printouts away.

He turned on his Amstrad, a present to himself on his promotion to the major enquiry section, and began to type out his report summary. It began with the formal words always used at the top of a Customs submission: 'To the Commissioners: Gentlemen, I report . . .' and he started to type the names of the men he had left in custody in Fetter Lane. When he had entered the fifth name, Muazzam, he paused, and then on an impulse he wrote Nadim Janjoa.

The joy of the Amstrad is that you can make your mistakes with the least possible inconvenience. If he was wrong he could wipe it.

He started to type the report but almost immediately a thundering sound began on the stairs. Soon it was followed by shouts of pleasure, the house came alive. He knew there was no more work to be done till after bedtime and he turned towards his children.

Chapter 10

There were two hours before the judge in court three would be free to hear Scott's complaint against Judge Wrigley, so Scott had strolled along to the magistrates' court at the other end of the building to see what Tozer was doing.

He found the court and wandered in.

He had forgotten he was still in wig and gown and he caused a bit of a stir, as though some fabulous beast had strayed into a farmyard.

There were three magistrates, two men and a woman sitting next to each other in a row about four feet above everyone else. They were not lawyers, just worthy people who enjoyed being called Justice of the Peace, and they looked suitably puzzled at what was going on.

In front of and slightly below them sat the court clerk. The court was full. Facing the magistrates in the front row was a Crown Prosecution Service lawyer, almost obscured behind a pile of files. He was thumbing distractedly through the first one.

As he watched him Scott recognised the symptoms. The prosecutor knew not the slightest thing about any of these case files. He had probably only been given them ten minutes ago and as a result the selection of facts that he gave to the court would depend entirely upon which part of the file he chanced upon first.

The chairman of the magistrates swelled up. 'Mr Donkin,' he said – already Scott felt sorry for the prosecutor, pitying him his name – 'we're ready, we're waiting.'

Tozer sitting in the second row laughed out loud. The magistrates all looked towards him but by then Tozer had his back to them and was talking to his solicitor. It was Monty Bach.

Monty was sitting there in a heavy coat with huge scalloped astrakhan lapels. Scott had not seen such a thing before save in pre-war cartoons of capitalists climbing out of large motor cars. What could have brought Monty and Tozer to court?

'Mr Donkin?' the magistrate said again. The prosecutor had a Customs case in his hand. Scott could recognise it even from the back of the court by its different-coloured files. He was clearly unfamiliar with its layout, and was quite unable to find his way around. Why were the Crown prosecutors dealing with Customs' work? It never became clear.

Just to Scott's left there was a scuffling noise and into the dock along the side of the court there filed a group of five dispirited Pakistanis.

'Mr Donkin?' said the magistrate.

Donkin stood rooted to the spot, unable to locate the relevant part of the file.

Tozer stood up. 'If Mr Donkin is otherwise occupied perhaps I might mention my case, "Vespasian". Both Mr Bach' – Tozer bowed to his right, and Monty Bach half stood up, leering at the magistrates – 'and I have appointments elsewhere this afternoon. I myself am due at the DTI and I say that every moment before our case is called on is a valuable moment lost to the department.'

What he meant by this was not clear to the chairman of the

bench, although it was obviously perceived as a very potent threat.

The magistrate leant across and started a hurried conversation with the lady to his left. At that Monty Bach got up and started towards the bench with a file of documents.

Tozer suddenly spoke very loudly indeed, bringing the magistrates back, as though upon the command 'SIT!', to seated attention.

'Mr Vespasian has had these documents printed for his son and he would care to have you see them before his case is called.'

Tozer was standing facing slightly to one side, as though he was addressing another audience, and Scott followed his glance. Then it became clear why he was there for £1000.

Behind him on the public benches sat a large gentleman in a flashing suit. He had an unlit cigar between his teeth. This was Mr Vespasian, head of one of the largest property companies in East London. Scott had read that his son had been arrested for fire-bombing a competitor's pub. It must have been his son whom Scott had heard talking in the next-door cell downstairs.

At that moment, Mr Donkin, who had found his place, started speaking, 'Five defendants, they were all arrested at a hotel in Argyle. There was the owner, the desk clerk, and the other three, who the Crown say, sorry, the Customs say, are couriers. Fifteen kilos of heroin. Can that be right?'

He interrupted himself, he was now completely out of his depth and barely staying afloat. 'No, one point five kilos of heroin. We object to bail.'

He looked up, pleased to have got out the main points, only to be met by the chairman of the magistrates saying, 'Please, Mr Donkin! Mr Tozer is speaking.'

At that the clerk of the court got to his feet and began a hurried conversation with the magistrate.

Scott watched as the clerk shepherded the magistrates into dealing with the case that was in front of them.

Tozer was pushed back down in his seat and the smugglers' case continued.

No – it was decided – the incident did not happen in Argyle, it happened in the Argyle Hotel. At this there was much knowing laughter at the idea of the Elephant and Castle magistrates' court dealing with a Scottish case.

The defendants watched in amazement.

It was confirmed there were no applications for bail. The three couriers were remanded in custody and waived their right to come to court every week.

Scott looked at the men. All looked dispirited. Remarkably one of them was crying. Silently tears were pouring down his face. He looked at Scott, who stood there in his wig, not more than an arm's length from him. For a moment the man seemed about to speak, then a prison officer laid a hand on his arm and turned him away. 'Well, that's all right then,' said the clerk of the court.

This must have been the case where one of the couriers thought that the heroin balls were travel-sickness pills, the explanation that had caused Monty Bach such amusement.

Scott had at that time no way of knowing that this case was to cause him such trouble, and he forgot about the men as they left the court.

'Call Vespasian.'

As the occupants of the dock changed over, Donkin searched feverishly through the files. One of them fell to the floor and opened out like a flower.

Young Vespasian came in; Tozer got to his feet. 'You will know about this case, gentlemen, madam.' He turned to the lady magistrate. He simpered at her. The magistrates watched him blankly.

'We offer twenty-five thousand pounds bail on behalf of

the defendant, at an address near Harrogate with the defendant's relatives. The Crown have not yet produced the forensic report about the scene of the alleged arson that they said they would. So we renew the application for bail. We take grave exception to the prosecution's unconscionable delay.'

These last two words he drew out to their utmost length, until no one had the slightest doubt as to their meaning.

The magistrate, who ought to have said, 'Sit down and wait till it's your turn to speak, Mr Tozer,' did not do so. He spoke to Mr Donkin, 'Is this right?'

Mr Donkin did not have a clue. He turned to a wary, well-dressed man in a blue suit sitting behind him. 'I will call Chief Inspector Thomas,' he said.

Tozer took his opportunity. 'No, he will not,' he said, 'the Crown Prosecution Service always refuses to call officers to answer questions about bail when the defence requests it, they say they are responsible for the proceedings, so why should they be allowed to call police-officers to attempt to explain their own broken undertakings? They shuffle off their responsibility, I say.' He began to speak like a nineteenth-century alderman, and his hand slipped into his waistcoat pocket. 'Shuffle their responsibilities off, I say.'

Scott could see from where he was standing that Tozer was wearing a watch and chain; when had he taken to that?

This was too much for the magistrates. They beckoned the court clerk. The clerk had his back to them and of course could not see their distress. For a few moments the court was in suspended animation as the chairman tried to attract his attention.

Tozer again took the opportunity to dominate the proceedings. 'I ask my friend, can he produce the documents he so fulsomely promised the court?' He was almost singing.

Of course Mr Donkin hadn't fulsomely promised the court anything. He probably wasn't even there on the last occasion.

If the promise had been made, then someone else had made it.

The chairman looked up from his conference with the clerk. 'Do you have this report, Mr Donkin?'

Mr Donkin was prompted by the policeman. 'No,' he said. 'Why not?' There was silence.

The chief inspector leaned forward, but Donkin did not turn around. Scott recognised the paralysis that comes from complete loss of control. It had been induced by the overwhelming presence of Tozer and the superb astrakhan coat behind him.

'This court will accept the surety offered, twenty-five thousand pounds, an address in Harrogate. Please give us the full details, Mr Tozer. We will grant bail.'

Mr Vespasian had got his £1000 worth for his son.

Scott left the court before Tozer could speak to him, though as he turned at the door to bow to the court, Tozer's eyes flickered over at him. Tozer was continually aware of what was going on around him. Like a lizard.

Scott set off down the passages to court three to see the Perfect English Gentleman. He had already obtained the prosecution agreement, they did not object to his application for Masida's bail to be renewed. After all, Masida had been on bail for months before the trial.

If the other side weren't coming that meant that he would be able to see the judge alone. He might even get a drink.

Court three had already risen and there was only the usher cleaning out water jugs. She had the court file marked Masida.

'He'll see you immediately, I expect he wants to get home for his tea, poor dear,' she said, and took Scott up through the curtain to the judge's corridor and into his room.

Scott liked this judge. He was exactly what his nickname said he was. His formal, courteous manner even startled defendants, who sometimes thought he was teasing them. But he was not. He was just treating them like real people.

'Hello, Scott. My daughter was speaking of you yesterday.'

Scott had on occasion been out with his daughter and the judge approached him in an avuncular fashion as a consequence.

'I had remarked to her that I felt her attachment to the Green Party was a matter of concern, since I consider them no more than a front organisation for militant lesbianism, yet,' he paused, 'I also remarked to her that she had, sometimes to my regret, all too amply demonstrated that her inclinations did not lie in that direction. I nearly had occasion to mention you as an example.'

The Perfect English Gentleman had three daughters who looked after him. He was surrounded by women who loved him.

For a moment Scott saw in his mind's eye his own sister, dead now, leaning over the back of his father's armchair brushing his dark hair. How we are unable to deal with the images that pierce us to the heart and yet we carry them with us all the time.

'Well, what's Johnny been up to now?' said the judge. 'What are you complaining about?'

Johnny Wrigley was the bane of the Perfect English Gentleman's life, sending him memos, documents and forms to be filled in, continually giving him directions on how to be a judge – directions that he totally disregarded.

'Well, I think he has perhaps made a mistake about a bail matter.' Scott was cautious, careful not to upset the fund of goodwill by any direct criticism.

'But how can I help? If he has made a decision, I can't overrule him, can I?'

'It may be you can, Judge, since he has not really made a decision – or at least not properly. He was feeling ill. He went home and unfortunately neglected to ask the defence to address him when he remanded the defendant in custody in the middle of the trial. If I didn't address him then he didn't really make a proper decision at all, did he? So really there's nothing to be overruled, just an absence of decision.'

Scott was trying not to confuse himself as well as the judge. 'The judge remanded my client in custody as he, the judge, that is, was running out of the car park.'

The Perfect English Gentleman thought for a moment. 'The Crown are happy with your application, are they? Well, that's OK then. Will this annoy Wrigglers, I wonder? I rather think it might. Give the chap bail. Now how about something to drink?'

Drink was their downfall. For about three-quarters of an hour Masida's file lay on the judge's desk with the bail form while the judge told Scott what he thought about things. But then the mood broke. 'God, look at the time!' Scott said. 'I've got to get to the cells.'

But by the time he managed to get downstairs the prison van had gone and Masida had been taken away for the weekend.

'How could you take him? You haven't even got a warrant of commitment. He got bail,' Scott said to the warder.

'We didn't know that and we couldn't just leave him here, could we?'

This was true.

'And we certainly couldn't let him out without someone saying we could, not your Mr Masida.'

This was equally true. 'Where's he gone?'

'It will be on the commitment warrant, let's go and look.' They walked down the long corridor underneath the court. On either side, rooms, interview rooms and offices stood open. In one there was a table with three or four prison officers sitting around playing cards.

'Not everybody seems to have gone,' Scott remarked.

The gaoler looked at him. 'You don't know the half of it, sir,' he said.

There wasn't really any answer to that. It seemed to Scott that the prison service operated on an entirely different set of rules from the rest of humanity.

The gaoler examined a large book. 'There's no warrant of commitment for him.'

'Of course not,' said Scott. 'I've just been trying to tell you, he got bail. He got it from the Perfect English Gentleman in court three.'

'Well, if there is no warrant of commitment there will be no record of where he went. We only keep a record of those we are meant to have.'

As an admission of false imprisonment, Scott doubted whether this could be improved.

'Well, are you sure you have got him?'

'Oh, we've got him all right. You don't think we'd let your Mr Masida go without a bail form, properly marked. We may be slow, Mr Scott, but we're not that slow.'

The gaoler was a family man; Scott knew him fairly well. He also had daughters, and a son who was a lawyer in a City firm of solicitors. In his spare time the gaoler made wooden stands for barristers to lean on when addressing juries. He was a fair and kind man who knew that most of the people he dealt with would not give him the time of day for his fairness.

He was mildly amused by Scott's distress.

'Where is he, do you think?'

'Well, it won't be Brixton, I know they are full tonight. It could be Belmarsh, but it's more likely to be one of the holding cells. That's whichever police station is not full. Then it's a police problem. Nothing to do with us.'

'How do I find out?'

'Well, now you're asking. I don't think you'll be able to.'

The phone rang, the officer answered it. 'Yes,' he said. He

listened for a moment. Then he shouted to another officer in the next room, 'Harrogate police on the phone, Chief. They've had the surety for Vespasian signed, could we tell the police room?'

He turned back to Scott. 'Your real problem is that there is no commitment warrant. Without that there is no record of his being anywhere. Technically we don't have him at all. If he wanted to leave now we'd have no power to stop him.'

'Is someone going to tell him that?'

'I don't suppose they are,' said the gaoler.

Scott went back upstairs to a telephone. He had no 10p pieces and by now there was no one to get change from.

The government department which installs phones at court had decided that they weren't going to subsidise lawyers, so the phones didn't accept cards, nor, he discovered, could you make reverse-charge calls from them.

How do people in films manage? They never seemed to have this sort of problem.

He got the car and drove down to the Old Kent Road and found a phone which worked and took cards; he rang the solicitors. Their answerphone said that they had gone home for the weekend and please could he ring on Monday?

As he stood in the phone booth he realised that he had taken the court file with him. It contained an original exhibit. Now he would have to go back to the court. If he lost the exhibit then Wrigley would probably put him in jail for contempt, or worse.

Of course when he got there the court was closed. He rang chambers. Everyone had gone. Masida was going to have to stay in prison, whichever one it was.

Scott went home. Where he lived was rather smart, but shabby smart, a little flat behind Sloane Square. The best thing about it, other than where it was, was the twenty-four-hour porter service.

Bill was on duty. 'Hello, Mr Scott,' he said. 'You been in court today?'

Bill was big, boney and old. He had a great grinning face, a frayed jacket and huge baggy trousers.

He'd told Scott with pride that when he was in Aden he was the only member of the regiment to have to apply for the special long shorts. 'They had them for those who have long peckers, Mr Scott.'

This was a piece of information about the ways of the world that Scott kept to himself, it might come in useful one day.

Bill climbed on his old bike to set off for Battersea, his knees sticking out, moving so slowly that it was a wonder he stayed upright. 'Simms is downstairs,' he said, 'he'll be up in a while.' Simms was the porter who lived in the basement.

Scott went up to his flat. With any luck he would not need to speak to anyone save Simms till Monday. He turned on the Grateful Dead. They whined and twanged into his head. Bill was gurning on his bike back to Battersea. Simms was downstairs. What was Masida doing?

The odd thing was that no one need ever know that his carelessness had got Masida locked up for the weekend. Indeed, it could be said quite fairly that it wasn't his fault. Masida ought not to have been taken. The prison staff should have checked with the clerk. The clerk would have checked and discovered who had the file, and that it was still with the judge.

The evening wore on. Scott still had thirty-eight assorted bottles of wine, bought when the smart wine shop on the corner went bust. He opened one that didn't have a label. The flat was warming up. It was dark outside.

The parade ground outside his window – he overlooked a barracks – was empty. It was beginning to rain. The lights shone on the dark asphalt, the row of houses at the back of the square began to stand out in black silhouette against the London sky.

Once, years ago, at school, he had seen a film of the life of Toulouse-Lautrec, and a hand – Toulouse-Lautrec's hand – had filled in just such a silhouette, black against orange, on a canvas he was painting. It was the only real thing in the artificial film. The memory of this assured, precise hand sketching in the firm, strong image had remained with him like a reassurance. He stood and watched night fall over London.

Gradually the wine took the edge off the day. He felt hungry.

Chapter 11

How Emily finally got rid of Plunkett.

He had driven her back from court. 'How about a drink?' he had said, and without waiting for an answer from her he had pulled up at the back entrance of The Savoy Hotel.

'The American Bar will still be under way,' he said. He pushed through the swing doors, leaving her to follow. For a moment she might have been able to break away and walk off and he would not have seen her go, but he was a senior member of the chambers and she couldn't risk offending him.

She followed him into the hotel. The back entrance had the same atmosphere of nylon and heat as any suburban house, but as they made their way up the staircase it changed and the calm space of money greeted them.

Plunkett headed across the hall and into the bar. It was packed. Couples sat perched like decorations on banquettes set against the wall facing outward in to the room.

On one bench immediately facing the door was a huge man; Emily recognised him, an actor, famous for his advertisements. His vast stomach seemed to threaten to topple him over if he leaned forward. He sat still and looked out at everybody through his glasses.

She was surprised to see Plunkett nod at him.

'Fat bugger,' said Plunkett as they moved away, then, 'What will you drink?'

Plunkett drank Martinis and they talked about Emily's attempts to get a place at the Bar.

'I don't think I can help you myself, I can't take you on,' he said, 'anyway, you're far too —' he broke off at the word beautiful, thought for a moment and substituted 'attractive'.

'The wife.' He stopped, one didn't say 'the wife' any more. 'My wife wouldn't approve.' He thought he had given her a compliment but he noticed that she didn't seem pleased.

'What's your wife got to do with it?' said Emily.

'My wife is a most intelligent woman,' he said. It wasn't an exact answer but it seemed right.

The Martinis were very strong and he waved for another plate of little toast things. They might give him a Marmite one, sometimes they put one out for him. He remembered lemon curd. No lemon curd here, wrong time of day, although if you asked for it maybe you could get it. It was amazing how many thoughts could go through your head while you were actually speaking to someone.

'My wife is a most intelligent woman,' he repeated. 'She is an adviser. She advises people. I have no doubt she would advise me not to take you as a pupil.'

He had made this joke while talking with Henry, the girl's pupil master, the previous day. They had both laughed 'neahh, neahh', emphasising the absurdity of it; he could still see Henry's throat shaking. But the joke didn't work this time.

He became serious. He realised that the girl might see him as what was called sexist, a sexist – what was it? – a sexist thing. That was unfair.

He knew all the arguments. He understood them. He was able to use them himself. What annoyed him amidst all this clamour for rights, blacks, women, was that there was no understanding of the difficulties of being a middle-aged man. That wasn't so easy, you know, there were things to be said about that. One day he would do the saying.

What he did say. He explained himself, 'I'm married. If I spend most of my time at work with a young woman, it'd cause trouble. Now that's not me being difficult, that's my wife.' He was being very reasonable, he thought; it wasn't him being ridiculous, it was his jealous wife. He was saving this girl problems.

'Anyway,' he changed the subject, 'do you really want to do criminal law? Isn't matrimonial work, or children's law easier? That's what people do, isn't it? That's what girls, you, I mean, women members of the Bar do, isn't it?'

She didn't reply to that. He felt very relaxed and more confident of himself now.

Another Martini arrived. 'How do you get on with Henry, then? Is he a good pupil master? I think he's a good sort myself.'

As he spoke a huge shadow fell over them. They looked up and she saw that the actor had moved over to them from his bench and was about to speak. 'Douglas,' the actor said, 'Douglas, we must speak.'

Plunkett's face was slack with drink. He looked at the actor amazed. The fat man looked around for somewhere to sit.

Emily saw her chance, 'I have to go anyway, you can sit here,' and she was on her feet.

The actor subsided into her place, almost bouncing Plunkett from the bench on to the floor. 'Douglas, I have a part as a barrister,' he said, 'and I have to talk to the real thing.'

Plunkett felt better. His mouth opened to speak. It was as though a button had been pressed. Noises started to come out.

Emily was able to move away unnoticed.

Maybe the fat actor would have been better talking to that Scott, she thought, you don't get much more real than that.

* * *

Evening was drawing in. She had been in the bar for two hours and the light and dark of the street came as a sudden transformation from the white afternoon which they had left when they entered. The streets were wet and the reflected lights from the shops and buses gleamed on the dark road. The sky was still light but gave out no light.

Above her, as she walked towards Trafalgar Square, huge flocks of starlings, thousands of them, twisted and turned to order, the fold of their turns rippling through their dark mass. They settled in and around the square and then for no reason rose again and dipped and soared in the growing darkness.

As she approached the square she saw the crosspiece of Nelson's sword standing out rudely, just as it had been described in *Under the Net*. She stood where they had stood looking at it.

A bus swept past her and she crossed the road to the centre of the square past the huge column. On her right was London's smallest police station, in the pillar of a lamp.

She remembered the tales of London that her father used to tell her, they had seemed permanent when she had been told them; over in that theatre there, proof that there was farce at both ends of Whitehall; just up the road was where he had bought cartridges and his boots had been made at the end of the street, he had the same size feet as Disraeli. She still had the lasts.

Over to her left the lions lay at the base of the column with their paws stretched out like dogs. When the sculptor had realised his mistake – cats' legs don't work like dogs', they have to turn inwards – he had committed suicide. Or was that wrong, wasn't it the man who had designed the Royal Courts of Justice? He went mad, didn't he?

'Hi.' Two young tourists stopped her. 'Do you know where we can get a drink?'

She turned instinctively to point to the pub at the bottom of

St Martin's Lane, and then they said, 'Would you like to come with us?'

For a moment she wondered what it would be like. Two young backpackers. Eighteen, nineteen? An evening of drinking lager. But she politely refused and made her way up Haymarket and over to Jermyn Street. On the right was the hairdressers, you could still have a barrister's wig made up there. Where had the Turkish bath been? The one Dr Watson had used when Holmes saw that his bootlaces had been tied in a different way.

Past Simpsons'. The man who owned it was a doctor, wasn't he? Fancy giving up being a doctor in order to run a shop. Strange choice. Past Floris, they had lovely big wooden jars of soap. She had once nearly given one to a friend's sister, but then didn't.

Left down into St James's Square and then turn right to the London Library. This was once the centre of the world, her father had said. At the door there was the umbrella that seemed to have been there ever since she had been given her life membership. The quiet of the downstairs room folded her in. She made her way up the stairs to the first floor where the magazines were laid out.

In one of the deep chairs she recognised another member of the Bar; he nodded at her but wouldn't meet her glance for more than a moment. She picked up a copy of *The Literary Review* and went to sit near the window.

Below her the square grew blacker. The lights round the green in the middle began to form a necklace of bright points. A cab drew up to the club next door and an elderly man got out. A porter came down the stairs to help him.

It could have been a scene from Conrad's *Heart of Darkness*: ' "And this also," said Marlow suddenly, "has been one of the dark places of the earth." ' For him it was the centre of the world too, but she wasn't sitting on a boat on the Thames reach watching a pipe glowing in the dark – but Conrad, he must have used this room, mustn't he?

The idea intrigued her. Had Conrad been a member of the London Library? – he must have been. It gave her something to do; she made her way to the shelves at the back of the building.

Biology, biography, she picked her way through the bookstacks, careful not to catch her heels in the metal slats. As she climbed to each new level she turned on the next light and turned off the one behind her, until she moved through the dark building like a pool of lamplight. Her shoe scraped against the metal.

She picked out a book and smelt it. Her father had done that, too. He was weighing on her mind. His books must be here, though she had never gone to look at them. Did anyone read them now? Thrillers date so quickly.

The book smelt sweet, it was made of thick paper with an almost cloth-like texture. It had been rebound in London Library colours – she turned to the spine, *The Other Bundle*, Lord Shaw of Dunfermline, *Memoirs of a lawyer*.

Could a piece of work summing up a man's life be so disregarded? How forgotten a life becomes almost immediately. Who but she remembered her father?

Four storeys below her in the metal racks a light came on and then was turned off. 'Good night,' said a voice. Another voice replied, 'Good night.'

She could see down through the metal walkways, and as she watched, momentarily she saw a face look up at her. He couldn't have seen her, could he? To him she would only have been a patch of light or a flash of colour.

Then she heard steps come back into the tower of bookstacks, a level nearer her she saw a light flash on and off and heard footsteps moving up towards her level.

She put the book she was holding back on the shelf and

moved towards the window. As she passed the switch she turned the light off. She stopped and listened, mainly she heard her own breath.

She was in complete darkness now, lit only by the faint glow of the night from the windows. If she looked back into the stacks she could see nothing.

Unless the man, she assumed it was a man, had seen her, he wouldn't know what part of the shelf section she was in.

He was still coming up and she calculated that he was at the other side of the passageway. She quickly made her way towards the nearest staircase and picked her way down it. If he stood at the end of the stack opposite the stairs then he would see her clearly outlined against the window. But once she was below him she could easily disappear into the darkness of the shelves towards the centre of the building.

She reached the bottom of the stairs and paused. Was the sound above her or on her level?

Then her heart leapt. It was astonishing, for a moment she could see herself from the outside and her heart had actually seemed to rise up into her throat; a foot scraped immediately above her, she looked up. Close as they were to the windows she could see the leg of a man standing no more than eighteen inches above her head.

She stood still, astounded that he could not hear the blood pounding in her ears. He must hear, mustn't he? Any second he would come down. In here, in the London Library. Should she scream now or only when he started pulling at her clothes?

There was a whispering noise and she realised that the man was speaking to himself. He was reciting something, what was it?

'*Quod fuit esse, quod est . . .*' Jesus Christ, he's talking Latin!

She wasn't going to let herself be raped by some muttering moron reciting Latin to himself. She snapped the complete set of lights on. There was a gasp of astonishment above her as the whole of her level became flooded with light. The footsteps retreated away down the metal shelving, she could see the soles of his shoes.

For a moment she stood, and then turned to the books. There it was, right next to where she was standing, *A Life of Conrad*.

Oh well, at least she'd found her book. She pulled it out and returned to the warmth of the chair by the window. The barrister she vaguely knew was still in the armchair. Had it been him following her? He didn't even look up.

Perhaps she need only raise an eyebrow at him and they could go off to the Latin section together. Sex in the book-stacks? Mills and Boon?

She need only kill a couple of hours before she could make her meet with the dealer.

Night fell.

Chapter 12

The men had been watching the young Asian cry for some time. He was young and looked even younger than he was since this was an adult holding cell. Certainly his body had not yet begun to fill out with the strength and weight that the early twenties bring.

They were annoyed by his crying and began to show their annoyance, at one point one of them roughly pushed him aside in order to reach over for a newspaper.

If he had not attracted the attention of their anger he might not have had to suffer what he did.

The cell door opened. 'You're going to be here some time,' said a head appearing around it, 'there are no more admissions allowed tonight at Brixton. You'll be sleeping here.'

They sat doing nothing. Then one of the men spoke, it was Masida, 'If you don't shut up, I'll have you.' Masida was angry at having his bail cut short so unfairly by the bastard judge.

Muazzam, lying on the top bunk, couldn't follow what was happening, but he could certainly understand the tone of voice. Again there were stares at the boy and the same annoyance. The two men sat side by side.

Suddenly the light went out, but the cell was still lit from the courtyard. After a moment the two men stood up together and took hold of the boy's arms. One of them bent him forward. He was surprised. At first he did not resist, but then he started to struggle. By now it was too late, they were far too strong for him. One of the men had him by the elbows, with the weight of his shoulder bending the boy back, the other had him by the waist.

There was a tearing sound; Muazzam could see that the boy's trousers were being pulled away from him. The younger man kicked but there was no resisting the sheer power of the stronger men.

His trousers were thrown into a corner, he was wearing nothing underneath. His shirt was dragged up and he was turned on his back. His face was wide-eyed and soundless. One of the men sat on the floor behind him, holding him back by his arms, a knee in the small of his back forcing the boy's groin upwards as though for some obscene inspection.

Masida grinned and took hold of the boy's penis. He started pulling and stroking it as the boy struggled trying to move away. Then to Muazzam's amazement the young boy began to calm and he saw that he was slowly coming to an erection. One of the men spoke to the other. They began to move the boy up and down. Muazzam could see his face, the boy's mouth opened and his eyes widened. His stomach rose and fell slowly and rhythmically, with a small jerk and a gasp at the end of every up movement. The man at his back loosened his grasp and ran his hands down to the boy's buttocks, pressing and stroking.

From Masida's half-open mouth there dropped a sliver of saliva. Then the young man came to a shuddering climax, unable to control his body, which shook like a wire.

Muazzam turned away, he could only hear the slow moaning below and the rocking of the men. Then he looked again.

At that moment the boy was turned over. A mattress was

dragged from the bed and he was placed across it, he lay there with his buttocks in the air. He realised what was going to happen and shouted, only to have his mouth stopped by the man holding him. Then both men began to undo their own trousers. They moved towards the boy, one at his mouth, one at his buttocks, and Muazzam turned in his bed and faced the cold wall.

He thought of the vivid colours of his village and the fluid motion of his wife's sari.

He listened to the movement below, on one occasion there was a cry. Then there was quiet, save for the gasps of effort. After a few minutes he heard the man who was on the top bunk opposite him climb down. He had clearly decided to join in. There was laughter, a grunt of pain and Muazzam realised it was starting again.

The next morning they were taken to Brixton prison, each contained in a separate compartment of a large white van. Muazzam had tried to speak to the boy in his own language, but had received only a vacant stare.

Again Muazzam repeated, 'I saw what happened.' The boy looked at him. He said nothing, it would have been better if no one had seen.

At the prison they were signed in, and Muazzam put his cross where the warder stuck his finger. They were paraded naked before a doctor. He spoke to each of the men before Muazzam, but did not look at nor speak to Muazzam. The doctor looked at the Asian boy, put his hand on the boy's head, pulled him round, touched his buttocks, and turned to the prison officer and said something. The prison officer nodded and the doctor passed on to the next.

'I think we've had another rape in a holding cell,' the doctor said later to the officer in charge of the landing. 'Do you want me to report it?'

'Is the victim reporting it?' he was asked in reply. When the doctor said no, the prison officer laughed and said, 'How do you expect the governor to believe it, then?'

'I suppose you're right,' said the doctor.

Muazzam was put in a cell with two young men. They did not speak to him. He was given a card and an explanatory document in several languages. He could not read any of them.

He sat on the bunk. After about three hours one of the young men in his cell attacked the other one, who, being bigger, managed to force him to the ground where he kicked him in the side of the head.

For a long time the young man lay still on the ground. In the early hours of the next morning some men in uniform took him away. Two hours later they came as a group and dragged the other man out of the cell. Muazzam never saw either of them again.

He remained alone in the cell till the evening, then three new men came in. One was Pakistani and spoke Muazzam's language, though badly. Even though he could speak to Muazzam he didn't bother. He had been arrested with two friends and wanted to be like them, not like Muazzam.

He laughed occasionally at him, but he mostly lay on the bed. The men passed the time farting and then laughing loudly.

Then the three men left. Muazzam never saw them again. He was moved. He found himself in a cell with three Pakistanis. All spoke his language. The silence had ended.

'What are you here for?' said one.

'I came to measure clothes,' said Muazzam.

'But why have you been arrested?'

One of the other men was watching the conversation. 'He'll be a smuggler,' he said. 'Cocaine, or more likely heroin.'

Muazzam said nothing as they spoke about him. 'When do I get out of here,' he said.

The men laughed. How long? That depended on what he had done. Ten years said another.

Muazzam was not sure that he had heard properly. 'Ten years,' he repeated.

'Maybe. Depends on how much you brought in.'

Muazzam started rocking on his heels. Ten years was inconceivable. Was it already decided? He assumed it was. He watched the other men. They laughed and talked, although sometimes they just sat quietly. Are they here for ten years? After a long time he asked one of them why they were there. 'We attacked a group of whites on the Penfold estate and the police took us all away,' he was told.

How long would they be here? About two months before their trial.

He asked, 'Did I have a trial?'

'Depends which court you were in. Which court were you in? In the magistrates' court or in the Crown Court?'

They argued about that between themselves. If he was in Brixton it must be before trial, they agreed. One of them, the friendliest of them, turned to him. 'In the court, how were they dressed, was there a man with a wig on his head?' He explained what he meant.

Muazzam thought back and then pictured the court. 'Yes, yes,' he was pleased that he remembered something that he could identify, 'there was a man like that. Something on the top of his head. There was.'

'Well, you've been in the Crown Court, you've been sentenced then,' was the reply, 'ten years, no doubt about it.' He laughed again.

So it was correct. Muazzam reflected on it. Ten years. There was no way he could even think about it, he lay on the bed. Then he thought about it. The cell began to rock, he felt himself falling, before he hit the ground he began to scream.

* * *

'Is he a danger to himself, doctor?' asked the officer in charge of the landing.

The doctor thought for a moment. 'I don't think so,' he said, 'although of course I can't ask him, since he doesn't seem to speak English.'

Chapter 13

The next morning at about six thirty the phone rang and Gregory answered it, straight out of his sleep.

The voice didn't wait for introductions. 'They're probably going to deport the smart man today,' said Merv Stockwood.

'What!'

'I rang the immigration office to ask how soon they wanted witness statements about his arrest and they told me they didn't.'

Merv Stockwood was very conscientious. Without his phone call the immigration authorities would probably have sent the man home and Customs wouldn't have heard till too late.

'They said that they didn't need statements since they were not going to prosecute.'

Gregory was amazed. 'But they said they would.'

'Apparently they don't think they have enough evidence. They can't prove he entered illegally. There was also something about not being able to charge him with actually being here illegally, because when they found him he had just come out of custody and that makes the proof that he is here illegally even more difficult.'

He went on, 'They said that if they proceeded they would

have to give him bail, and then he would have been able to draw social security payments and no doubt he would disappear. So they gave him the option of going where he wanted to.'

'That can't be right. What about our agreement?'

'The damn duty officer said that was not his concern. He had nothing from their head office to confirm it.'

'Bloody people!' said Gregory.

'Well, anyway, they're going to release him any moment. You better think what to do.'

'What I have to do is get him back,' said Gregory. He jumped out of bed.

Stockwood had been working on a night shift, and it was only by a lucky chance that he had contacted the immigration duty officer. Gregory was going to have to move quickly or they'd lose the smart man.

The immigration service infuriated Gregory. They seemed to operate without regard to anybody else's concerns or worries. Dear God, he thought, what must it be like to be on the receiving end of their smug indifference?

He left the house at a run, into his car. Bentley holding centre was not so far away and he would certainly get there before it was really operating.

As he pulled out of the drive he was already trying to phone the Customs lawyers. From the bend in the road he saw his curtain twitch and caught a momentary glimpse of his wife's face.

Of course the legal department wouldn't be in, so he phoned Merv Stockwood at Fetter Lanc. 'It's me. I'm on the way to Bentley now. I need an arrest warrant, or at least an application for one on the surveyor's desk. In the name of Nadim Janjoa.'

'Where did you get that name from?'

'There was a Nadim Janjoa on the aeroplane sitting behind Muazzam.'

'And on that you're going to arrest him? That's not enough. Why not arrest the people sitting either side of him as well, just for fun?'

'Because they weren't found on the steps of the Argyle, with no identification at all – which means it was got rid of. They weren't, our man was.'

Gregory corrected the car on a bend. He slowed down. Five minutes was not going to make that much difference.

'How do you know the man we found is a Nadim Janjoa?'

'I don't know how I know, but I know. I'll spell the name for you. Then you get to Heathrow, I'll go there afterwards.'

Bentley is run by civilians not the prison service and is where people arrested under the immigration laws are detained. Although run by civilians, the centre emulates the prison service – at its worst.

Gregory's first problem was that he did not have the name of the man he was looking for. Neither of course did Bentley, since the arrested man had given no name, neither to them nor to the Customs.

'Without a name I can't even begin to process your coming in,' said the man on the gate.

'But the whole point about him is that he has no name.' Gregory was beginning to get angry. 'It's the reason he's here at all. It can't be the first time you've had that problem. You must have a section for people with no names.'

'I'm sure we have, but without a name I can't even start looking. The computer says "enter name".'

'Well, try Janjoa, then.' He spelt it out. The gatekeeper turned on the computer.

'No, no Janjoa. Nor Nadim neither, I'm afraid.'

'Are you able to look at detainees by date of arrest on that thing?' Every time Gregory spoke he had to lean down and speak to the guard upwards and sideways through the thickened glass.

'Yes, I think I can, now I've got it going. Here we are. Two people taken in on Thursday evening. Loona doc Wadi and A. N. Other.'

'Well, I'd like to have a word with Mr A. N. Other,' said Gregory, marvelling at the persistence of school culture.

'You can't, he's gone.'

'Where?'

'Home,' said the gatekeeper, 'an hour ago. At his own request and at the taxpayer's expense. Pakistan.'

Gregory headed for Heathrow.

There were two Karachi flights a day. If he was lucky, Janjoa – what name would he use? – would be on the afternoon flight not the early one.

On the way to the airport he rang Stockwood again. 'Check which flight has received an immigration deportee, it's either the nine a.m. or the afternoon flight. I'm going to talk to Janjoa before he can leave, and depending on what he says I'll take him off. Leave a message at departure for me.'

Gregory pulled into the restricted area outside the terminal and flashed his warrant card at the traffic warden who was on to him instantly.

'I'm on business and it's urgent. If you want to tow it, then tow it,' he said. 'We won't pay, and my office will demand a report from you for interfering with a Customs operation.'

Asking a traffic warden for a report was the easiest way of making them look the other way; she backed off.

'I'll get someone out to move it as soon as I can,' he shouted over his shoulder as he ran into the terminal.

At passport control there was no trouble, the officer recognised him. As he came into the departure lounge he saw that the nine thirty-five departure for Karachi was boarding, he also saw his code number flashing with a message.

He ran to gate twenty-eight where, as he turned into the lounge, he saw the check-in closing. There was no time for the message now, he had better go straight to the plane, and he dashed past the barrier flashing his warrant card and into the tunnel.

At the end he could see the last stragglers waiting to be shown in by the cabin staff. 'I need to speak to the chief stewardess,' he was panting with effort.

It was an American plane, and despite his sexist mistake of talking about stewardesses, he thanked his stars for it. Americans are much more able to deal with the unusual.

He looked down the jumbo jet, almost all the seats were taken.

What was he going to do?

Until now, save for the traffic warden, he had not behaved outside normal procedures. But he was about to take someone off an aeroplane, and not an English one. To keep a jumbo jet on the ground in London costs, when he last heard, £45 a minute. A delay leading to losing a take-off slot could cost thousands of pounds. And on what evidence could he take the man off? He had none. He didn't fancy justifying himself to the commissioners. What could he say . . . ? 'I was acting on a hunch.' It was a depressing thought.

'Yes,' the cabin staff answered his question, 'we have a Pakistani national who is being deported, he has no documentation. He is sitting there, row H3. Be quick, please, we leave in seven minutes.'

The stewardess looked at him. She would help him, he thought.

He appealed to her, 'Hey, I have a problem. I need to get that man to say his name. I need to hear him say it. I have evidence that a man called Janjoa is involved with importing heroin and I believe that's him.'

The girl, no, not a girl, the woman watched him. She rather approved of what she saw, a lean, hard-looking man, soft Glasgow accent.

'Yes,' she said after a pause, 'I can help. Does he know you?'

'Probably not – dressed as I am.' Gregory suddenly became aware of his clothes, old jeans, a sweater and an old jacket. For a moment he saw again the look in people's eyes when he had demanded things of them this morning. He understood their reaction now.

He followed the stewardess, and busied himself apparently settling into a vacant seat behind Janjoa.

'Excuse me, sir,' the stewardess spoke to Janjoa, and in response Janjoa's eyes swivelled up to the stewardess. He did not move his body. It was the gesture of someone used to transferring his attention momentarily to a servant.

'We will have a problem at the stopovers. Unfortunately we will not be able to allow you to leave the plane, since you have no escort, no papers. May I ask, did you have a ticket when you came to this country? Is there a reference to a ticket, or even a name that we can put in the computer files?'

She spoke softly; gaining his confidence, openly demonstrating to Janjoa that she intended that what she said would not be overheard by the other passengers.

'I have a computer terminal available. We can interrogate the switchboard in Karachi. If there is a reference on it then we can allow you to leave the plane when we arrive there unannounced.'

Janjoa watched her. Her American accent encouraged his growing feeling of security.

She paused. 'If we have no reference then we are bound to announce your arrival, so that the local authorities will certainly find out the circumstances under which you have arrived.'

Again she paused, before producing the phrase that clinched the argument, 'This is a service we offer.'

Janjoa stood up. Gregory busied himself, opening the overhead locker, moving other people's bags about.

'I had an open ticket, bought six days ago. I bought it at Janjoa's Travel, Karachi.' He was speaking slowly and quietly. 'My name is Nadim Janjoa. The ticket agency will confirm that the ticket was bought for cash. My family can meet me at Karachi.'

That was enough to arrest him. The name fitted, he could prove he had travelled with Muazzam. Gregory turned away from the locker. 'Hello, Mr Janjoa,' he said.

Janjoa straightened up, he looked shocked.

'I said I'd visit you, didn't I? Please come with me, we can't allow you to leave. Say nothing for a moment, please.'

He led Janjoa off the plane. He passed the cabin staff and said thank you to the woman who had helped him.

'See you again,' he said.

'I wish,' she said.

That surprised him and he looked back at her to catch her look.

At the door of the aircraft he saw Stockwood, who said, 'Did you get my message? The surveyor says you have no grounds for an arrest.'

'I have now,' said Gregory.

Gregory took Janjoa back to Customs headquarters and then went to his office. The prisoner was being entered into the custody records system downstairs as Gregory rang up the surveyor and told him he had taken Janjoa off the plane.

The surveyor was a man who put paperwork and proper operating methods before everything.

No, said Gregory, the plane had not been delayed for one minute. Yes, he said, he had already done all the paperwork at Heathrow dealing with the airport authorities.

The machinery had had to be put into motion backwards to cope with someone coming back out of the exit channels. Any move in an investigation created a bow wave of paperwork.

It was only then that the surveyor asked what evidence

Gregory thought he had to arrest Janjoa. When he was told, he wasn't over-impressed. 'You think that's enough?'

'Yes,' said Gregory, stopping there.

He said nothing more. He knew that the surveyor hadn't the grasp of the case to be any more enquiring than that. And he was right.

'Oh,' was the final response. 'Put it in the report then.'

Gregory put the phone down and then notified the duty solicitor that there was an arrested prisoner to be seen.

Monty Bach was the duty solicitor. Gregory groaned when he saw the name, but he was bound by the roster and he had no good reason to risk disregarding it as he had with Muazzam. So he rang the firm.

It was Saturday morning, but Monty was there – probably avoiding his wife, thought Gregory, who had heard the stories. Yes, he would come and would be there in about an hour. Gregory arranged for Monty to be admitted downstairs.

'I can tell you, Mr Janjoa is not going to say anything. Yes, of course I would like to be present when Mr Gregory interviews him,' said Monty the moment he arrived.

The interview began with Monty breathing heavily in the background.

'Please introduce yourself, Mr Janjoa.'

Janjoa looked at Monty. Monty nodded. 'You can say your name.'

Gregory recited the introduction: 'Present here are Paul Gregory, Mervyn Stockwood, both investigation officers from Customs and Excise investigation department; Mr Janjoa and Montgomery Bach, Mr Janjoa's solicitor. Please identify yourself for the benefit of the tape recording, Mr Bach.'

Monty Bach said that he was present, and added that he had advised his client to say nothing until both of them knew precisely what all of this was about.

'Thank you very much, Mr Bach,' said Gregory.

116

'Now, Mr Janjoa, you have been arrested for being knowingly concerned in the importation of drugs. One and a half kilos of heroin were imported into this country last Tuesday by three men. We say they are couriers. Is it correct that you travelled on the same plane that they did, that is a PIA flight arriving at six thirty-five a.m. at terminal three, Heathrow?'

'I have been advised by my solicitor that I need say nothing and I would be foolish to disregard his advice.' Janjoa spoke with only a slight accent.

Where did he go to school? thought Gregory to himself. Was it in this country?

'Mr Janjoa, we can prove that a man of your name travelled from Pakistan on that flight, sitting right behind one of the couriers, a Mr Muazzam.'

'I have been advised by my solicitor that I need say nothing and I do not wish to disregard his advice.'

'Mr Janjoa, you were originally arrested on the steps of the Argyle Hotel in Earl's Court. Had you travelled to that address with the three couriers who were there?'

'I have been advised by my solicitor . . .'

'Mr Janjoa, when you were arrested on the previous occasion you refused to give us your name. Why was that?'

'That is not an acceptable question,' said Monty. 'If he was told he need say nothing, as he should have been, then he didn't have to say anything, and you can't ask him why he said nothing, nor can you imply that he ought to have answered.'

'OK, OK,' said Gregory, momentarily forgetting that he was being tape-recorded, letting his annoyance show.

'You're not going to say anything. We suggest to you, Mr Janjoa, that you were minding, that is, looking after the couriers, which is why you were on that plane.'

Janjoa said nothing.

Monty Bach was breathing so heavily that he was being picked up by the tape recorder. The interview ended.

They had started going through the rigmarole of signing off with names and timings for the tape when Monty Bach spoke, 'Muazzam, the man you say was a courier, thought the stuff he'd swallowed was for travel sickness. So if he didn't know he was carrying heroin he wouldn't have needed minding, would he?'

Monty was laying the ground for a defence, it was one of his trademark techniques.

Merv Stockwood looked at Gregory, Gregory looked at Stockwood and said to Monty, 'Where did you get that information from?'

'I overheard him say it,' said Monty Bach.

'Where?'

'In the magistrates' court cells at Elephant and Castle yesterday afternoon. I was there for my Mr Vespasian. I saw you upstairs, Mr Stockwood, in the magistrates' court, don't you remember?'

'You talked with Muazzam?'

Monty said nothing, only his heavy breathing continued.

'So Muazzam does speak English,' said Stockwood. 'All his behaviour here was an act. The police-officer was right.'

Chapter 14

The Monday after Masida had been locked up by mistake, Jeremy Scott got to court early. He had to explain, if he could, why it had happened.

But of course Mr Masida wasn't there.

'He's not on our list. We haven't got him,' said Charlie, the duty prison officer, refusing to open the cells' door.

He and Scott had to conduct the conversation through the keyhole, while Scott bobbed up and down looking at Charlie's face through the Plexiglas window.

'He's coming in off bail, isn't he?' Charlie said.

It was so obvious that this was bound to happen that Scott kicked himself for not foreseeing it.

If Masida hadn't been on the list of people who had been taken into custody from the court the previous Friday night, then he wouldn't be on the list of people who had to be brought back to the court this Monday.

'We can't let you in, Mr Scott. You've got no reason to come in here. You've got no one to see,' said Charlie gleefully.

Scott decided it was better to be a bit down-to-earth. 'Oh, piss off, Charlie, I've got to get in to speak to the chief about this cock-up and you're only holding things up.'

Charlie let him in. Scott went along the same corridors he had walked on Friday, the same prison officers were playing cards and sitting at the same tables.

'Look,' he said to the chief prison officer, 'you took him away from here on Friday evening. Remember I was here at about five, trying to get him out.'

'Oh yes, so you were,' said the CPO. 'Now, where's the warrant of commitment?'

'There isn't one,' Scott said. He should have said nothing.

'Well, if there isn't one then we haven't got him.'

Give me strength, Scott thought, but he didn't say it. 'But just a moment ago you remembered taking him away from the court on Friday. You saw me here on Friday evening complaining about it, didn't you?'

The CPO thought for a moment. 'Yes, we did. I remember now. Have a seat, Mr Scott, while I sort this out. This may take some time.'

Scott knew precisely what that meant. They would have to find out where Masida was. They would have to notify the prison holding him. That notification would have to come from an official source before he could be allowed to go anywhere. Then they would have to get an order for his transport. Next find the transport. Get him to court. Never mind that Masida actually being on bail could have caught a bus, he had to come in a spare prison van. There is no such thing as a spare prison van. They would all have to wait.

'No, I won't stay, thanks all the same, I had better get upstairs. I'll need to speak to fag-ash Gertie.'

Fag-ash Gertie was the list officer. Her power was so extensive that, Judge Wrigley apart, she, and she alone, could say what anybody could do. She, and she alone, could allow a case to be called on, if the defendant had not turned up, in order to release all parties waiting. More often than not she would refuse to do either and everybody would have to wait.

Everyone was terrified of her. Everyone that is save Judge Wrigley. Between them there was an armed truce.

Scott thought that it was sensible to let Gertie know of this cock-up as soon as possible, since she had the habit of blaming anybody for anything, and to leave her unaware of what was going on in her courts was the greatest sin. He also had another reason for seeing her.

He went upstairs to her room. 'I'm in court one,' he said, after he had stood in front of her, completely ignored for a minute or two. She started coughing. He took the opportunity of her inability to interrupt him and ploughed on. 'The prison service haven't brought Mr Masida.'

'He's on bail,' she coughed. Here we go again, he thought. 'No, he's not on bail, Wrigley remanded him in custody Friday lunchtime.'

'Where's the file,' she said, and started searching around in a pile beside her.

He slipped the file out from his bag, put it on her desk and picked it up again. 'Is this it?' he asked.

'Yes. That's it. How did it get there?'

Gertie dropped her cigarette into a waste-bin behind her where it smouldered.

At least he was off the hook for that one. What were the consequences if he had been found taking an exhibit home? God knows. It was probably an offence against the Official Secrets Act.

'There's no commitment warrant.'

'No.'

'There should be. Then he must be on bail.'

'Gertie, believe me,' he said, 'he is in custody.'

She looked at him for the first time. She knew him quite well; they had known each other for some time, ever since she once caught him sleeping overnight in the Bar mess when his wife had kicked him out.

'Oh, all right, I believe you. How long's it going to take to get him here?'

'Hours. I'll go to court and tell the judge. Shall I take the file?'

'No,' said Gertie, 'we've had a directive not to let the defence take files any more. There's been a clamp-down. They mustn't go anywhere. Pain of death.'

That wasn't a punishment he had expected, though, come to think of it, now she said it he wasn't surprised.

His Honour Judge Wrigley was already sitting in court when he got there. It wasn't half-past, but the judge had decided to come in nevertheless. The jury were coming in as well. Scott tried to get to his seat without any fuss, but he was noticed.

'Oh hello, Mr Scott. You've decided to favour us with your presence?' said Wrigley.

It was better not to respond. 'Your Honour,' he said, doing a little dip at him, just lifting himself off the seat.

'Well, where is everyone? Come in, come in,' the judge said, as some more jurors arrived at the door.

Prosecution counsel slid into his seat.

The lawyer from the Crown Prosecution Service slipped in behind him. There was a pause. Then Scott's solicitor's clerk, Bethany Thomas, wandered in.

She had not noticed that the judge was already sitting and started flapping her umbrella to get rid of the water. That done she took off her raincoat, spread it out and folded it up. She got out her thermos and put it on the floor. She opened her bag and pulled out the case file, her book, a magazine, a hairbrush, a little mirror and a bag of tissues.

Everyone in court followed her movements in horrified fascination as she slowly unwrapped herself.

Wrigley watched her like a snake.

'Hello, Mr Scott,' she said, noticing him in the seat in front, 'no sign of Mr Masida.'

Scott whispered slowly and urgently, 'Bethany. Sit down. Say nothing. Don't look up. Believe me.' That was twice in one day he had said 'believe me'. She sat down looking puzzled. Wrigley saw his prey vanishing.

'No Mr Masida, eh! Mr Masida not here?' he said loudly. What the effect on Bethany would have been without Scott's warning he feared to think, as it was her body jolted like an eel.

'Oh my God! I didn't see him,' she breathed.

'I am afraid he has not been brought to court,' Scott said rising.

'Brought to court! Brought to court! Do defendants need to be brought to court nowadays? Where will it end, ladies and gentlemen?' The judge turned to the jury. 'Perhaps defendants will want to be paid for loss of earnings, loss of burgling time, perhaps?

'He is on bail, is he not?' the judge continued. 'Pass me the file.'

The clerk of the court, not the same man as last week and who therefore probably knew nothing at all about the case, handed it up. 'Yes, he is on bail,' he said.

The judge was clearly pleased at the opportunity this offered him.

'Well, Mr Scott. We shall proceed whether Mr Masida graces us with his presence or not. Where had we got to, Mr Plunkett?'

Even Plunkett was able to recognise a mistake when he saw one as big as this. He looked with astonishment, 'Does Your Honour suggest— ?'

He was interrupted by the judge. 'That we carry on? Yes, I do. Mr Scott has only cared to say that his client has not been brought to court. He is on bail. It says so here. There is no commitment warrant in the file.'

This was the first time Scott had heard that same remark with something like pleasure.

The judge was painting himself into a corner. He had not paused to listen. If he went on much longer then Mr Masida would have, well, not a cast-iron appeal based on the judge's behaviour, but at least some good fun at the judge's expense in the Court of Appeal.

'If Mr Scott's client takes the attitude that he has to be brought to court then we shall carry on without him. Look at Archbold on *Criminal Pleading, Evidence and Practice*, it's all in there, it's all in there, Mr Plunkett.'

Wrigley always called the criminal law bible by its full name. 'Now, don't stand there gaping, call your next witness.'

Scott thought he ought to try again. 'He is in custody, he has not been brought by the prison staff, Your Honour.'

'Nonsense. Is he in custody, Dock Officer?'

The prison officer sitting in the dock was jerked into wakefulness from his Sven Hassell book. 'Uh, no, Your Honour, we've no commitment warrant,' he said, checking his list, which of course showed Mr Masida on bail.

'There you are, what did I say, Mr Scott?' The judge had obviously totally forgotten last Friday.

Scott saw Murphy, the usher, sitting beneath the judge's raised dais, swivel his eyes up to heaven as he watched his judge putting his foot right in it.

Wrigley took the opportunity of having a go at Scott. 'Your client has been on bail all the time. He was on bail after arrest. I don't know why, given he was charged with such a serious offence. He was on bail after committal. He came here on bail. He was probably born on bail.'

At this old joke he was rewarded with a titter from the bystanders. The jury sat astonished at the eruption.

'He spent last weekend on bail. He is just being insolent, and indifferent to the proper administration of justice. And you, Mr Scott, are pretending that it is not his fault. Now what do you have to say to that?'

At this Scott let go. He had put up with this judge long enough.

'Your Honour is entirely wrong. Your Honour remanded him in custody whilst you were running out of the car park at ten past one last Friday to catch the next train to Kent.'

A tremendous hush descended over the court.

'You were completely wrong in doing so since you did not invite the defence to address you, even in the car park, which I would have been perfectly willing to do. I have not been able to get him out of prison over the weekend. He is now lost in the system.'

There was complete silence. It went on and on and on. Eventually it was broken by a Welsh voice at the back of the court, 'Silly bugger. He's gone too far this time.' Scott turned and saw Tozer watching from the back. The judge rose and left the court.

'Come in, Scott. Come in, Plunkett. Come on in. Good to see you. Miss Phillips, you've come too?' Judge Wrigley spoke to the shorthand writer.

They had both, Scott and the prosecuting counsel, been invited to go and see the judge, but Scott wasn't going to go without a shorthand writer being there to record what was said.

The judge had released the jury till twelve o'clock and had sent the clerk of the court to call counsel in to see him.

'Did you hear the latest story going round? There's no need to write this down, Miss Phillips.' Despite the rather strained atmosphere of the gathering, Wrigley set off on one of his funny stories.

'We had a two-month fraud case in here and towards the end of it everybody was getting a bit bored. A bit bored? Very bored! Go on, Murphy, go on, coffee for everyone,' he said, as

Murphy his usher came into the room with a coffee pot, cups and biscuits.

Wrigley was clearly intent on getting out of the problem into which he had forced himself by sheer good humour.

He went on with his story, 'The Bar started playing the silly word game. You know, they had to get a strange word into their speeches without it seeming odd. Mellors had "armadillo", he got it in but cheated a bit. And Marshall, you know him? very amusing man, was given the word "clitoris".

'Well, no one thought he could do it, in fact there was quite a lot of money saying he wouldn't manage it. The case involved a valuation, a man not involved in the dishonesty, mind you, but mentioned in the case, Clutton. I think he gave a valuation of some stolen property.

'So Marshall comes to the point and says "Now, ladies and gentlemen, we have to remember the evidence of the expert valuer . . . Clit-or-is . . . it Clutton?"

'Well, Soapy Joe Greaves actually fell off his seat laughing. Murphy had to help him out of court.'

Everyone listening laughed. Miss Phillips blushed and Wrigley looked pleased with himself.

'Now, Scott. How are we going to sort this out? Do you want a retrial? After all, I said some fairly strong things about your client?'

Scott looked sharply at Miss Phillips, who wasn't writing but started the moment she noticed his glance.

'No, I do not.'

With astonishing speed the judge executed a 180-degree turn. He turned to Plunkett. 'You saw your officer, your main witness Williams, flayed by Scott on Friday. Do you really want to proceed? The jury clearly won't believe a word he says.'

Plunkett boggled at him. He still had a perfectly good case against Masida. He wasn't about to drop it.

'If you proceed, I shall stop the case and tell the jury to acquit,' said Wrigley. 'Take instructions. Let me know what is happening in ten minutes, gentlemen. Drink up. Drink up.'

The court reassembled at twelve o'clock. The jury came in, puzzled at the atmosphere, and settled themselves in the jury box. The trial as far as they were concerned was just getting interesting.

Plunkett stood up and said that he had taken instructions from the solicitors for the prosecution and, 'Given the circumstances that now obtain since the unsatisfactory evidence of PC Williams last Friday, I do not think it proper to proceed any further against the defendant.'

He had given in to the judge's threat. There was little else he could do. If a judge says he is going to stop the case then that's that. The prosecution can't argue.

The jury gaped. PC Williams got up and left the court. The judge said, 'Can I direct the jury to return the verdict of Not Guilty while your client is not here, Mr Scott? I don't see why not.' And the trial finished.

Courteney Masida arrived just before lunch in a special prison van. Scott went to tell him what the judge had done. He listened and said, 'Well, I've never had a judge behave to me like that before.'

Then he said, 'That's two new things that's happened to me this weekend. Both of them different from normal.'

Part Two

Chapter 15

Monty Bach's office was at the top of the old ambulance station in Peckham. There was no sign. Unless you needed it you wouldn't have known it was there, but if you were local and you needed a solicitor then you had always known where it was.

Monty's office was as much part of the neighbourhood as the primary school, the police station and the rural deanery next door. The firm had been started two generations before when the founder arrived from the Welsh valleys to end up, fifty years later, in the House of Lords.

But the new young partners didn't find the Peckham office sexy enough, in fact they thought it plain down-market and spent their time jostling in the West End for company work, hoping that one day a contested take-over bid would land on their desks.

Monty was left in Peckham to get on with it, and between times he helped the grandsons and great-grandsons of the people who had started off with the firm, when the firm was as poor and vulnerable as they. His main business was heavy crime.

The front entrance was blocked by a small market. There

were three or four fruit and vegetable traders and an aggressively patriotic man who sold West Indian food.

He marvelled at how his stock went. 'Don't look much, Monty, but they all buy it, you know.'

There was also a stall whose main stock seemed to be imitation sellotape, plastic toy cars, screwdrivers and packets of curtain hooks.

John Howard picked his way to the entrance through the discarded vegetables, the cardboard boxes and the crush of the market to climb the cold, ringing concrete steps to the top floor.

The smell of an old-fashioned office greeted him – Mansion House polish and linoleum; for a moment he was taken back to his first school.

The frosted half-glass doors at the top of the stairs opened into a waiting-room the size of a small flat. Around the sides of the room there were old park benches, varnished and then mottled with age. On the far wall there was a painted hand with an index finger pointing at a brass bell. The sign said 'Reception; please ring'. For a few moments Howard looked at the semi-colon.

On the walls there were mementoes of cases in which the firm had been involved, each as poignant and dated as a regiment's battle honours.

He peered at the names; Buster Smith, Mifsud, the Cope brothers. There were cartoons of judges, some by Spy, others were modern. At the end of the row there was a case of butterflies with, in the middle, a large hairy spider. A silver plaque underneath said Witwatersrand: Bangor College Expedition 1921.

He pressed a brass bell-push which pealed gently in the distance and sat down on one of the benches. To his left there was a cartoon, roughly drawn on lined paper and touched in with crayon. A judge was pictured in the act of sentencing a smiling prisoner to gaol. Underneath it was the caption, 'You have been convicted of arson of a dwelling house. But it must be said in your favour you warned the occupants of the danger by shouting "Come out you coons and fight." '

Opposite him the frosted glass separated the waiting-room from the offices. Through the glass he could make out individual offices and occasionally a figure moving against the light. All the rooms were formed of partitioning, wood below, frosted glass above, but each opened up to a huge timbered roofspace that covered the top floor of the building.

Everywhere there were piles of papers, tied in red ribbon. There were files marked 'Correspondence', 'Letters sent', 'Letters received' and one file lying discarded on the wooden bench marked enigmatically 'Things To Do'. Howard picked it up. It was empty.

A secretary put her head round the door and asked who it was he wished to see. He said he had an appointment with a Mr Bach. He was asked what name, but replied only that his appointment was at twelve o'clock. He sat and waited.

He sat for about ten minutes in absolute silence. Sunlight filtered in through a skylight and the air was full of floating dust rotating gently in the light. Howard began to drift into sleep.

Then there was a bustling noise, he glanced at his watch – it was twelve o'clock and a man came out rubbing his hands.

No jacket on, the man was wearing a grey moleskin waistcoat, unbuttoned over a shirt which looked as though it were made of mattress ticking. In his left hand he trailed a large khaki handkerchief, unable for the moment to tuck it away into a coat sleeve. His hair was greying at the tips and hung wispily over his collar. He paused as he crossed the room. Howard watched with astonishment as he took a pinch of snuff and then flapped at his nose with the handkerchief.

'Mr John? I think we have never met.' The man put out his

hand, and as Howard took it Monty Bach's other hand went round his shoulder and he was led into one of the offices.

It was stacked on every surface with papers, some grey with age. All one side of the room was opaque glass, a lattice of small panes held in a peeling metal frame.

'Well, how can I help you?' Monty Bach slipped into the chair behind his desk and reached for a tin of snuff. He became a shape against the blinding light from the window and when he spoke his voice, until Howard got used to the light, seemed to come out of darkness.

'I am concerned for one of your clients, Mr Bach.'

He pulled out a cheque-book and placed it on the desk in front of him, where it lay, assisting the conversation.

'I understand he has been arrested for offences involving drugs. His name is Nadim Janjoa. He is from Pakistan.'

'Yes, that's right,' said Monty.

'I should like to know a little of what has happened, and I would also wish to contribute to his expenses.'

'There are none,' said Monty. 'He was granted Legal Aid almost immediately on his arrest. Legal Aid means he has a state-appointed lawyer.'

Monty was straining to place this Mr John, he thought he detected a slight accent. If he was American he would respond to the phrase 'state-appointed'.

Howard did not react.

'Oh, I understand that, of course,' he said, 'but in any undertaking there are always matters that need that extra bit of financial assistance.' He spoke slowly and a little pompously to give both himself and Monty Bach time to think.

He went on. Monty Bach said nothing.

'If I give you five hundred pounds towards expenses, then you need not be worried about getting permission from the Legal Aid authorities for every extra bit of spending.'

It was now clear to Monty that Howard knew precisely what

he was talking about, that he didn't want him to interrupt or even take part in the offer that he was about to make. He said nothing.

'For the moment, Mr Bach, I need another set of the depositions.' Howard paused. Was the word too technical, was he showing too great a familiarity with the process? He felt it might reveal too much of what he knew.

'Depositions?' he repeated. 'I mean, the evidence that is to be given in the case. The prosecution have to give you that in advance, don't they? Have I got the word right? – the witness statements, I mean.'

Monty Bach said nothing.

Howard came to the point, he was clearly safe. 'Here is five hundred pounds, Mr Bach. I need no receipt, I don't bother with records. Could I have a copy of the witness statements and copies of all the court exhibits which have been sent you, please?'

Howard leaned forward. He did not write out a cheque but took ten banknotes from the back of the cheque-book. 'You must take this, Mr Bach.' They lay on the desk before him. 'Perhaps you could tell me a little about the case, too.'

Monty Bach paused. He would be doing nothing wrong telling this man what the case was about. He wasn't surprised at his appearing in his office asking questions. In any big trial there are always people on the edge who are interested in exactly what is happening.

'Well, here are the case papers.' Monty Bach pointed to a large bundle on a shelf behind him. 'It will take some time to copy them all, but it can be done. Perhaps for the moment I can give you our selection, the central part of the case.'

He went on, 'Mr Janjoa was arrested about a month ago, outside a hotel in Earl's Court, west London. He was not carrying any drugs, but he's been charged with smuggling heroin.

'There were three others in the hotel who were carrying heroin, and the prosecutors say Janjoa was involved with them. The others had swallowed two-thirds of a kilo each before flying here from Pakistan.'

He paused. 'Two-thirds of a kilo, that's a lot.' Howard did not react. By now Monty had a good idea the man was involved. 'The owner of the hotel and the booking clerk were arrested as well.'

'Are they all in prison?'

'Yes. No bail for any of them. No one's going to get bail on a charge like this.'

'Did any of the others mention Nadim Janjoa when they were arrested? Did they blame him?'

'No, I don't think so.'

'Who's doing what?' said Howard. 'Are all the defendants fighting the case? Are they all pleading not guilty?'

'I'm not sure,' said Monty. 'Nadim Janjoa is pleading not guilty. The hotel owner is. I don't know about the desk clerk. Two of the couriers are pleading guilty, but one of them is fighting the case – his name is Muazzam. He says he's not guilty, although I don't see how he can when they've actually found drugs in his belly.'

Howard listened. 'Who's representing who? Who are the lawyers in the case?'

Monty Bach pulled the file in front of him. 'Well, the hotel owner, I don't know. The couriers are represented by Farakian – good firm. Save the one who is fighting the case. I nearly acted for him, he's with Stanhope's, Bill Squire.'

'Who's prosecuting?'

'Well, it's a Customs case, not a police prosecution. The Customs officer is called Gregory.'

'No, I mean who is counsel, the barrister for the prosecution?'

Monty was surprised. He had never been asked this question

136

before, nor thought it important. 'Well, I don't know.'

'Can you find out?'

'I can ask.'

'If you did that it would help,' said Howard.

Monty picked up the phone, dialled and waited for a reply. 'Can I speak to your reference AJK, that's Mr – ?' he paused, 'Mr Khayat, thank you. Can I speak to Mr Khayat?'

He sat waiting while the Customs and Excise telephone exchange played Elgar to him. He watched Howard's face. He thought that he had seen him before, but could not place him. A face he had seen in court? Perhaps.

'Mr Khayat? Monty Bach here. Could you tell me which barrister you are instructing to act for you in Janjoa? We would like to speak to him before we go to court again.' There was a pause.

Monty spoke to Howard, putting the phone down. 'He doesn't know yet, but he said he would let me know after lunch. If you ring later I'll let you know. The next hearing of the case is Friday. At the magistrates' court. Elephant and Castle. Will I see you there?'

'I'll be there. What time?'

'Ten thirty,' said Monty. 'Mr John, I said we hadn't met before,' Monty decided to try to find out who this man was, 'was I correct to think that? You must tell me whether my memory is playing tricks with me.'

'No. No tricks, Mr Bach. You remembered correctly, but you must forget people as quickly as you meet them.'

It was as much an order as a comment.

'I shall be back for the case papers in a quarter of an hour. I shall be in a taxi at the end of the street.' And he left.

Just over ten minutes later an office boy with slicked hair appeared at the end of the street. He was looking for a taxi, saw it and handed the papers he had copied to the passenger. 'Mr Bach said this is as complete as he could manage.'

Howard looked. It was very complete. It even contained a copy of Nadim Janjoa's explanation of the events to the solicitor.

He slid the documents into a case and sat back in the taxi to continue reading the *Spectator*.

The cab took him to Soho, to the French pub. He went upstairs to the restaurant. He took a table by the window, asked the waiter to clear a space and spread the papers out. He ordered lunch and a bottle of Brouilly, and sat back in his chair.

To eat a meal on his own, with time, with something to read and with matters to occupy his mind was a version of perfection. He leaned back, enjoying London, and his attention wandered to the other tables.

Next to him there were five people. He vaguely recognised one of them and studied his face, trying to remember where he had seen him before. The man had a high forehead and a permanent smile. He watched the man talk. As he formed his words his whole face took part in his conversation, at one moment laughing, the next self-deprecating, as if to echo and emphasise his awareness of what he was saying and its implications.

Howard watched him. He was sure the man was part of his past, but for the moment he could not place him. He could hear what was being said. 'Yesterday I had lunch at the Temple with a barrister. I spent the afternoon at Brixton prison. And the evening at a police station, and I reflected when I got home' – the speaker's mouth pursed to express reflection and then quizzical detachment – 'and I realised that I was the only person in London to have undertaken that journey that day.'

Howard thought, who could he be? A barrister, a probation officer? A solicitor? Less likely, since neither a probation officer nor a solicitor would go to the Temple. If he was so pleased with what he had done, and it was something he

138

regarded as special, then he couldn't be a professional, just an amateur out to experience real life.

Then Howard remembered where he had seen him before – at Cambridge, reading English, one of the group he had known. He had heard he had become a writer.

The waiter brought him some food and Howard turned away, feeling certain that he himself would not be recognised. He started to look at the court documents.

The solicitors had prepared a summary of the case for counsel and had pointed out the weakness in the evidence in the case against their client Janjoa.

They accepted that it could be shown that the others had carried heroin, but pointed out that the main question would be whether the prosecution, that is the Customs, could prove that Janjoa was involved in the conspiracy.

At best they could prove that Janjoa had arrived at the hotel where the drugs were found at much the same time as the drug couriers.

Even then it couldn't be shown that he had travelled with them all the time, only that he must have left London airport at about the same time as they had and that he had arrived at the Argyle Hotel, in Earl's Court, where they were arrested, a short time after them.

There was nothing else connecting the drug-runners with him save the coincidence of the name Janjoa on the travel-agency tickets the couriers carried. It wasn't much to prove a conspiracy.

The crowd at the next table began to laugh and Howard's attention was distracted from the papers.

'But we know that politicians are corrupt, why write a play to demonstrate what we already know?'

The playwright (Howard strained to remember his name) answered, 'But the real corruption we should fear is the corrupting effect of the ordinary, isn't it? That's where we must make our stand.' The remark was greeted with respect and the voices dropped again.

Howard went back to the court papers. In the description of events that Janjoa had given to his defence solicitor the journey from India was hardly touched.

Howard checked the interrogations, no, Janjoa had said nothing when questioned about the offence. He hadn't tied himself down to a defence. He had not said anything that he might later have to contradict.

The wine was good, rich and thick, the sun was filtering in, the people next door were as good as a show, he felt at ease with himself. He would stay in the house in Ovington Square tonight and get to work tomorrow.

There was a telephone in the passage outside the dining-room. He stepped outside and dialled. 'Mrs Roberts,' he said, 'I am in London, I shall be staying in the house for a few weeks. Could you get it ready?'

He listened. 'Yes, I shall be in tonight. No. Just me. Nothing special, Mrs Roberts.'

He dialled again, this time a portable phone number. It rang, a voice answered. 'Scully? Howard here. Yes, I know, I shan't be long. I was told you have someone. Someone at the Bar. A barrister, yes. What's the name? Emily Clarke, a girl? Does she owe you anything? Yes. I'll pay it off then. Have you her address?'

He wrote it down. 'OK, I'll be in touch.'

He dialled another number. 'Mr Bach, it's me. I came to see you a little earlier today. Have you managed to get the name of counsel in the case. Yes? Jeremy Scott. He practises from Tasker Walk in the Temple?' He wrote the name down next to Emily's.

'Oh, you know his clerk? Is there a chance of an introduction?'

Chapter 16

Right from when Peter Khan put his brass plate up – Khan and Co., Criminal Solicitors, Stockwell, South London – he had a man on the inside in Brixton prison. He got £50 for every client referred to them. He worked in reception, the best place for it, processing the entry of new arrivals. When he saw Muazzam and picked over his possessions, he inevitably saw the papers requesting a change of solicitor from Stanhope's to Monty Bach. It took only a moment to switch names for Khan and Co. on the form instead.

Muazzam had signed, or at least put his cross, just as he put his mark on the three other prison entry documents, one acknowledging the rules, the second recording his clothes and the third declaring his faith.

The prison officer left the reasons for the request as Monty Bach had drafted them and the complaint about the service that Muazzam was being given by Bill Squire was on its way to the Legal Aid office by the time Muazzam had been locked into a cell.

Muazzam was going to earn someone a lot of money: the fight for the right to earn it was now on.

The magistrates' court received the request for the change

of solicitor and telephoned Bill Squire.

'Your Mr Muazzam is not satisfied with your firm,' said the clerk.

Bill Squire was amazed. 'He's only been in custody for a short time, he's not had time to *be* dissatisfied with us yet. What's his complaint?'

'Let me see. Failure to take instructions. Failure to contact family. Failure to follow up instructions.'

'Hang on,' said Bill Squire, 'I haven't been to see him yet. How can I have done all that, or at least not done all that?'

'I don't know,' said the clerk, 'but he says you have – or rather haven't.' The clerk was on a salary, he wasn't in the slightest bit interested. 'Do you object?'

'Damn right I object,' said Bill Squire.

'Well, you'll have to take it up with the magistrate when the case comes on at committal. For the moment I shall tell the other firm that you object.'

'Who's the other firm?' said Bill Squire, but the phone had been put down.

Peter Khan was told of the refusal to transfer Legal Aid not long after he had been told the client wanted him. Now it was a matter of principle, he was going to make absolutely sure that Muazzam received proper representation from counsel who understood his problems.

It was something he felt deeply about. Two nights later he was talking about it on a late-night television conversation show, receiving a sympathetic hearing from those gathered on the studio sofa.

The secretary and president of the Ethnic Lawyers Association had been present to help the argument along, and the conversation was led by Miss Moira McRae, a radical lawyer.

'We think it essential,' said Peter Khan, 'that defendants from an ethnic background receive ethnic assistance from those who appreciate the problems that are unique to the situation in which they find themselves.'

He looked around at the bright circle in which they were sitting for support. He noticed that behind Miss McRae, outside the brightness, a technician was picking his nose. 'Everywhere it is clear that defendants are being mistreated by people who aren't like them,' he said.

Miss McRae leaned forward with an encouraging smile. Khan could see the powder on her face cracking. Her lipstick glistened.

'It is important,' he pointed out, 'that if this is to be done, then it should be done by people who understand what it feels like.'

There was general agreement and a shared sense of satisfaction amongst them all that they had shared the burden.

'We in Ethnic Lawyers,' the secretary took up the argument, 'being ethnic ourselves, are continually aware of the psychological power of other people's preconceptions. Black equals bad, white equals good.'

Miss McRae pointed out that the Irish shared the same difficulty. For a moment she hesitated on the edge of speaking of a prism or rainbow effect, moving from green towards black away from white, but she found that the analogy could not be pressed to any sensible conclusion and so she turned to encourage Peter Khan to talk more.

'I presently have a case,' he remarked. He interrupted himself and leaned over to Miss McRae, touching her on the arm. 'You need not worry, I shall not identify anyone.' She coughed a smile at him. 'I presently have a case where the defendant speaks no English at all. He has been remanded in prison. He has never been seen by a solicitor who speaks his own language. Indeed, I understand he has said nothing to anybody at all, despite being in a foreign country with no friends.'

He paused. 'Imagine that. Imagine one of your family being imprisoned abroad, in some awful place. Thailand, for example.'

The producer squawked in Miss McRae's earpiece and she exclaimed hurriedly, 'Not that Thailand is awful, of course, they have their own ethnicity.'

Peter Khan was quick enough to see what he had done wrong. 'No, I only meant let's imagine that someone might quite unreasonably think that Thailand is an awful place – and your, or rather his or her, relation is arrested there. What about that, then?'

He had lost his way as a result of the interruption.

'You'd expect the High Commissioner to come?' Miss McRae prompted him.

'Yes, or rather no,' said Khan, wishing he had not got down to specifics, 'the High Commissioner didn't come, but I shall go and I shall speak to my client in a language that he understands.'

'No, you bloody well won't,' said Bill Squire, 'you scaly little bastard. So it's you, is it?' Bill Squire was sitting at home in front of the television. 'You're not getting anywhere near my client.'

But Peter Khan went to Brixton to see Muazzam and there was nothing Bill Squire could do about it.

He went through the X-ray machine, leaving his keys and money in a plastic cup. 'Number four,' shouted the officer at the desk, and Khan sat and waited in the cubicle while Muazzam was fetched.

He was offered tea by a prisoner doing orderly work and after a while Muazzam was shown in. Muazzam approached Khan, puzzled at what was happening, and when Khan signalled to him he sat down at the table.

'I am able to help you,' said Khan.

Muazzam started and looked up at him. This was a revelation. The man spoke his language and offered hope.

'I have not yet got the full papers in the case, but I will be given them soon. Am I right that you have been charged with smuggling?'

For the first time Muazzam found himself speaking about his case to someone in his own language, to someone who seemed interested in what was happening.

'Yes,' said Muazzam, 'and I have been locked up for ten years.'

This puzzled Khan. 'But you are on remand waiting trial.'

It was clear Muazzam had no idea what was happening so Khan went to speak to the gaoler on duty.

'He says he is serving a sentence already – ten years. Can that be right?'

The officer checked the file. 'It doesn't look like it,' he said. 'It looks to me as though he is on remand awaiting committal for trial the week after next. I'll check with the office.'

Khan returned to the small room where Muazzam was sitting and they sat and looked at each other.

There was nothing in the room except the table, the chairs and some notices on the wall. The notices reminded readers that nothing was to be given to prisoners. They also remarked, rather hopelessly it seemed to Khan, that the aims and duties of the prison service were to educate those in the prison's care in a useful way of life.

Another sign said 'Do not smoke', underneath that was written, 'Joe Keenan. Looking at fifteen years'.

Peter Khan got out a cigarette and lit it. 'They'll be here in a second. I told them to get some information for me.' He sat looking at Muazzam.

Muazzam looked at Khan. He saw a well-dressed, lightly built man. He had on elegant spectacles and carried a slim leather briefcase. His shirt was snowy white and his shoes shone in a way that said only one thing, money. And his suit, Muazzam, the tailor, had never seen anything of that quality. He sat there on the other side of the table, playing with a gold pen, poised over a pad of paper, smoking a long American cigarette. For Muazzam this man was an apparition and a moment later he was to discover, a saviour.

The prison warder came to the door. He spoke to Khan and, what was remarkable, he spoke politely to him. Muazzam noticed that he even called him 'Sir' – a word that Muazzam had heard only when prison officers were being addressed.

The warder seemed to be taking orders. Perhaps, thought Muazzam, this man can get me out of here.

Moments later his wish almost came true. 'You are not here for ten years,' Khan said. 'I have spoken with, ah, I have arranged with the officers, and the ten years no longer applies. We shall have you in court next week when we shall start to organise your defence, and we hope to arrange' – he leaned forward and binding Muazzam to him with hoops stronger than steel, he touched his hand – 'we sincerely hope to arrange your release.

'We shall be appearing in the magistrates' court in about ten days. That court has to consider whether there is sufficient evidence for you to have to stand trial. In your case I fear that there is such evidence. However, I shall be arranging for a barrister to be there to represent you.'

He explained what he meant, 'A barrister is just a lawyer, like myself, but he works for us. Now you must do exactly what he says. We will have someone there who can speak your language. I shall prepare some documents for you to sign, to give to the court. I shall be organising bail for you. That means you could leave here to await your trial. Unless the court is very unreasonable, and I fear that sometimes they are, then you will get bail.

'Now, please, you must refuse to see other lawyers. They may not have your best interests at heart.

'Meanwhile,' he went on, 'is there anyone whom I can contact for you back home? Have you a wife? Have you a family?'

The floodgates burst and Muazzam told him about his wife and the child about to be born. It felt to him as though he were allowing someone into his secret life, into the tiny defended place where he had protected the memory of his wife from the horror surrounding him.

'Be ready for next week, I shall write to you, I shall be representing you from now on,' said Mr Khan, 'and I shall be in regular contact.'

He wrote to each client on remand in prison at least twice a week. Most of the letters were a standard repetition, but he tried always to add a few words of encouragement to each in ink at the bottom. This took time but less time now that standard letters could be stored on the computer.

As a result his clients thought themselves the best cared for in prison. He had often found that people came to him because they had shared a cell with one of his clients and that while there they had been impressed by the amount of attention they had seen their cell-mate receive.

Each letter contained a visiting card. It meant that at least twelve to fifteen business cards were going into Brixton and Belmarsh prisons each week.

He reflected on this as he walked across Brixton Hill to his car. It was attention to detail such as this that enabled him to own, as he did, a bright-red Ferrari.

Chapter 17

John Howard's dinner guest leaned forward and placed both his elbows carefully on the table.

As he spoke his hands were occasionally unclasped and the heel of his palm was thrust outwards and upwards in a sweeping gesture. When he did so a diamond bracelet swayed on his wrist. He was wearing a lavender shirt, open to the third button, a pair of beige trousers, and soft leather pumps over white silk socks. His name was Frans.

The girl next to him was watching him nervously. She both longed and yet feared to catch her friend's eye in case they laughed.

'I find that I am very forward,' Frans said, 'and there is no doubt that this girl was very beautiful, very poised, very elegant,' he turned the word into three swooping syllables, 'but of course this did not touch me, and I just asked her, "My dear, where did you get that jewellery?" '

Howard transferred his attention to the man on his left and watched him for a moment. What he was saying did not at first sink in and he watched as the man spoke.

It seemed to him that he was not watching only one man but the last of a line of men, that the man spoke for all those whom he had been before, who made him speak as he did now.

Frans's voice cut through to the present again. He was telling a story. 'I was offered the picture for two thousand pounds. Do you know the type, rococo but done in art-deco style? Very finely painted on amethyst. Beautifully done. It is not a style that is important in this country, but in Germany, in southern Germany, my dear, they go crazy for it,' he turned and spoke directly to the girl next to him.

She did not know how to react.

'Well, I looked at it. I have a photographic memory for pictures, it is a trained memory, I see them clearly. Look at that picture.' He pointed at an oil on the wall behind the buffet to his right where Mrs Roberts stood momentarily serving a sauce. 'I walked past and immediately I said to John here' – he turned and gestured to Howard – 'that's Manuela, that's Manuela Roberts – and of course he said yes – well, if you look you can see sometimes she holds her eyes just so.' The guests all looked at the picture and then turned to look at Mrs Roberts, it was only when they did so that they saw the likeness in the picture's eyes. She remained completely indifferent to their inspection.

'But I have a good, no, that is wrong, a totally correct memory. And I knew I had seen the picture I was offered before. It was a *fête-champêtre,* you know.'

His eyes lighted on the man sitting opposite him, as they had throughout the story, picking out this or that person to be for the moment the listener for whose benefit the whole story was told. He paused as if for an answer.

'I don't. No. I don't know actually,' the man said, and everybody laughed at this piece of philistinism. It was not clear whether Frans was distressed at the reaction; he continued in exactly the same tone.

'Well, as I say, I knew this picture from somewhere, but

the signature I had never heard of. I tried to read it, Camob, it seemed to be. The man selling it said it was French. Naturally he didn't know. He is no expert, he only knew the provenance of the picture and of course he wouldn't tell me where he had found it. I would not have asked him.

'I had seen this picture before, but I knew of no Frenchman Camob who was working at the time. So I didn't buy it, but I said please hold it for me, I will let you know.'

By now the whole table was listening to this story. The calm of the room enveloped it. Plates were gently placed before the guests and the wine was occasionally moved from one to another.

Howard sipped the claret and it pierced his taste with a fugitive sourness, then sweet, then slightly salty, then gone.

A car passed outside, and the rushing in the air it caused died away. A word filled his mind 'crepuscular', the rustling of the sound of it complementing the quiet of his table.

He spoke the word out loud, and when eyes were turned towards him he said nothing, not moving, as though he had not spoken.

'So I went home,' Frans continued, 'I thought about it. Now, in order to tell this story properly I must tell you about another time completely. When I was seven I had measles and had to spend time in bed. As soon as I was able I asked for the magazines I loved. They were bound copies of *Klasse-Arte*,' he spoke the German precisely, obviously it was his own language, 'what you would now call a fine-art magazine. I had read these magazines since I was three, mind you, three, and I sat in bed turning the pages over.'

He had lain in the dark room, lit only by a soft bedside light. The curtains had remained half-drawn, and outside he could hear the rattle of the trams. Occasionally, for these were very bad times, he could hear marching steps on the cobbles, and once when the marching steps appeared, his mother and the nurse had come to his window to stand and look out.

He remembered his mother speaking to the nurse in the soft Schleswig German that, when he heard it now, still brought her back to him. And he saw the nurse turning from the window wiping her eyes. The gesture was as mannered and tragic as that of an actress.

He knew that what was happening outside would eventually burst into the quiet room, but for the moment in the calm that awaited the chaos he turned over the leaves of the book. They were in black and white, printed on a glossy paper that smelled of wax polish. He could still see them vivid in his mind. They were from another world, poised, peaceful, balanced, and he seemed also to stand as if at a window looking out at that world beyond the curtain.

'It was in that magazine that I had seen that picture!' Frans spoke forcefully, now reliving this journey of the mind before the audience at the dinner table.

'I no longer have that magazine, but I am able to check the index of such a publication. And I went to my private library. Hatchards in Piccadilly.' He smiled at his fellow guests. 'No such name as Camob in the index.'

He paused triumphantly.

'But I know that I am correct. I can see that picture. So why cannot I find the name? And I start thinking. What do I remember of that picture, and I remember, and I remember' – here he pressed his fingers to his temples to demonstrate his effort of memory – 'and then I wake up one morning remembering Russia – and tea. And I think why do I remember Russia and why tea? What has tea got to do with it? And again I cannot remember. Then I think to myself perhaps it is not the tea I remember, as I reflect and reflect upon this picture in my mind, perhaps it is something other.

'And then, of course, I do remember. I lived in Berlin at that time, when I was seven, and going to the railway station I used to see the trains with the running boards: Paris, Brussels, Aachen, Berlin, Potsdam, Lvov, Kiev, Moscow – so romantic, you know – and of course the Russian names are written in Cyrillic, MOCKVA.

'And I see this name is written in Cyrillic, it is not a French name Camob but Cyrillic "*Samov*".'

He turned to the girl next to him, she had been listening to this story, made placid by the silence but not part of its magic. '*Samov*, samovar, don't you see? Tea. That's why I thought of tea.'

Clearly she neither understood nor cared.

'I knew Samov. This was not his style of painting at all, how can this be? But I checked, and found – of course! – he had moved to Paris later in his life. This was unlike any work he had done before, but he was an able designer and he took to the new designs and worked with them, he was a refugee, he had to do it to live.

'It is worth fifteen thousand pounds at least. I am tempted to go to King Street immediately to sell it. But I don't speak of that, that is mere nothing.' He touched the girl on the arm lightly with his fingertips and then brushed his mouth with them in a gesture of negligent disdain.

The girl shrank from him in dismay.

She had understood the idea of £2000 being turned into £15,000, and had now grasped the point of the story – the profit.

'I don't speak of that, not profit, it is mere nothing, I speak of the mind. Where does this live, this memory? What does it do to us?'

There was silence.

John Howard spoke to fill the gap, 'Had your story been by Borges, then in his stories each of these men Camob and Samov would have existed, pursuing each other perhaps, or sharing the same lover at different times. They might have been different people but part of one mind, as the characters in a novel are all parts of one mind and therefore parts of each other.'

He smiled at Frans, who watched him, relieved to be lifted of the burden of speaking to those around him but puzzled by this intervention.

Howard went on, 'Perhaps one would have knifed the other, in a blinding moment, on a beach maybe – we must involve Camus – and then the killer would have painted in the dead man's style, taking his life first and then stealing his art.

'But I am sorry, Frans, I am intruding upon your life and am turning that into fiction. That is unforgivable, is it not? Perhaps to do that has the same effect that photography has upon a primitive people, it steals their soul, or part of their soul?'

Frans laughed, slightly nervously. He felt uncomfortable at the turn the talk had taken away from the solidity of his own experience.

'But fifteen thousand pounds,' said the girl. 'You will make thirteen thousand pounds for a week's work.'

'No, I shall not sell in this country, I shall sell in Cologne and then I shall make more than that. But it is not the week's work, it is the experience that I am paid for.'

He smiled. It was not clear whether his English, perfect but sometimes slightly incorrect, had led him to say 'it is the experience I am paid for', when he might have said 'it is my experience I am paid for'.

'I've never enjoyed that, I've done it, of course,' another voice cut in from across the table, the man who had said no to the question about the *fête-champêtre*. 'I've done it, of course, bought here, carried there, and put the profit in my pocket. Enjoyed spending it, but not enjoyed making it. Now, if I had worked and worked on something, and then sold it, that's different.'

Mrs Roberts moved soundlessly round the room, leaning over the guests' shoulders as she gathered the plates.

Howard reflected that Mrs Roberts was the most elegant woman there. She left the room and his guests sat quietly. Soon they would go.

Emily Clarke sat next to the man who had last spoken, and felt the contempt with which Frans had looked at him after his comment. Clearly the story Frans had told was not about profit, but, for a moment, she felt protective and her own contempt for the man who had misunderstood lessened.

Obviously there will be some people who won't understand, who don't even want to bother with such experiences. Who's to say they are wrong? she thought.

The door opened, Mrs Roberts spoke to Howard, 'There is coffee in the other room now, sir.'

'Who's for coffee and who's for afters?' said Howard, half rising. His guests took it as an instruction and got up as a group for the other room, but Emily found herself sitting still.

She had not expected this.

Her pupil master, Henry Strachan, who had brought her to Howard's, had told her that Howard was rich, indeed had laughed about how he had inherited five million in shares when his father's chemical business had been sold. She had therefore been partly prepared for an opulent lifestyle but had not expected the offer of cocaine to follow.

She found herself sitting alone at the table with her host. 'I'm John Howard,' he said, 'Henry introduced us, but we haven't spoken yet.'

Emily smiled. A candle guttered on the table in front of her and she saw the reflection of her hand as it lay on the polished mahogany. A table so highly polished that it would reflect what lay on its surface. A silver candelabra. A housekeeper who was also clearly this man's mistress. There were paintings of her hanging on the wall. One had already been pointed out to her as a Kitaj.

'I have a line here,' he said, 'are you happy to try some even though Henry is here?'

Emily remembered who she was with. She was thankful to Howard for thinking of it. It was only later that she realised how it betrayed how much he knew about her.

'I have a small sitting-room next door, perhaps we should step in there,' he said, rising. There was a door set into the panels of the dining-room.

She stepped through it. It was a small room with a desk, the walls completely covered with books. There were two armchairs drawn up before a fire which was set and alight.

Howard pulled out a small pipe and placed a little piece of whitish crystal in its bowl. 'Have you tried it this way?' he said, offering it to her and smiling. 'You really should, you know.'

The smoke took Emily straight away. The white lady. The lady's drug.

She remained very still. Outside she could hear in precise detail the movements of the trees. The coal fire burning in the hearth occasionally roared, and now and again the air rushed against the window as a car passed. She was aware of voices laughing outside at one point and a door shutting.

For a few moments she became very frightened and she was sure that there were people outside looking for her, then with a change as complete as a curtain rising in a theatre she felt better again.

Later she saw John Howard sitting opposite her. 'The others have gone,' he said. They sat there for a while.

'Henry tells me that you are looking for chambers.'

Emily wished he wasn't talking, but fought to be polite. She nodded.

'I know a man called Vinnie Moran, a barrister's clerk, he

might be able to help you. Look, you will want to get home, let me give you a lift and I'll tell you on the way.'

Emily began to feel very sleepy. They left the house and climbed into a car parked outside. He set off down behind Harrods.

'I'll be in touch with Vinnie soon. He's at number six Tasker Buildings. I think I can persuade him to help you. And if he says he will then it's all settled. After all, it's the clerks who really run barristers' chambers, we all know that.'

The next day Emily found the note of the address in her bag. She didn't remember getting back. She only remembered that John Howard had given her a lift, that she had been in a mini-cab with a radio and crackling messages. She also dimly remembered Scully, but that seemed unlikely.

Chapter 18

John Howard walked through the Temple past the barristers setting out home after the day's work. He felt the need to pull his collar up, though he knew no one would recognise him.

Both he and the Temple had changed.

The huge space of the Inner Temple courtyard stretching down to the river was full of cars where before only a few had parked there. People had travelled by tube and train in his time.

The great plane trees had gone, the result, he supposed, of the storm. They had been replaced now by saplings, though it would be another thirty years before the whole area would again be in the shade of wide branches on a summer's afternoon.

But the most dramatic change was the stonework of the buildings. It was white now where he had known it black, the soot had been washed off. He'd always assumed it was black stone, that it was meant to be black. Had the dark wood of the law courts' benches and desks once been white and bright? That was difficult to imagine, it was an intolerable image of innocence.

The names on the staircases leading to the various sets of chambers were much the same as he remembered them, now and then he recognised one. Generally there was still the same sprinkling of the aristocracy and double-barrelled names, often Welsh.

No one here wanted to be honest Tom Jones. But then he noticed a real novelty, a set of chambers made up entirely of foreign names: Adiposo, Kmayoto, and here was a great name, Tuesday Thompson. Through the windows he glimpsed black faces.

He turned through the arches of the cloisters and passed the Temple Church. He checked his watch. He had a little time left so he turned into the church.

It was as though he had stepped into the quiet of the country straight out of the centre of London. The echoing silence of the interior and the still crystal light soothed and slowed his movements.

His attention turned inward. He became aware of his feet as he stepped on the stones, and aware of his hands as he grasped them behind his back. His previous busy hurrying movements became superfluous.

He gently pushed the second door closed and it clicked shut, the noise reverberating from the roof. To his right there was a desk with papers on it, pamphlets with pictures of grateful people gathered at water wells.

He picked one up and supposed that the Kalashnikovs were out of sight. The pictures had just the same detachment from reality as the space he was now in had from the reality of the insurance companies and wine bars of Fleet Street.

As if to emphasise his last thoughts he became aware of a tapping noise, a sharp command and a treble choir started singing softly away to his right.

He turned away from the sound, not wishing to interrupt it, and sat down on one of the chairs at the back of the church. By a hassock near his feet there was an old, soft leather book, a catechism, discarded, displaced now, he assumed, by the *Good News Bible*.

He picked it up and opening it, smelt the pages. It smelt as rich as beech woods, but drier. The voices at the far end of the church suddenly lifted in urgent supplication and then fell away. The print of the book swam slightly before his eyes.

There was a time when there was an entitlement to these things but their validity was in question now. Was affection for something that had endured necessarily a rejection of the new?

His mood pricked at him, and gradually he began down the old route of doubt and disgust, one following the other.

First, honesty, then sentimentality, indulgence, then disbelief in the honesty of his own affections and last – again he did what he had always done – he shook the whole sorry mess away from him, stood up and looking not to the right nor the left strode out of the church into the evening.

He turned back the way he had come, through the Inner Temple and up towards the Clachan. The noise of the pub and the hard lights greeted him and swept away his mood. There was redemption only to be found in action, not reflection.

A pall of cigarette smoke on the stairs, something he had not seen in London recently, was unfamiliar enough to affect his eyes. He pushed his way downstairs, looking around. Over in one corner he saw Monty Bach drinking with another man. That must be Vinnie, the clerk.

Monty said he could get him there to meet Howard and he had. Monty was gesturing with one finger lifted towards his listener's face, who was following what he was saying closely – with the slightly stupid attention of one who has had too much to drink.

Howard watched them for a moment, gauging the situation.

Monty picked up a glass of whisky, he gestured again, and the other man raised his glass in reply – yes, Howard could see they were both drinking whisky.

Howard pushed his way to the bar and ordered three drinks,

large malt whiskies, and then, clutching a packet of peanuts between his teeth, he threaded his way over towards the men.

As he approached he lifted the glasses up in front of him, avoiding the press of the crowd, but demanding attention and welcome and getting just that.

'Hello, Monty,' Howard said, and gave him the drink, then he turned and offered the other glass to the second man.

'Thanks for that,' the man said, leaning forward, swaying slightly. Howard turned away from them both and deliberately began to organise a space for his glass on the shelf next to him.

It was a pause calculated to allow Monty to remind Vinnie who he was and he could hear Monty taking the opportunity.

Howard swivelled back, and he leaned forward, a huge smile on his face. 'Well, Vinnie, it's good to meet you, Monty's spoken of you often.' He paused, raising his voice as though he had just asked a question.

Monty intervened, and repeated what he had said earlier, 'Mr John here' – he took Howard's shoulder and looked at Vinnie – 'he gets me, can get us, Vinnie, a lot of work.'

'Good stuff,' said Vinnie, and raised his drink. Howard raised his and winked. They were friends. 'Monty tells me that this girl who is coming to see me tomorrow is coming on your recommendation?'

Jeremy Scott, watching from the window with a pile of papers in his hand, had seen Vinnie, his clerk, set off up the car park hill for the Clachan and then seen Monty Bach cross the car park to greet him.

He wondered why Monty should be meeting Vinnie. He didn't send much work to chambers, but then gave it no more thought. He returned to the papers he was holding.

There was a circular from an insurance company, an offer of some wine, a man from Hong Kong who could make him a suit, an incomprehensible document from the City of London with a picture of a man wearing a stiff collar and an unctuous smile.

Also there was a brief from the Customs and Excise solicitors. A prosecution brief. He opened it, six defendants smuggling heroin. Nearly a million pounds' worth. Even accounting for the natural enthusiasm of the Customs to overstate their case, it was still quite a haul.

There were photographs, some, incomprehensibly, of a lavatory, and as he leafed through the statements he came across a statement from a man who called himself the Appointed Plumber to the Customs and Excise.

There was a thick pile of documents, a lot of reading. But he wasn't going to do it now. Now he was going to have a drink. He left his chambers and set off up the hill.

He stepped into El Vino's through the back door letting a blast of cold air in with him. The people next to him glared while he carefully shut the door. When he had done so they instantly turned away and carried on their conversation, 'So Timothy told him that the Settled Lands Acts did not apply. Well, you can imagine what the reaction was.'

Scott caught their conversation. He recognised one of the group.

He picked his way past the chairs looking to see if there was a place. Over in the corner Willie Watkinson waved at him, there were chairs free next to him.

'Wine?' Watkinson asked. Scott nodded agreement and squeezed into the chair under the picture of La Veuve Clicquot. William was one of the last people Scott knew who, when he said wine, meant champagne. It was going to be expensive if he stayed any length of time.

'When are they going to make you a judge, Willie?' Scott asked.

'Well, I'm not sure I'd want it. Frightfully lonely. All you do is sit in your little room all day. The only people you ever see are the others at lunch. And they're just as bored as you are.'

Willie breathed deeply after producing such a long sentence. He was hugely fat and even found sitting down a strain.

More champagne and glasses arrived. He fished out a handful of crumpled notes which he put on the table. The girl who had brought the bottle leaned over and fished around for a moment before taking some of them.

'Anyway, I'd never pass the medical. You've got to pass the medical, otherwise you could drop down dead after six months and your wife would collect the pension. Not that that would affect me.'

Willie wasn't married and lived the life of a nineteenth-century bachelor. In about an hour he would heave himself into a taxi and make his way to his club.

After that it would be another taxi home, read a complete book every night then bed. Four hours' sleep before breakfast at the Savoy and then the whole day over again.

'But Willie, life would be easier, wouldn't it?'

Willie snorted. 'We'll see.'

There was a movement beside him and more people arrived.

'Here you are, here you are,' said Willie. Two figures sat down at their table; the man Scott knew, Henry Strachan, but not the girl. He remembered seeing her before –but where? She was ravishing.

'Well, Henry,' Willie welcomed the new arrivals, 'who is this charming lady?' While all this stuff went on Scott was able to look at the girl.

She was bright blonde, with violet eyes.

'Emily Clarke,' Henry introduced her, 'my pupil. Been with me for six months. She needs another place now.'

Scott watched with amusement as she flushed in embarrassment. 'Look, Henry,' she said, 'don't talk like that. This isn't some slave market, you'll have them pinching my arms next to see if I'm strong enough.'

Both the men laughed. The idea obviously appealed to them.

'Now, Emily,' the man with her went on, 'Willie can't take you to the Garrick, can you, Willie?' He turned to him. 'I told her you couldn't take her, since they don't let women in. So we're going to have to leave you.'

'And I told you that I didn't want to go. I'm quite happy to sit here for a while.'

'I don't know if that's allowed either,' Henry laughed, 'this is El Vino's, you know. El Vino's doesn't like unaccompanied women. At least you're not wearing trousers.'

Scott listened to the banter. It was apparently light-hearted but then he noticed there was a serious note in her tone, it bordered on anger, made worse by the man's flippancy. The girl was on the verge of losing her temper.

The two men became immersed in a long anecdote and Henry grabbed the arm of someone passing behind them to listen. Scott watched the girl. Where had he seen her?

She seemed very self-possessed, looking directly at him, not reacting. Not asking for his approval.

'I'm not going anywhere,' he said.

'That's good,' she was quite neutral.

They had been thrown together, so he turned away to allow her the opportunity to shift her attention. A wave of laughter from near the door gave him something to look at and he grinned at a face he knew. Then he turned back.

She was still looking directly at him. She had not taken the opportunity he'd given her to shift her attention. It felt good.

'I'll have another drink then if you're the man at the table,' she said.

'Oh, I don't think it really works like that,' said Scott. 'I think he was joking.'

'I'll still have another drink,' she said.

'Have the bottle,' a voice interrupted; Henry and Willie Watkinson finished their story with more laughter and Watkinson pushed the champagne towards Scott as they began to heave themselves up.

It was difficult to move, the chairs were so close, but eventually they pushed and pulled themselves free. 'See you tomorrow, Emily,' said Henry, and then Watkinson surprised them, 'Don't forget there's another bottle on the way. Have fun.'

A new bottle and fresh glasses came. Scott was able to push his chair back a little and he put his foot up on the rail of the next chair. He felt relaxed. Some biscuits arrived.

'So,' he said, 'we're going to have to drink this together?'

'There's no "have to" about it,' she said, 'I don't have to. But I will.'

There was a pause, and then she said, 'Well, you know who I am. Who are you?'

He looked at her. 'I'm a criminal hack. I do simple crime.'

'Yes,' she said, 'I think I've seen you.'

That was always flattering. 'What was I doing?'

'You were turning a policeman inside out.'

'Why was I doing that?' asking for more.

'Because you're good at it.' She laughed at him. 'Do people often tell you that?'

'No,' he said. It wasn't what he had expected.

'But you hope they will?'

What could he say now? 'No.' He thought about it. 'No. I'm being honest. I don't think about it. I sometimes think about whether I could have done better.'

What was he doing talking like this? He didn't even know this girl.

'But I'm not sure I ever think about it. Anyway, what about you?'

'I'm a pupil still, didn't you hear Henry saying that?'

'Yes. Yes, I did, but what I meant was how are things? Are you anywhere near finding a place?'

'Well, I'm seeing your clerk tomorrow. Your chambers are in Tasker Walk, aren't they?'

'Yeah. But I can't' – he waved his hands – 'I've got nothing to do with the way they run it.'

'I wasn't asking you to help me.'

'No. I know.' Again he was embarrassed. 'At least, I mean, that isn't what I meant.'

This was supposed to be an easy drink, yet every time he opened his mouth something stupid came out. 'Look, I didn't think you were asking me to help you. But it's naturally what I thought.'

He had done it again.

'I mean, I thought immediately of how I couldn't help you since I don't know what is going on in chambers, I don't have much to do with it. I don't know whether there's a place there or even a temporary place for a pupil.'

'Oh, that's OK,' she said, 'I just felt I had to tell you that I had an introduction to your clerk tomorrow. Someone told me he might be able to help. I'd have looked a bit silly if I hadn't told you and then we'd bumped into each other, wouldn't I?'

There was silence. Then she said, 'Anyway, let's at least finish the bottle.'

'Good,' he said. 'Let's start all over again. I'll get another bottle. What do you say?'

'Well, if you want. It's very expensive . . .' She stopped. It was her turn to feel embarrassed.

He laughed. Now he was in charge. 'No. You're right, it's too expensive.' He took a breath. 'I'm hungry.' He stopped. They looked at each other. She was so beautiful that he felt quite calm.

'Come out to dinner with me.'

'Yes,' she said.

Chapter 19

'Then you asked him, "Well, if you can't answer that, how about this one then?" Honestly, I thought the policeman was going to die. Plunkett could hardly control himself he was so angry.'

He had taken her to Leonardo's in the King's Road.

As they filed past the tables the men looked up at her. Scott could see why, he could not stop looking at her himself. He helped her take her coat off when she returned from the lavatory and he brushed her arm as he did so. There was a snap of electricity.

'Nylon in the coat lining,' she said, and she stroked her suit down over her hips. The cocaine she put back in the coat pocket. Behind them on the wall there was a photograph of a motor-cyclist dressed in red leather leaning on a racing bike. Scott's eye caught it and he remembered it.

She had no need to smooth her jacket down. Clothes hung on her with extraordinary fluidity.

He looked away from her jacket and there were those cool violet eyes watching him. He felt she was amused by him, as though she were saying 'You too?'

With a curl of her skirt she followed the manager to a table. She turned and sat on the offered chair in one movement. Scott felt clumsy just watching her. Then she disappeared behind the menu.

'They serve spaghetti in a paper bag,' he said.

'I won't ask why, but I'll have it.' She put the menu down and looked at him. 'Now let me tell you what I think of you.'

He caught his breath. Then he thought, we've both had a little too much to drink.

'I saw you at Elephant and Castle, in a case called Masida.'

'Oh, yes.' Scott remembered her now. That's where he had seen her. He had done that well, that case.

'You were with Plunkett.'

'Plonker, as you called him,' she said. 'I saw you cross-examine the policeman. It was wonderful.'

'You shouldn't say things like that,' he said, 'you'll make me vain.' This was great.

'You already are,' she said, 'save that you don't show it. You think people will laugh at you, so you keep your feeling of superiority hidden.' Suddenly she hiccupped. 'Anyway, I'm allowed to talk like this since you've got me tipsy. And especially since I don't know you from Adam.'

She had her hand up to her mouth, holding the linen napkin, her eyes were open very wide and she started to laugh.

'But we're both members of the Bar, so I'm automatically a friend, not a stranger,' he said.

'That's a joke,' she said, 'you should see what some of your "friends" have done to me. That man Plunkett put his hand up my skirt in a taxi while a friend of his, one of your "friends" was watching.'

Scott's mouth dropped open. He was genuinely shocked. 'He didn't, did he?'

'The trouble with you, Scott,' she said – she could feel herself talking to this man as though she had known him for years, she couldn't stop herself – 'is that you're too innocent.'

'How do you know?' he said. 'Just a moment ago you said

you don't know me from Adam.'

'Well, innocence – that's clearly a characteristic you share with him. We shall have to see about that,' she answered.

They both burst into tears of laughter at their own wit.

The waiter picking up their plates remembered how when he was young, in a café in Como, he had had dinner with the woman who was now his wife, and how they had laughed and laughed.

'More wine, sir? Madam?' he said.

The bubble of pleasure which surrounded them even survived the cold air on the street when they emerged from the restaurant.

'So,' he said, 'I only live down the other end of the King's Road. Don't let's say goodbye yet.'

A taxi pulled up and they got in. The cabbie had to turn back the way he had come and he pulled a sharp arc in the road.

She was thrown against Scott as they sat in the back, and his arm went round her shoulder with no effort on his part.

She didn't resist the slight pressure which kept her leaning against him. He could smell the sweetness of her hair.

For a moment he felt a tremor against him, but before he could be sure the cab pulled around the Royal Hospital and he had to free his arm to get the fare ready.

Upstairs, for a long time they just lay and talked.

'The trouble is that they don't take women seriously. Sets of chambers are groups, mainly groups of men, so when you're allowed in it's not because you can do your job, but because you are acceptable to the group, and we know what that means if you're a woman.'

The bedroom was dark and she couldn't see his face, she was talking into the darkness. Then he moved and ran his hand through her hair, backwards from her forehead, slightly crooking his fingers.

Her father had done the same, the night she left for school, the last night she had seen him.

'Do that again,' she said. As he did so tears started on her cheeks; he leaned over and kissed her.

'You're crying,' he said. 'Am I frightening you?'

'No, no,' she said.

His hands traced the curve of her neck and her shoulder, cupped her breast and stroked the flatness of her stomach.

Then she felt the movement of his thigh against hers, and the pressure of his body on her. She slightly arched her back as her legs parted and her mouth opened.

'So, you're not so innocent, my Adam,' she said, and then she couldn't speak at all.

She woke in the middle of the night. The orange glow of the London night filled the room. The man next to her was breathing heavily. His hand was still in her hair. He had tricked her with a movement which reminded her of her father.

No, he hadn't, of course he hadn't. She had done this to herself. She could smell the alcohol on his breath. Hoggish sleep, that was it. For a moment she was revolted, then she remembered their laughter. She had told him everything. She had cried in his bed.

Then she knew what he would think of her. She was applying to his chambers tomorrow. How could she have let herself do this, when she had been strong enough to fight all the others off?

The obvious answer didn't occur to her; love is a weakness, we are all vulnerable.

When Scott woke she was gone. The scent of her body still clung to the pillow, but the bed was cold where she had lain.

She wasn't in the kitchen. He looked for a note. Nothing.

Why had she gone? He had certainly taken advantage of her. He was older than she and she wasn't a happy person. He could feel it.

He was just another man in a taxi with his hand up her skirt, making her pay for her supper. He had turned her into a crude boast in a saloon bar. He was angry with himself.

Chapter 20

The main entrance hall of the Elephant and Castle court was already beginning to fill with people as Scott made his way past the groups waiting, the policemen and the lawyers mostly white, the defendants and their families mainly black, to the notice-board where cases to be heard are listed with their court number.

He was in court six. This morning there was no time for coffee. He had to go straight in to get everything organised.

Most of all he needed to finish reading the brief. He had only opened the papers the night before, too late and now he was paying the penalty. He had only until ten thirty a.m. to get the story completely clear in his mind.

At ten ten he had another half an hour's reading done, when the Customs officer in charge of the case arrived. He was a lean, pleasant-looking man with a soft Scottish accent.

'Paul Gregory, sir. Is everything in order?'

Scott could sense the officer's unspoken question as he stood watching him reading the case papers, Have you got a clue what is going on?

Gregory had prepared these papers, no doubt, with huge effort and care and now he was having to give them to someone else to play around with – someone whom he had no reason to trust, who might, for all he knew, not even have read them properly. And to cap it all he was obliged to call him 'Sir'.

As a consequence, Scott rather overdid his response, 'Yes, yes, it's a beautifully prepared brief, Mr Gregory. I think everything is in good order.'

He paused and chanced his arm, 'It seems to me that the evidence against Janjoanadim is a bit thin, though.'

As he spoke he realised he had sounded reproachful, and wished he had not – as though he had any right to reproach him, he hadn't meant to.

'Ah, that'll be Nadim Janjoa, sir, two names.' Gregory paused, giving the lawyer time to catch up. 'It's two names, sir. Nadim Janjoa.' Gregory said it as if he were spelling out a word to a five-year-old.

'Yes, I hadn't appreciated that,' Scott said, marking his notebook.

Gregory went on, 'I'm afraid we couldn't find much evidence against him although he was certainly involved. I don't suppose there's even enough evidence to have him stand trial, is there?'

Scott had seen the name of the magistrate before whom the case was listed. It was Sarson, he never threw any cases out – unless the prosecuting lawyer annoyed him and then he might dismiss the case out of sheer spite. If Scott avoided that problem he would get the case through.

'Well, I don't think that this court will say there isn't enough evidence against him. My guess is,' he emphasised the word 'guess' because you really could never be sure, 'that there's enough.'

Scott changed the subject, 'The one who really intrigues me is the man behind it. In your case report you give him the name Lockyer, you know, the one with the bank accounts.'

Gregory began to relax. It was clear that the lawyer had

done his work and was interested in the case. In his experience that was a change.

'Well, wherever we went into the evidence we found someone else's footprints.'

Scott watched him, he sounded like Sherlock Holmes. He was an attractive person, a bit more interesting than the investigating officers he often had to work with.

'I think there's a man behind the whole organisation. The money they were making had to go somewhere, and it wasn't being sent back to Pakistan. The people who ran the hotel hadn't set it up. You saw the accounts?'

Scott turned to the section of the brief that dealt with the money going through the hotel. He had marked it with a tag and his ability to go straight to it increased Gregory's confidence.

'Look,' Gregory pointed at the wads of credit-card bills, 'you saw we found these accounts in the hotel, eighteen credit cards, over eight thousand pounds a month going to Bermuda and Jamaica, all paid for in cash this end. The hotel wasn't making anything like this money.'

He pulled out another section from his case. 'We haven't included these.' This set of bills reads like a sex 'n' shopping novel. Someone has arrived in London, using the name Lockyer, and set off round the West End. Look, early morning drinks at the Connaught. Then a stroll down Bond Street. Lunch at the French House – the bloody wine cost thirty-five pounds a bottle. I got the copy bill.'

Scott took the credit-card account from him. It was astonishing. In four days the man had spent nearly £16,000, culminating in a bill to a freight company to deliver stuff to Bermuda.

'We've checked Bermuda. It was sent on to Jamaica, but by then it was classed as a mammy shipment and so no records were kept. It disappeared. I tell you, it was beautiful stuff.

This lot here,' he pointed his finger at the name of an antique shop, 'was a set of eighteenth-century twist-stem rummer glasses. Twenty-four of them. That's no mammy shipment.'

'What's a mammy shipment?' said Scott.

Before he could get an answer they were interrupted. The clerk of the court came in and said, 'Not before twelve now. We won't be sitting in this court before twelve o'clock. Mr Sarson has had to go to the dentist.'

One of the lawyers sitting behind Scott laughed, 'He's bad enough already. I can't imagine what he's like with a toothache,' and the court began to clear.

'What's a mammy shipment?' Scott repeated.

Gregory smiled. 'The name started in Nigeria. Mammies, large Nigerian ladies, fly over and buy clothes, mainly children's clothes at Marks and Sparks, and return with a big bundle.'

He paused and tried to find an inoffensive way of saying it. He wasn't going to presume on this lawyer's prejudices. 'They used to look like mammies, like Epaminondas's mammy coming back from the market with a bundle on her head. A mammy load is a private importation that no one bothers with.'

'Epaminondas,' said Scott. 'I didn't know anybody had still heard of Epaminondas. What do you know about eighteenth-century twist rummers?'

He meant it as a joke but Gregory capped it. 'Well, I know that there's a history of fine glass in Jamaica, and I think we might be able to get access to recent auction records out there.'

Knowledge was just knowledge for Scott, stuff he had gathered up in large quantities along the way, but for this man it was a tool. Knowing something had a purpose for him. Scott rather envied him. 'The creature hath a purpose and his eyes are bright with it,' he said to himself, more useless knowledge.

Out loud he said on a sudden impulse, 'How about a coffee?'

Immediately they faced a difficulty. Scott couldn't take the officer to the Bar mess, the lawyer's restaurant. The public canteen was awful, and Scott couldn't go to the police restaurant. The very layout of the building was designed to emphasise distinctions.

'Look, there's a Costa coffee place just down the road. Why don't we go there?' he said.

'Real coffee?' said Gregory. 'That's a good idea.'

'The credit-card bills don't show any payment for hotels or accommodation. So we have to assume that the guy who comes over has a house here.' They had got two coffees and Gregory was talking. 'None of the shops where things have been bought have delivery addresses, save on occasions to a shipping office. The shipping office say they know nothing. The banks only have a poste restante address for the account. Lockyer. An address in New York. The bills are paid from there with cash. I know everything about the guy. Look. He favours Yves Saint Laurent grey flannel double-breasted suits with shoes from Ling and Attwood.'

Scott looked at the credit-card statements: three suits – £2000. Two pairs of shoes – £600.

'Good God,' he said.

'I know everything about him,' said Gregory, 'save who he is.'

He pulled out a black cloth-bound notebook. 'He buys books at auction. His favourite poet is a man called Gerard Manley Hopkins – whoever the hell he is.' Gregory wasn't about to let Scott tell him, although he obviously knew, 'I went and checked up. He was a weird Catholic monk or something.

'And,' he plunged into his briefcase again. 'He bought a Cezanne painting for cash. We've got a photograph of it from the insurance company who shipped it to Bermuda.' He showed Scott the photograph. It was a sketch of a mountain. Scott was astonished.

'How much?'

'Thirteen thousand.'

'Can you buy a Cezanne for thirteen thousand?'

'Not this one any more,' said Gregory, 'it's been exported.'

'Are you going to give this lot to the defence?' Scott asked.

'Am I hell!' said Gregory. 'It's an ongoing investigation. Public interest immunity. Anyway, it's too interesting, too good for them, they would never appreciate it.' He laughed.

They drank their coffee.

'Well, we may not get him, but we'll get some of his men down,' Gregory said, 'as long as we get them through the lottery.'

'The lottery?' Scott did not understand. He had the impression that Gregory was trying something out on him.

'The court lottery. I draw you. They draw Monty Bach, and we see who wins.' Gregory pretended he was being light-hearted. He didn't want to offend. But he wanted to say what he meant.

'How can it be otherwise?' said Scott. 'If you have a system of courts – and you have to have a system of courts – then some people will work them better than others.'

'Of course,' said Gregory, 'but maybe it's gone too far. I've been let down a little too often.'

'What do you mean let down?'

'Well, once the lawyers have got hold of it, I've got no control at all.'

Scott knew he couldn't be completely honest. Just to agree with him, though he felt like it, would be too jarring and wouldn't sound sincere.

'Well, I don't pretend to be anything special. But if I can help you then I'll try, and if you don't like it then you tell me.' Did he sound too offhand?

Gregory watched him. This man was speaking honestly to him. He hadn't taken offence.

They changed the subject.

'Do you know who is representing the defendants?' Scott asked.

'Yes, Monty Bach is for Janjoa. Farakian's are for the hotel staff and the couriers. Muazzam has got Stanhope's, although I'm told that Khan and Co. are sniffing around.'

He went on. 'Bill Squire rang me to say Peter Khan had approached Muazzam to change his Legal Aid order over to them. I suppose there's a fair amount of money running on it.'

Scott knew all the names, there weren't that many criminal lawyers in London. He said, 'Yes, but Khan's different, he wants the political satisfaction as much as the money.'

'What do you mean?'

'Well, he's got a mission to show that blacks should be represented by blacks. He calls it defendants being represented by people who understand them, but it's just another way of his getting business as far as I'm concerned. Good luck to him.'

He went on, 'Now, Muazzam, he's the one who hasn't spoken at all?'

'Yes.'

'Sorry, I haven't got the names entirely pat yet, it's difficult to remember them only from seeing them written down.'

'Well, I've seen the people.'

'Of course that's the real difference,' said Scott. 'A lot of the trouble starts from there. For me the whole thing is just an idea, like a story in a book, for you it's something you've experienced. And yet we try to pretend we're talking about the same thing.'

Gregory had never thought of that before. Maybe that's why lawyers sounded so glib.

'Khan is trying to get Muazzam to change to him, is he? What have the Legal Aid people said about it?'

'Apparently they've refused. But will that stop him?'

'No. You're right there. I wonder who will come this morning?' said Scott.

He went on, 'Do you know who is contesting the committal? Are any of them saying there is not enough evidence to send them for trial?'

'I think only Janjoa, Monty Bach's client. Obviously. Do you think there's enough evidence against him to make him stand trial?'

'Do you want me to be honest?' said Scott.

Gregory smiled. 'Why not? You have so far.'

'No,' said Scott. 'There's not enough evidence. Not by a long chalk. But Sarson will commit him. He'd commit a pudding if he was asked. Especially with toothache. Sarson that is, not the pudding,' he added, smiling.

The two men laughed and stood up to leave.

As they arrived back at court the lawyers' seats were beginning to fill. Scott set about getting everyone's name and finding out how they wanted the case dealt with.

Scott got the names of four of them. Then confusion set in. Two lawyers had turned up both representing Muazzam. Scott wasn't surprised given what Gregory had been saying.

At the last moment Tozer swept in. He was at court, he informed Scott portentously, on other business as well as looking after Nadim Janjoa – so he could not yet give this case his full attention. Could Scott please let the magistrate know that he was next door if he was needed? 'We agree to the committal,' he said.

Scott was astonished. Even in front of Sarson, Scott thought that Tozer would have to try to get the case against Janjoa stopped. At its very strongest the evidence against him was only that he happened to be outside the hotel at the time of the raid.

'Well, what witnesses will you need at the trial?' Scott said as Tozer left, but either he didn't hear him or he wasn't interested. He didn't reply.

Scott was furious: Tozer always did that to him.

Scott turned to the two lawyers who were claiming to represent Muazzam. 'Now, have you worked out who I should tell the magistrate is representing Mr Muazzam?'

That was a little malicious, but Tozer had always got under his skin, ever since they were students together. He half suspected that in the past he had made a pass at his wife.

The court clerk stood up. 'Put up Muazzam, Janjoa,' and he read out all the other names.

The dock officer organised a great clanging and shuffling of keys and doors, and the six defendants arrived and attached themselves to the names that had been bothering Scott all night.

Scott got up to introduce the lawyers to the court. He wanted to do this quickly. The confusion over Janjoa's representation and Tozer's absence would probably send Sarson berserk, and Scott wanted that to happen after he had sat down.

'Speak up!' said Sarson gracelessly.

Scott named the lawyers, said that Tozer, who appeared for Nadim Janjoa, was not here but next door, and then pointed out there was some doubt about who was representing Mr Muazzam, Wesley Divall or Fred Greer.

When Peter Khan had got back to his office after seeing Muazzam in Brixton prison he had immediately rung Wesley Divall's chambers.

'I've got a committal Thursday after next. Biggish drug importation. I expect to be briefed at court privately, would Mr Divall be interested in accepting the brief?'

'Of course he would,' said the clerk, 'he'll be free.' He made a note in the diary. 'South London magistrates sitting at sessions, that'll be Sarson probably. If there are problems, and he can't get there at the last moment, who else in chambers would you be prepared to accept?'

'It had better be Mr Divall. If not I'll pop over there and do it myself,' said Khan.

The clerk didn't like that. Come to think of it, he didn't like Khan very much either. His wasn't at all the type of firm that the chambers normally dealt with.

That night Wesley Divall's phone rang at home. 'Peter Khan here, Wesley,' the voice said.

Wesley Divall had been practising for only about a year. He had met Khan at an Ethnic Lawyers Association meeting. He had not gone again, sensing that it was not for him, but Peter Khan had latched on to him and had sent him a number of briefs.

'It's Peter Khan here. Look, Wesley, there's a client who is going to need representation. He's been on Legal Aid until now, but he has told me that he wants me to look after him. He'll pay directly, and has decided not to use Legal Aid. Could you handle it?'

Wesley Divall said he was sure he could if he was free. He wondered why Khan had bothered to ring him at home.

'The reason I've rung you is that you're going to have to tell the court that you are now instructed privately, and that the client doesn't want Legal Aid any more. I thought I ought to let you know.'

'Right,' said the magistrate, 'let's sort this out. Where's Mr Tozer?'

There was no one else to answer, so Scott had to.

'He's next door, sir, he asked me to tell you. He also told me that he accepts that there is a case against his client, and that he doesn't oppose committal.'

This was the cue for Sarson's first outburst of the day.

'Mr Scott,' he squeezed the name out into a long hiss and hit the 't' of Scott like a doorstep. 'The law says that I may decide that a man should go for trial before a jury without considering the evidence, if,' he spread the word out over three beats, 'the defence lawyers' – he was shouting now – 'not the prosecuting lawyers say that they accept there is enough evidence. If it's the prosecuting lawyer who says there's enough evidence,' and these last words he spat out, 'there's not much point, is there, because he would say that, wouldn't he?'

Scott wasn't going to put up with this and instead of answering he just sat down.

'Fetch Tozer,' said Sarson. An usher left the court.

'Now, Mr, uh, where are we? Mr Wesley Divall,' Sarson picked up the paper in front of him and read the name out, making it clear that it was unfamiliar to him, 'now, Mr Wesley Divall, now, Mr Greer. What's going on with Muazzam?'

Fred Greer got to his feet. He was an elderly but energetic man, always with several ideas spinning in his head, and keen to get as many of them out at soon as possible. The result was that he rapidly became incoherent. He began fairly well but then lost it.

'I understand that my client wishes to change lawyers, to have Mr Khan, who went to see him, who, it was on the thirteenth, I think, if I am not mistaken, yes, here it is, I have a note, and there's a letter to confirm it, we received it about a week ago, to ask whether you, sir, agree with this.'

The whole central part of what he had intended to say, his objection to the change, had gone missing in the rush. He started again, but was prevented by Sarson. Bill Squire could see his case disappearing.

'Sit down, Mr Greer.' The magistrate could be astonishingly rude.

'Now, Mr Wesley Divall.' Sarson did not like black men and he showed it. 'Where do you come into this?'

'I have been instructed to appear on behalf of Mr Muazzam. Khan and Co., who instruct me in the case, invite you to note the change of representation. I am asked to give you this letter with the documents attached.'

He handed up a letter to the magistrate and gave Scott a copy.

There was no doubt whatever about the quality of Peter Khan's preparation. The letter was beautifully written. Mr Muazzam, it said, wished to dispense with the services of Bill Squire of Stanhope and Partners, and he now wished to instruct Khan and Co. to represent him. He would pay the fees himself.

There was a letter and two copies, signed and sworn by a commissioner for oaths, from an interpreter saying that Mr Muazzam had received help with his understanding of the language and that he had made an informed decision.

This was a complete shut-out for Sarson. He was bound to discharge the Legal Aid order, and Stanhope and Partners would lose their client. That Stanhope's were losing a client didn't worry him at all, but Sarson knew precisely what was happening. Khan and Co. were snatching the client. Later, when the money ran out – if there was any money – they would apply for Legal Aid again.

Sarson could do nothing about it – or at least he could do one thing.

He turned to Wesley Divall and said, 'So, Mr Divall, you are representing Mr Muazzam on a cash basis. He is paying you out of his own pocket. Mr Muazzam is, I understand, a tailor from an Indian village. I wonder where he has got the money from? Two months ago he didn't have a sheet of paper to wipe his arse with.'

The calculated obscenity shattered the atmosphere of the court.

He went on, 'I see he made an application to change his Legal Aid certificate to your instructing solicitors which was refused, or rather referred to me to decide. So now he is doing without Legal Aid entirely, and by coincidence going to those very same solicitors? I hope he's got the money to pay you, and that your solicitors don't come back to this court in six weeks asking for Legal Aid to be reinstated.'

He was warming up by now, 'Let me ask you this, Mr Divall, what is your fee? Let me see your brief, please?'

Wesley Divall's world rocked. In a rush he understood what was going on, why Khan had bothered to ring him. This wasn't a simple change of representation but a scam to snatch the client from another firm.

His brief was not marked, it did not have a fee on it.

Scott watched with interest.

The very first rule of the barristers' code of conduct says that all private briefs, those not funded by Legal Aid, should be marked with a fee – he had never known why, but it was the rule.

Wesley Divall had never even seen a privately paid criminal brief. Private payers don't accept young and inexperienced barristers – all his work had been state-funded. It hadn't even occurred to him that there should be a figure marked on the papers.

For a moment time stood still. The possible consequences of what was happening stretched out before him in clear detail.

There would be a complaint, a hearing before the professional disciplinary tribunal. The idea that he was 'sharp', that is, willing to break the rules, would attach itself to him like a smell. It would hurt him badly, especially since he had enough of a handicap already.

'Well,' said Sarson.

Divall had met prejudice and dislike, he'd been dealing with it for years. But he didn't think he had ever been at the end of such concentrated anger.

Scott watched Divall. He couldn't say that he honestly liked him. He looked and behaved as though he were someone out of a television serial about smart lawyers. He was too well-dressed. He was always a bit too friendly. Scott had met him only once and yet Divall always greeted him by his first name.

On the other hand, Scott disliked Sarson even more.

He got up, trying to help Divall, 'Sir, to deal with a brief fee in open court might well put the Crown in a difficult position if there was eventually to be cross-examination on the defendant's means.'

'Shut up, Mr Scott. Well, Mr Divall?'

Scott had done more harm than good, by emphasising Divall's inability to reply.

But he had broken the spell, and Divall at last noticed that the solicitor's clerk sitting behind him was poking him in the back. He turned around.

'You've got the copy brief by mistake, sir. Here's the original.' The clerk handed Divall a brief.

The fee, marked on it in red ink, stood out like a signpost; Scott could see it from where he sat. It was passed up to the magistrate.

Peter Khan had thought of everything.

Gregory, sitting behind Scott, whispered, 'Well, that Muazzam's not all he seems, is he, if he's got that sort of money?'

'Don't you believe it, Muazzam's got no money. The brief is a dummy,' Scott said, turning round. 'That brief would not have been produced if it had not been asked for directly. Then Divall would never have got his money. He probably won't anyway.'

As Scott turned he saw Tozer coming in, holding the door open, he was accompanied by Emily Clarke, the girl from the restaurant.

'Ah, Mr Tozer. How kind. You've arrived,' said Sarson, turning his fire against another mark.

But Tozer was a different opponent entirely.

'Good morning, sir,' he said. He was completely

unapologetic. 'I am here as I said I would be. I don't think the court has been delayed?'

Since it had not there was little Sarson could say.

He turned back to Wesley Divall. 'Mr Divall, it seems you are properly instructed on behalf of Mr Muazzam. Mr Greer, Legal Aid is discharged, we shall not be needing your attendance. No costs for your attendance today.'

Poor Fred Greer wouldn't even get paid and Scott knew he needed the money, he had school fees to pay.

Tozer sat down. Emily sat behind him whispering, 'Where's Jeremy Scott, can you see him?' She couldn't see his face, since she was in the row directly behind him.

'Here he is,' said Tozer. Scott turned slightly and Emily saw him.

She blushed. Tozer was on to it like a flash. 'Oh, you know each other, do you?'

'Yes, but I didn't know where he was,' she said, not making any sense.

'We've met,' Scott said.

This was an unnecessary piece of information for Tozer. He had only to sniff the atmosphere. Natural selection seemed to have endowed him with senses undreamed of in ordinary men.

The case was finished by twelve thirty p.m.; all the defendants were committed to stand trial for importing drugs, and all were sent back to prison to wait the trial.

Scott went to the phone. 'Vinnie, I'm finished here. Is there anything else?'

'No, that's it for the day. Oh, by the way, I sent a girl down to you. Little blonde-haired thing. She's a new pupil started today, name of Clarke. There's been a mix-up, so I've arranged for her to come to you instead. Could you get hold of her and fix her up?'

Yes, Scott said, he would.

When he came back from the phone he found Emily talking to Tozer.

'You've got a new pupil?' said Tozer.

'Yes,' said Scott.

'Well, it happens all the time,' said Tozer, 'and the first thing to do is to get to know her. Unless you know her already. Let's go to the Bar mess and you can buy us a drink.'

At first Scott was pleased that Tozer was there, it made it a little easier. Scott didn't know what the etiquette was after a one-night stand, especially when you become the boss.

The more quiet Scott and Emily were, the noisier Tozer became.

'You're going to see how the ordinary barrister works,' he said to Emily, 'there's nothing flashy about our Jeremy.'

They were both silent.

'But he knows what he's doing,' said Tozer. 'At least in court, he does. Outside it he's a bit lost.'

Scott bought the drinks. What makes Tozer think he can talk like this?

As he went back to where they were sitting, he heard Tozer saying, 'I've known him for years.'

'Known who?' said Scott.

'You,' said Tozer.

'I suppose that's right,' said Scott gloomily.

'Don't be so sad about it,' said Tozer, 'you used to be quite happy then. You changed a lot, you know.'

'All right, Tozer, all right,' Scott said. He glanced at Emily.

Emily smiled. She tried to let him know she wasn't listening to this stupid man. Scott looked away, she was laughing at him.

He got up in anger and displaced it by walking to the bar to get some nuts. As he left the table he heard Tozer say, 'His wife left him, you know.'

188

He couldn't believe it, he turned and said, 'We're going now. I have work to do. Come with me, Miss Clarke.'

He had never given an order to someone who was an employee before.

Part Three

Chapter 21

Muazzam came up, blinking, into the light.

The dock, where the prisoners sat behind a Perspex screen, was already full. To his left sat a prison officer filling in a ledger. There were eight other people in the dock and to Muazzam, who had spent the last months waiting the trial in an old Victorian prison where the cells only take two people – however hard the governor tried to get more in – it was as though he had been catapulted into the middle of a busy market.

Barristers and solicitors leaned over the barrier talking to their clients, and there were even two women sitting amongst the defendants, knitting and chatting.

Muazzam looked round.

He was hoping to see Khan, he hadn't seen him since the man had come to Brixton. Only once had he had any contact with the firm when another man came on Khan's behalf.

The clerk had produced a pile of papers and had started to ask Muazzam questions.

Muazzam repeated again what had happened, about his wife, about the child which must have been born by now, the offer he had received to go to London to use his skills as a tailor, the villa near Karachi, and the pills he had been told to take for travel sickness.

Then two days later he had received a bill from the solicitors.

A prisoner who had grown up in Southall translated it for him. It was a bill for £2894, plus tax, for care and control of Muazzam's case, and for partial payment of counsel's fees.

The bill represented, the accompanying letter said, sixty hours of work on his behalf 'perusing the papers', taking instructions, travel, and an 'uplift to reflect the complexity and gravity' of the case.

Muazzam sat still for a few moments. 'How much?' he said.

Ditpak Siddiqui, known in the gaol as the dippy Paki, repeated the figure.

'That's two thousand, eight hundred and ninety-four pounds, plus VAT, which they say is four hundred and thirty-four pounds, ten pence. So that's' – Ditpak screwed up his face in a grimace that his friends had christened the divvy-dippy-Paki look, and added it up – 'three thousand, three hundred and twenty-eight pounds, and ten pence.'

Had Ditpak wanted he could have gone to university on his maths ability, but he preferred market trading and stealing.

'I don't suppose you can even afford the VAT,' he said, translating VAT freely as the 'extra bit for the government'.

Muazzam sat and looked at him in astonishment.

'Well, I wouldn't worry about that,' said Ditpak, 'perhaps they'll let you off that bit.'

He flicked the letter back and laughed manically. He wasn't much interested in this rather pale and very stupid peasant.

Muazzam dealt with the figure in the same way that he treated his prison sentence. He turned his face from it, refusing to look, and retreated into the business of making each minute pass.

He even experienced the extraordinary phenomenon of finding that his empty, purposeless life was overcrowded with details, that he was too busy. But after a while he realised that this curious feeling was directly related to the intensity with which he shut out any other thought than the moment.

The instant he raised his eyes, hopelessness flooded in, as overwhelming as a tidal wave.

A week later another letter arrived. It was in the same form as the one before, white crested envelope, clear purple type, and Muazzam took it to Ditpak.

Ditpak opened it and read it. 'Well, that's it, they're sacking you, unless you pay before the trial. That starts Tuesday.'

Muazzam had brought the bill to court with him and was holding it as he blinked in the bright light, standing in the crowded dock.

He was looking for Khan. Perhaps he might come despite his letters. It seemed to him that perhaps Khan had misunderstood his circumstances.

But most of all he was afraid that Mr Khan, perhaps feeling cheated by not being paid, might arrange with the prison officers to cancel the agreement he had so effortlessly made the first day they had met. He was afraid that Mr Khan would give him back the ten years' imprisonment because he had not paid the bill.

He had never, even just before meeting Khan, felt so alone.

Suddenly Khan appeared at his side in the dock. Muazzam had not seen him come. Without a word he took the letter containing the bill from Muazzam's hand and said, 'These letters mean nothing. We can disregard them. It was necessary. Merely a necessary arrangement to manage the judge, he must in the end decide who gets paid. And I have to get paid.' He smiled at Muazzam, leaning his head closer in a confidential gesture that for a moment shut out the court, the pain, the world.

'For I also, as you have, have duties and demands upon me that I must meet. You must, please, trust me.'

Muazzam was happy.

He looked no further than Mr Khan, the whole world beyond him was unimaginably distant, and it did not surprise him at all that the people who inhabited it had to be handled in strange propitiatory ways.

Scott was watching the dock from where he sat in the front row of the court.

It is possible to prosecute a trial without ever once looking at the faces of the defendants, save when they step forward to be cross-examined. But the result is a curious emptiness, it is better to have their faces, frightened, angry, self-confident, whatever they are, before you.

As far as he could see, all the defendants had arrived. At least he could see six men in the dock, not counting those who were obviously lawyers, and the two lady interpreters knitting as though they were sitting on a park bench.

He could see Monty Bach and Peter Khan, and the man from Farakian's. 'That's the great Monty Bach,' he said to Emily, who was sitting behind him. Scott pointed to Monty leaning over speaking to Nadim Janjoa.

Emily was wearing full barristers' robes; she was entitled now after six months of pupillage to speak in court.

She had on an old horsehair wig which sat incongruously on her shining hair. It had slipped forward slightly giving her a rather puzzled expression.

He had seen her address a judge, and had watched entranced as the colour rose in her cheeks and her eyes sparkled, all set off by the fusty clothes, the starched collar, the wig and the gown.

That judge had given up all resistance by the end of the third sentence she uttered, and had listened to her argument as though hearing a favourite story from his youngest daughter. Emily had been asking for an adjournment, but could have thrown in a request for the whole world without greatly affecting the course of proceedings.

'Yes,' she said, 'I know him, Tozer introduced me.'

He would have, thought Scott. And then he thought, there you are, already Tozer was affecting him, and the damn man hadn't even arrived yet.

Then, as if on cue, Tozer walked in. 'H'lo, Scott,' he said as he passed.

He grinned at Emily, who smiled back.

'He tried to get me into bed once,' Emily whispered to Scott, 'what a putz.' Scott stared at her for a moment, and then realised how good that made him feel. His face relaxed as Emily watched him, and she wanted to touch his cheek.

The evening they had spent together had never been mentioned, as though it were an accident, or mistaken identity, or perhaps had never happened. Scott thought maybe that it hadn't.

The effect was curious, creating a reserve, preventing either of them from putting too much warmth into anything they said.

Scott praised her ability and was pleased at the speed with which she understood the subtleties of the work.

He taught her to breathe slowly from deep in her stomach as she spoke, to watch the witness and listen properly to the reply before asking another question, to visualise the scene which was being described and yet to be aware that her picture of what happened was only her own and had to be changeable at a moment's conflict with the evidence – in short, not to snatch at the case.

But he wasn't able to show anything other than a gruff indication or a direct complimentary remark to demonstrate his pleasure. He wasn't going to have her think he would use his position as her teacher to his advantage.

She in her turn enjoyed the way he handled clients, teasing the detail from them and using it in court; admired the ease with which he drew different parts of the case together to demonstrate inconsistency. But she could not say so. Or at least if she spoke it had to be phrased as a formal expression of interest in the work she was learning.

But her confidence grew and when she first spoke in court she could feel his encouragement calm her. Something solid was beginning to replace the emptiness at the centre of her life.

Slowly the court assembled. There was no feeling of hurry, nor, surprisingly, even of expectation.

Piles of papers began to arrive behind Scott in the solicitors' row, six copies of everything, exhibits, interviews between defendants and Customs' officers, and schedules. Six copies of the indictment – the formal allegation of the crime – six schedules of defendants, six so that there could be one between each two members of the jury.

Then there were spare copies for the witnesses, for the shorthand writer, for the judge, so that he had the same numbering as the jury.

As Scott was sorting them there was a movement beside him, he turned and found Peter Khan standing next to him. 'I have a letter for the judge, here is a copy for you.'

He handed Scott an envelope.

'They are the same,' Khan said unnecessarily.

Perhaps the remark wasn't unnecessary and was only made for emphasis. It was Khan's way of saying, You don't trust me. He was right, Scott didn't trust him.

The letter contained copies of the letter Muazzam had received in prison warning him that the solicitors could no longer work for him if they were not paid. Attached to it there was a record of a conversation with a court official who was warned that Muazzam may turn up at court unrepresented.

A covering letter to the judge said that Khan and Co. were

unable to act any further for Muazzam as he had not paid them, but that they wished to make an application for Legal Aid so they could continue to do so.

Scott was just digesting the implications of this when there was a sharp rap on the door.

It was the signal for the judge.

The judge entered staring straight ahead of him like a monk in a procession. He took two strides and then swivelled to his right. It was as if he were trying to imitate a robot.

When he got to his chair he stood beside it, quite rigid, and did not move until Betty, the flustered court usher, pulled it out for him.

As the usher opened the court with the daily invitation for anybody who had business there to step forward, the judge rocked on his heels as though he had just been hit with a giant gong stick and was only now letting the final vibrations of the blow leave him.

It was a ritual that Scott was to watch being repeated twice a day for the length of the trial.

This was His Honour Judge Stebbing. He was, as far as Scott could gauge, barking mad. It was going to be a very long eight weeks.

The court quietened down. Stebbing turned his stare towards Scott and said, 'There are interpreters? They should be sworn immediately.'

As he said this Peter Khan got to his feet and spoke, 'You got the letter, milord?'

Stebbing registered exaggerated dismay, then puzzlement, then surprise. He ignored Khan and spoke to Scott. 'Who is this man?' he said.

'Khan, Your Honour. Peter Khan, Solicitor of Khan and Co.,' said Khan before Scott could speak.

'I will not be addressed by anyone other than counsel in my court.'

'That's the problem,' said Khan, who was obviously quite at ease, and not at all upset by the display the judge was putting on. 'I am afraid you can't hear counsel. Only me, since I am unable to obtain counsel for Mr Muazzam. He has no counsel.'

Had Stebbing possessed a thunderous 'Silence!' he might have been able to handle Khan. But he could not.

Khan's main strength was that he was behaving quite normally, he had something of importance to say to the court and he was saying it.

'Mr Muazzam cannot afford now,' he lingered slightly on the 'now', 'to instruct counsel or solicitors. I can no longer act for him.'

'He never could,' whispered Scott to Emily. 'This is stage two of the plan to get Legal Aid changed from the original solicitors to Khan.'

'I have filled in an application for Legal Aid on his behalf,' said Khan. 'Without Legal Aid he will have no lawyer; no doubt the court would not wish this man to stand trial on such a serious charge without a lawyer.' And he walked forward to the clerk's bench below the judge and gave him a document.

He made no reference to the fact that it was only his intervention that had made it possible that Muazzam might appear unrepresented by lawyers.

'We should swear the interpreters,' said Stebbing disregarding him.

The judge was quite prepared to carry on without a lawyer. He had seen the magistrate's report and when Khan's letter arrived had decided that neither Muazzam nor Khan were going to manipulate the court.

Khan paused, his bluff was being called. He said quite conversationally, 'Here is the application, it may be that the court should consider it.'

He turned and left.

'The interpreters,' said Stebbing. The two ladies came

forward, carrying their knitting, swore they spoke Punjabi and that they would well and faithfully interpret it. They identified Muazzam and two others as needing help. Then they returned to their needles, occasionally whispering to the men sitting beside them and sometimes to each other.

Their attempts at interpreting, fitful at first, later died away into complete forgetfulness.

'We have to deal with representation, Mr Scott. Mr Muazzam has no lawyer. Is that right, Mr Muazzam?'

The question was translated. Muazzam and one of the interpreters fell into a long conversation while everybody waited expectantly. At the end of it not much came out. 'He said, he doesn't worry, everybody has to get paid.'

'I am sure that's right,' said the judge, 'but that means, does it, that you have no lawyer?'

Again the conversation with the knitting ladies, who now both joined in.

'He has no lawyer. No lawyer than Khan. Who is the best lawyer?' they relayed back.

The judge spoke directly to the interpreters. 'Madam, please do not turn what he says into reported speech. Say it directly. If he says "I have no lawyer", then say "I have no lawyer", not he has no lawyer.' The interpreters looked at each other and discussed this.

The judge turned to Scott. 'The indictment should be put.'

The owner of the hotel and the desk clerk both pleaded not guilty. Nadim Janjoa pleaded not guilty, two of the couriers pleaded guilty. Muazzam said nothing at all.

The judge told all the other defendants to sit down and directed the clerk to put the question to Muazzam again.

It was read out, 'That on the seventh day of November you were knowingly concerned in the fraudulent importation of drugs, etc. etc. contrary to the Customs and Excise Management Act 1952.'

The formal language was quite beyond the ability of the interpreters, who normally did not bother themselves with this part of the case; 'knowingly concerned in the fraudulent importation', slowed them up, and 'Customs and Excise Management Act 1952' completely floored them.

They continued speaking for some time after the clerk had finished, discussing exactly what was said, and then asked, 'What was the date?'

'November the seventh,' said the clerk.

'No, no, the date of the Act of Parliament, was it 1952 or 1852?'

'Nineteen fifty-two.'

The two women turned to Muazzam and told him, 'Nineteen fifty-two.'

Muazzam was not helped by this.

Now and again the people in the main part of the court would turn round and look at him. He was aware that the man in the front was reading something out, but he had not the slightest idea who he was, no one had ever bothered to tell him. He was expected to know.

Could he be the judge? Again the man standing read something out. The women on either side of him started a discussion about what had been said. They eventually spoke to him and asked if he brought drugs here and did he wish to tell the court.

'They told me they were drugs,' he said. This was translated.

The clerk of the court stopped, not quite sure whether this counted as a plea of guilty or not guilty.

The judge launched himself into Muazzam. 'I would advise you not to play fast and loose with this court, young man,' he said.

The court shorthand note would not have betrayed the snarling nastiness of his voice.

'Mr Scott,' he turned to the prosecution, 'is it the prosecution case that Mr Muazzam speaks English?'

Scott turned to the bundle of statements. 'Yes, Your Honour. At page fifteen you will see the statement of PC Williams, who says that the defendant spoke quite clearly to him, before he struck out at him and tried to run away. The prosecution say that Mr Muazzam speaks good English.'

Tozer interrupted, 'Evidence will also be called on Mr Nadim Janjoa's behalf that Muazzam speaks English.'

The judge ignored Tozer. He leaned down towards his clerk and had a whispered conversation.

Scott turned to Emily. 'So it's going to be a cut-throat.'

She looked at him puzzled and he explained.

'It's clear from what Tozer said that Janjoa is going to blame Muazzam for this. One defendant cutting the throat of another in order to defend himself, it's called a cut-throat defence. Janjoa's going to put Muazzam forward as the guy in charge.'

'But that's crazy,' said Emily, 'he's an illiterate tailor from a village.'

'Repeat something often enough in the right tone of voice in a court and however extraordinary it is it eventually becomes believable,' said Scott. 'You just watch Tozer.'

Muazzam standing on his own at the back of the court was unaware of the role into which everyone was casting him – the organiser, a man moreover concealing his grasp of English, a man playing the court system to the limit. Even his transparent innocence was a cynical and clever act.

The judge started again, 'Mr Muazzam, you were minded to dispense with counsel provided by Legal Aid' – the interpreters were lost immediately – 'and I have here the documents in which you did so, making it clear that you knew what you were doing. Now you have again dispensed with counsel by refusing to pay the proper fees. I think I should make it clear that you are now speaking for yourself, and that this court will brook no prevarication. Do you plead guilty or not guilty to this charge?'

The interpreters eventually came back with a reply.

'I was told these were drugs.'

'That is not a proper reply,' said the judge. 'Guilty or not guilty?'

The interpreters thought that this was some sort of criticism of them and they discussed for a moment why it should be that what Muazzam had said was not a reply. It had seemed just that to them.

'You will either reply guilty or not guilty,' the judge was almost shouting.

He paused and when there came no immediate answer, he said to the clerk, 'Enter a plea of not guilty.'

Tozer was on his feet immediately. 'I should like it clearly recorded that Mr Muazzam has admitted that he was told that what he was carrying were drugs.'

Muazzam, who had meant that the Customs had told him that what they had found in the little packages were drugs, had not begun the trial, upon which fifteen years of his life might depend, particularly well.

'I don't see what I can do,' said Scott, 'the judge has got it into his head that the defendant is a fraud, that he obviously speaks English though he pretends he doesn't and that he has got rid of his lawyers just to delay the proceedings. But it's clear as a bell that this is one of Peter Khan's snatched cases where the plan has gone wrong.

'Any of the other judges there, Maxie, the Sucker obviously, even Screaming Jack Madden, would have given him Legal Aid lawyers immediately.' He paused, he was really quite angry.

'In the end it'd be cheaper. What's more it's a cut-throat trial. Tozer is going to suggest that Muazzam has organised the whole importation and he hopes that will acquit his client.

'He's even using what the man is saying now against him

when he has no lawyers to help. It's obvious who Muazzam is, he's a simple peasant just like the other two couriers and he has been taken for a ride. It's going to be slaughter, and if Muazzam comes out as the ringleader playing the system against the court he could end up with fifteen years.'

His anger was making him moody. 'And what will the Court of Appeal say to him if he appeals? "Bugger off!" Especially after I've stood up there on behalf of the Crown and said how fair everything was, and what a lovely judge Stebbing is.'

Emily watched him across the table. They were having a drink in El Vino's. Scott was with a friend, Ronnie Knox, from his old set, a man particularly good at listening.

'Tell the judge you're worried,' said Emily.

'You can't,' said Ronnie. 'Jeremy's not meant to be concerned. He's prosecuting. If someone that he's prosecuting wants to behave stupidly then he's pleased, not upset. There are limits to being a bleeding-heart liberal.'

In court Scott had spent the rest of the day after the bad-tempered start opening his case to the jury, that is, describing the evidence that was to be called against the six defendants.

As he had told the story he became aware again of how strong the evidence was against Muazzam and how weak it was against Janjoa and yet a feeling that in fact the truth was the other way round came even more strongly than before. It was a feeling he had had while preparing the papers. He could not account for it since the evidence was quite clearly the other way.

At one moment, when he turned towards the dock to emphasise the point of Muazzam's assault on the arresting officer, he saw the man's eyes on him.

He was reminded of another moment a few months ago when he had stood near to a man, an Asian, in a dock, who had reached out to touch him. But he was fully occupied with his speech and could not spare the time to retrieve the memory.

'Oh, so what, at least it will make the trial last longer,' he said, finishing his wine, 'and it's all money.'

'More?' said Knox, waving towards the latest Australian girl serving in El Vino's back bar. He said, 'Another bottle of Velvin, please.'

The girl climbed on to the wine box to lean through the hatch and call the order. As though it had been the sole reason for ordering the wine Ronnie's eyes never left her bottom.

'No,' said Emily, 'no more, thanks, but I have to go.' She got up.

She paused as she left. 'I may be a little late tomorrow.'

'Of course, no problem,' said Scott.

Emily threaded her way through the crowd of men in dark suits standing in the main section. Ronnie's weren't the only eyes that followed the back of her suit and the flash of her calf.

'Coo, what a corker,' Ronnie said, and he began to laugh.

It was a frightening noise, the whole of his chest heaved, giving off the sound of a heavy object being dragged across a pebble beach. It sounded so painful that Scott was amazed that Ronnie ever dared find anything funny.

'Bit dangerous, eh?' Ronnie asked.

'Dangerous?' Scott in his bad mood didn't want to play word games. But Ronnie's good nature was too much for him, 'Well, yes. I suppose so.'

'In fact,' Ronnie leaned forward, 'I meant a bit more than that. She is actually a bit dangerous.'

'What do you mean?'

'Well—' Ronnie paused and for a moment he thought, was his friendship with Scott up to this, then he decided to go ahead anyway, even an argument was fun. 'Well, she has got a reputation as someone who uses cocaine.'

'Where on earth did you get that from?'

'Well,' Ronnie found himself saying 'Well' again.

But before he could go on Scott hit the mark. 'I bet it was Tozer said it. That self-righteous little shit. Just because,' he remembered to add 'probably' in time; 'probably just because she wouldn't go to bed with him, not like the rest of the female Bar. So he's spreading stories. And he knew, you duffer, that you would tell me. Well, you tell him from me that he's a great tosser.'

Ronnie smiled broadly and rubbed the ring on his hand, showing it to Scott as though it were some sort of benediction. He began to laugh and the shingle in his lungs began to move again.

Just behind him sat a huge man in barristers' pin-stripes telling a joke at the next table. He also began to laugh with the same effect, only in his case his whole body began to quiver like a jelly.

What sort of a madhouse is this? thought Scott. 'I'm going to screw Tozer for that,' he said.

Emily went to Howard's house. He had some cocaine for her.

After the two occasions when she had smoked crack with Scully and with John Howard the night of the dinner party, she had refused more crack, but only at the cost of a regular trip to Howard's small sitting-room for a line of powder.

She found him there regularly in the evening. He sometimes spoke of needing to go out later in the night, but he never seemed hurried nor pressurised by any particular time to be observed. Nor did he ask for money.

On the other hand, things fell apart with the drug so she could not be entirely sure what was happening anyway.

Chapter 22

The next day Scott walked along the long corridor towards the court. The building had been a hospital once and it was still possible to make out its old shape. The long corridors must have led to the wards, now converted into courtrooms, with sluice rooms, laundry rooms and nurses' offices being turned into interview rooms.

The building somehow still shimmered in hygienic hospital light.

At the end of the passage Scott's prosecution witnesses, mostly uniformed, were gathered. They had not been needed the day before, the first day of the trial.

He stood slightly apart as he waited for the door of the court to be opened but found he was near enough to hear their conversation.

One or two of them glanced over and a voice said, 'Is he appearing for one of the guilty ones, or the very guilty one?'

There was a snigger and the officer who spoke, Scott could not see him clearly, was encouraged.

'He charges more to get the really guilty ones off. Then they need to commit more crime to pay him. It's a business expansion scheme.'

Scott sat down, making it seem that he was preoccupied with his papers. He watched the group. He was curious who was speaking. Amongst the Customs officers' uniforms he could see a police-officer. He was sure he recognised the sneer but couldn't remember where he had heard it before.

The court doors opened. As the jury were brought in Scott stood up to call his first witness. He discovered that it was the police-officer who he thought had laughed outside.

PC Williams made his way to the witness-box and started reading his evidence.

'I made my way to the third floor of the hotel and on the directions of Mr Paul Gregory, officer of Customs and Excise, I arrested the defendant Muazzam, I cautioned him.'

'Could you repeat the caution for the jury, please, Officer?' Scott asked.

It was a question he had asked hundreds of times and his mind was far away, trying to remember where he had seen this officer before.

'I warned him that he need not say anything but that if he did so then what was said would be taken down and used in evidence.'

The officer looked up from his notebook and turned to look at Scott. Then Scott realised who he was. He had last seen him while cross-examining on behalf of Masida.

The officer carried on with his evidence. 'I asked Muazzam if he knew what he was carrying, and he replied, "Of course I bloody do," and at that point the prisoner Muazzam pushed out with his left hand and swung round with his right hand hitting me on the jaw. He broke the crown on my tooth.'

'That must have been painful?' said the judge.

'I was off duty for five days.'

Five days, the memory of his previous encounter with Williams was suddenly clear to Scott, and the evidence that he had given against Masida then came back to him: 'He swung his right fist at me and hit me in the face . . . I was off work for five days.'

Scott knew he was lying.

For a moment Scott stood saying nothing. The witness, puzzled by the silence, turned and looked at him. The moment their eyes met each knew that the other knew the evidence was a lie.

'So the defendant Muazzam spoke English? And not only that, but rather good English, Officer?' said the judge.

PC Williams looked away from Scott at the judge and nodded. Then he remembered where he was, 'Yes, Your Honour,' he said. He hadn't realised outside the court that this barrister was the prosecutor, he had assumed he was defending.

Scott sat down.

Tozer got up to cross-examine, and immediately signalled the line he was going to take in the case on behalf of Janjoa.

'Did it surprise you, Officer, that this man Muazzam, apparently a penniless visitor to this country, could speak such good idiomatic English?'

This was too much for the judge.

'Oh, really, Mr Tozer. Whether this officer was surprised is neither here nor there. We are not concerned with his opinion.'

This only gave Tozer even greater opportunity to make his point and he completely disregarded the purpose of the judge's intervention. 'Well, Your Honour, I would be surprised if the officer were not surprised,' his voice began to take on the sing-song tone that Scott had heard before so often, 'since the defendant Muazzam pretends to be a poor tailor who speaks not a word of English. And yet here he was, effing and blinding like one of my magistrates' court clients.'

Stebbing still had memories of being defence counsel himself. Perhaps those memories were rapidly disappearing under the weight of his present self-importance but he realised he had to protect Muazzam.

After all, there was no one else there to do it; he Stebbing had seen to that.

'Mr Tozer, it is not your task in this court to tell us what you think. Your role is to put what your client says happened to the witness, so the witness can say whether it is right or wrong.'

Tozer again took no notice of the judge's correction. 'Well, my client says that Muazzam is a fraud, and that despite his denials he speaks English, as you would expect, like a native.'

He sat down, leaving this curiously ambiguous comparison in the air.

The judge addressed Muazzam across the court. He spoke slowly and carefully as though addressing a deaf mute.

'Now it's your turn, Muazzam. You must ask any question you want to ask.'

There was silence as the interpreter comprehended this and then translated it.

There was more silence.

Muazzam had nothing to ask. He had no idea who this man who had come into the court and who had talked about him was. He was not aware of having seen him before. He had been describing a fight it seemed. He knew he had not been involved in a fight and had not paid much attention to what the man was saying.

The court waited.

As the silence continued it began to weigh more heavily on each person sitting there. Although quite neutral the silence allowed suspicions to gather.

Here, it seemed to say, is the very event, this man is pretending he can't speak English.

'Muazzam,' the judge spoke sharply. 'Do you have nothing to say?'

The interpreter translated, 'Did you have nothing to say?'

'No,' said Muazzam.

'No,' the interpreter repeated.

Tozer immediately got to his feet. 'If Mr Muazzam does not contradict the officer when the officer quite plainly described him speaking good English, then I object to his having an interpreter. It misleads the jury.'

The judge showed surprising decisiveness and almost shouted, 'Sit down, Mr Tozer.'

Then he turned to the jury, 'Perhaps you could leave us for a moment, ladies and gentlemen.'

They got up and filed from the court, some smiling, one or two looking worried.

'Now, Mr Tozer,' the judge said, 'this trial has barely begun and already you have made two remarks in front of the jury that can only prejudice the defendant Muazzam's case. Some might say they were calculated to prejudice his case. I must ask you to refrain from any such comment.'

Tozer remained standing. 'I object to this defendant unfairly using court procedures to his advantage. He is sheltering behind a lie. I can call the evidence of someone who heard Muazzam speaking English. My solicitor was present' – Tozer pointed to Monty Bach – 'with a client, a Mr Vespasian, when Muazzam was speaking English.'

The name Vespasian jerked Scott back to the cells at Elephant and Castle Crown Court.

He remembered. Monty Bach had been next door handing out hamburgers. Vespasian was the man who was trying to get clients for Monty. It must have been Muazzam who had been upstairs in court when Donkin dropped the brief – he was the defendant who had been crying and who reached out to him. Again a memory fell into place.

Gregory tapped Scott on the shoulder. He had been going through the same process of recall, although he had remembered the conversation with Monty at the Customs headquarters, 'Monty Bach told us that he had heard Muazzam speak English,' he told Scott.

The judge interrupted Tozer, 'Mr Tozer, I am not going to risk a man being prevented from understanding his trial. I can't take away his interpreter. And I certainly won't do it on evidence provided by a co-defendant who may well have his own purposes to serve.'

This was a remark so self-evidently fair that it reduced even Tozer to silence.

Scott thought back to the events in the cell. He was sure he hadn't heard Muazzam speak, in fact, now he could remember, Vespasian had translated for him. He could still hear the bird-like language twittering in the next cell. Yes, he remembered now thinking of the Welshness of the accents. He could remember Vespasian saying that Muazzam spoke no English and he would hardly have been making it up – who would he have wanted to make it up for?

The judge spoke to him, 'What do you say, Mr Scott? Do you say I should hear Mr Tozer's application to remove this man's interpreter?'

The judge was covering himself against any appeal by asking the prosecution's opinion, by hearing all sides to the argument.

'I do not support Mr Tozer's application. If a man says he needs an interpreter then it's not for the court to hear other people's opinion. It's a matter for the judge to decide and eventually for the jury to consider. Mr Tozer is entitled to suggest what he likes to Mr Muazzam in cross-examination when the time comes.'

This answer was so clearly what the judge needed to get on with the trial that Scott took the risk of going further. He wasn't going to stand by and let this unfairness go on, especially if Tozer was doing it.

'What's more, I think Mr Muazzam ought to be represented.

He should have a lawyer. This trial is clearly going to be a cut-throat.'

The slang expression brought home to the judge the situation he had created by refusing Khan's application for Legal Aid the day before.

He paused, then changed his mind. 'I suppose we had better send for Mr Khan,' he said.

Peter Khan had taken a risk by persuading Muazzam to sack his other lawyer, but not, he thought, an unreasonable one. Who could have imagined that a judge would make a defendant go through a trial of this gravity without a lawyer? That he would refuse to grant a resumption of Legal Aid?

On reflection, the judge's behaviour was yet another example of the court's indifference to racially differentiated defendants.

Obviously the court had seen it was him defending as well. He was too well-known as a radical lawyer. And he was black. It was prejudice at its most glaring.

So the telephone call, when it came from the clerk of the court, was only confirmation that he had been right all along and that the trial could not be conducted without lawyers. He was completely vindicated.

On the phone he was reluctant, just to show them they couldn't order him around, but provisionally he agreed to come back into the trial. He asked to see the judge that afternoon. If he was coming back it was going to be on his own terms.

Smiling he put the phone down and called Wesley Divall's clerk. 'Khan here,' he said. 'We've been granted Legal Aid now in the Muazzam case. I told you we would. Can Divall get there tomorrow?'

He was told yes.

'It'll be three weeks of work, or maybe more,' Khan said. 'The case will be listed at two o'clock so Mr Divall can get himself organised. It started yesterday so he's got some catching up to do.'

Khan put the phone down and went to see the judge.

His Honour Judge Stebbing was annoyed. He had agreed to see Khan late in the day and so had had to remain at court long past his normal train.

He passed the time by continuing with his tabulation of the minor county cricket scores. He was busy with County Durham when there was a scuffling noise at the door. Durham was a difficult county, not least because it was no longer minor, and his annoyance was redoubled by the time the court clerk introduced Peter Khan.

'We need a shorthand writer before we can discuss the matter,' said the judge, and he motioned Khan to sit down. Both of them sat in silence.

The judge's eyes kept flickering away to his figures and tables but his manners would not allow him to continue the work. He and Khan stared at each other in simple dislike.

Khan had already noticed the copy of *Wisden* lying open on the desk. He took in the room. It was oak-panelled. Around the walls there was a complete set of law reports, there were sets of *Criminal Law Review* and Criminal Appeal reports. There were editions of Archbold going back to the tiny blue copies of the late 1950s, but more numerous than any of the law reports there was a complete set of *Wisden*, of *Cricket Magazine*, and racks of the *County Cricket Observer*.

Khan took a breath and then said, 'My grandfather knew Gubby Allen well. He hit him back over his head for six twice in an over at Karachi, and then entertained him to dinner. Gubby would have been past his best then, though.'

Stebbing could hardly believe his ears. Here was the authentic tone of colonial cricket at its best – and from a Legal Aid solicitor from Stockwell.

'Gubby Allen,' he said softly.

He had a copy of the photograph of the famous bowling action, and was about to get it out when he was interrupted by the stenographer's awkward arrival – shuffling through the door sideways in order to accommodate the legs of her machine.

She had been kept at court too and wasn't pleased.

'I shall need to go to Pakistan,' said Khan – the judge looked startled – 'before I can undertake to defend Mr Muazzam properly. Do you wish me to tell you why?'

Khan used the momentary pause he had created to carry on.

'I shall tell you only what would have been in the formal application had we been able to make one in good time.

'There is a witness there who can prove Muazzam's defence. She has to be seen. The case cannot be defended correctly without that. I need you to indicate that it would be a proper thing to do given the degree of urgency. If you do that I shall be paid, I can't take the risk of the expenditure without it.'

So Khan's acceptance of the case depended on this request. It would be cheaper overall to accept it than to abort the whole trial and obtain a different solicitor who would have to start reading the case papers from scratch.

But much more importantly, Peter Khan had with that one comment about cricket put himself into a different category. The judge said, 'Can you get counsel able to start tomorrow at two o'clock?'

'Yes, I can.'

'Then I agree to your request.' The judge turned to the clerk. 'Let the court papers be so marked.'

Chapter 23

Ronnie Knox was in the same place still, or so it seemed, watching the same waitress.

'We've been at it six days now and this damn case is going from bad to worse,' said Scott. He signalled for a wine. 'Not only is Tozer cut-throating Muazzam, but now I know that one of my witnesses is lying and —'

'How do you know?' Ronnie interrupted him.

'Because he lied in another case that I was in.'

'How do you know he lied?' said Ronnie.

'Because the judge threw out the case.'

'How did the judge know he was lying?' Ronnie had got hold of the conversation like a Rottweiler.

'I don't suppose he did,' said Scott. 'He just threw the case out.'

'Then you don't know that he was lying.'

'Yes, you're right,' Scott admitted, 'but I know as in *I know* that he is lying now.'

'Fat lot of good that is to anyone,' said Ronnie.

'What's more I know that Muazzam doesn't speak English.'

'How do you know?' said Ronnie.

Scott became exasperated. 'Ronnie, can't you behave like

a human being for a moment?'

'Are we talking about a court case or what?' was Ronnie's reply. 'How do you know this about Muazzam?'

'I overheard someone say it in a cell.'

'So what?'

'Look, the guy who said it had no reason whatever to lie. He didn't know he was being overheard.'

'That proves that he believed it, but that doesn't prove he's right – does it?'

'No.'

'What are you going to do? Tell everyone you're going to be a witness for the defence? What you overhear isn't even admissible evidence. How do you know who was speaking? You're only guessing.'

'You're right.'

'It's perfectly normal and proper to prosecute someone you think is innocent. Do you really think that prosecuting counsel in the Farrell appeal case thought that they were all guilty. After that evidence? After a washerwoman described cleaning blood off the walls of the police station? Do me a favour. Anyone can get a guilty man down, it takes skill to get an innocent man convicted.' Ronnie laughed, it was an old joke, but all the same a little worrying.

The pebbles on the beach moved across Ronnie's chest, 'The first question people always ask me at dinner parties is how you can defend guilty people. They never ask me how I can prosecute innocent ones.'

The shingle reminded Scott of the beach at Dover, where ignorant armies clash by night.

Emily woke up with a shudder. She seemed still to be in her dream, and though she was awake, the fear of it remained.

Her back and neck were damp with sweat and instead of being warm, her bedclothes were as cold as the room around her. She got straight up and stood silently facing the curtains.

From behind them the orange glow of the London night sky swelled up. It was very still. The furniture, especially her father's great wardrobe, loomed indifferently in the half-light.

She had hidden in that wardrobe that night she came home from school and found her mother gone. The house was filled with strange noises and she had been afraid.

How old was she? Six.

She had burrowed into the corner under the suits and coats, a pair of trousers had fallen from its hanger and she had sat trying to fold the huge amount of material. It was more than her small hands could manage.

A rough tweed jacket hung down by her cheek and she had rested her head against it, reassured by its connection with her father. She had often felt its roughness against her bare legs when he was wearing it, when he lifted her up.

She had held the cloth close to her. The smell of it had made her swoon. The dark, the muffled quiet and the smell; the reminder of him, the scent of his body, his hair and his shoes all swam together in her memory.

Then the door had opened and a sharp voice had called her name.

It was a woman who later came to live in the house. Emily had seen a hand, thin and narrow, with long nails, pull the clothes aside. She shrunk back from contact and the voice had gone away, dismissive, 'You better deal with it, Charles'; it was a phrase she was to become familiar with later. Then her father's arms reaching for her through the clothes, his voice reassuring her. If he was so strong why was he allowing these things to happen to them?

There was no movement, she was entirely alone, she turned and faced the wardrobe.

There was a drawer in that cupboard, a secret drawer that opened into a hidden space. In it she kept a jumble, a silk scarf, a pair of dress gloves and a rough knitted pair of socks. They all belonged to him. She had darned them once at school. She remembered burying her face in the scrap of wool and shutting out the world. A badge, an old pair of spectacles, a pencil. The rag-and-bone shop of her heart.

She felt empty and in need. Suddenly she started moving, jittering up and down, touching her arms and elbows, she began to walk round the room. She picked up a china doll and put it down, then a shoe, then a little tin containing pins. She watched herself touch and move the pieces on her desk. Without a break in her movements she climbed back into bed, then as suddenly she stood up and pulled the bedclothes to the floor, picked them up and folded them, laid them out, smoothed them, tucked them in, got back into bed, then out again and stood facing the window.

She remembered something that had happened to her years ago at school when she had made a fool of herself. She coughed and pushed out her fist as if to push the memory away. She stopped, looked at her hand, it seemed to be beginning to swell.

She sat down and picked up a book. In the dark she could not read it. So she threw it down.

Moments later she discovered that she was convulsively scratching her knee, only the pain stopped her.

She fell back into the bed and pulled the blanket round, down over her shoulder, and twisted herself into a ball, forcing her hands under her arms until her fingers began to bend back. For a while she became preoccupied with the growing numbness in her wrists.

She moved her arm then felt the pins and needles overwhelm her fingers and hand, then creep up her forearm. But soon they stopped, and her attention was left to wander back to the – what was it? It wasn't an emptiness. It wasn't hunger. It was more like dissatisfaction. It became hunger, then cold, then thirst, then boredom, then fear. And then all of them together.

She looked at her clock, it was 3.52. The numbers glowed indifferently in the dark.

Where was John Howard? Could she ring him at this time of night? She lay thinking, then she realised that she didn't care whether she woke him or not, what she needed was some cocaine.

She reached over to the phone and dialled his number, after two rings an answerphone clicked in and her heart fell. Then she heard the familiar voice giving a portable phone number; she memorised the number and, repeating it to herself, she put the phone down and dialled again.

The phone rang just long enough to make her think he would not answer, then his voice came on.

'Yes. Car ninety-three.'

She didn't pause to think what that meant but told him who had called, 'It's Emily.'

'Hello, I'm just near you.' It was as if he already knew what it was that she needed.

'I'm in need.' The words as they came out seemed wrong, and yet she had said what she felt, and the slang no longer sounded artificial but a statement of the simple truth.

'I'll collect you in ten minutes.'

She got dressed; jeans, sweater and soft shoes. It was cold out but she did not bother with a coat. But her bag, yes, it had her cash card. As she paused by the door she saw her briefcase with her court robes, her wig and the white bands spilling out of it. Next to it a notebook and pen lay on the floor. She had thrown the bag down when she arrived home and hadn't touched them since. It had been some time since she worked on any papers at home.

Then the bell rang and she left.

At first she did not see Howard, until she realised that the old beaten-up car right in front of her was his. She climbed in front and he pulled away. On the dashboard of the car in front of her there was a no-smoking sign and hanging from the mirror there was a three-colour traffic-light air freshener. There was a radio, and stuffed between the front seats an A to Z map of London. He was driving a mini-cab.

'Why?' she turned towards him. The radio crackled.

'I've always wondered what it was like. Haven't you?'

But she had already lost interest in the idea.

'I hope you don't mind me ringing you.' She knew that everything she said was false with the message, get me cocaine.

'No, no,' he said, 'I have been expecting it. We need to talk, anyway.'

His house shone into the dark square where the leaves on the road glistened in the rain. The trees opposite the door dripped gently on to the cars parked beneath them. The cobbled gutter dipping towards the railings surrounding the small garden in the middle of the square reflected the drooping street-lamps.

He parked outside and they dashed up the stairs to the front door. It opened as they reached it, light poured out and there stood Mrs Roberts.

'You needn't have waited up,' said Howard. But Mrs Roberts said nothing, only taking his coat from him and closing the large door against the night wind.

'In here,' he said, and they went into the small book-lined room. A fire was burning and there was a coffee cup waiting by the hearth.

Despite the welcome of the room, the warm glow of the wood and dappled books, she felt no better. The only effect of this immediate calm was to increase her expectation.

'You wanted a line.'

It wasn't a question. Howard sat down by the fire.

She said nothing.

He turned and started to pull things from a drawer beside him. 'In fact, you need a line.'

She looked at him blankly, he was repeating what she had nearly said out loud an hour ago in her darkened room.

It was startling to hear someone else acknowledge exactly what she felt, uninvited, as though they were comparing independent memories of the same book.

She had time to reflect on the oddity of her situation. Her personal experience, despite being so intensely her own experience, was straight out of the manuals on addiction. Every strand of it was at the same time both new to her and yet banal and could be read anywhere.

Suddenly he said, 'Scully told me you owed him money.' Howard looked up at her and smiled.

It was a method he had learned before; send two different messages at the same time.

The cocaine, her need for it, had stripped away everything from her save direct understanding. There were no manners left. She responded, 'What do you want?'

It was clear to her that he was about to deliver the bill, for the drugs he'd given her on account.

'Do you want to sleep with me?'

'Of course,' he said. 'Who wouldn't? But I don't want to buy you.'

He turned to the table between them and laid out the piece of paper on which he had been chopping the crystals. 'I do want something, though. I want some information.' He laughed. 'Not just want, I shall insist on it.'

He paused, as though to allow their altered relationship time to settle.

'Are you managing all right at the new chambers?'

'Yes.'

'Is Vinnie all right? I have heard he can be a difficult clerk.'

'I don't really have anything to do with him,' she said. 'I spend most of my time working with Jeremy Scott.'

'Are you working with him now?'

He gave her the drug.

As he did so she knew what it was he wanted.

'You want me to interfere with the trial.'

'Yes,' he said.

'I would prefer not to.'

The remark seemed absurd; it was absurd but was the strongest thing she could find to say. Part of her remembered 'Bartleby the Scrivener'.

She watched the white line of powder on the table by his hand. Nothing seemed important beside this heaven, this earth.

'All I am asking is that you place a piece of paper in one of the unused bags of exhibits. It will not even be telling an untruth, in fact quite the opposite.

'See, I have it here.' He held it out towards her.

She took it to look at, out of curiosity, and in the same moment accepted the task. The line of cocaine sweetened everything around her, and she stared unobserving at a mini-cab card with the name Bill written on it in pencil.

Chapter 24

Tozer would rather have been a prosecutor. He felt most at home when he was amongst CID and Customs officers. He enjoyed their rituals and the reassuring atmosphere of their loyalties, their male clubbishness, the safety of their assumptions.

As a result of his friendships he already had a small collection of ties, printed by various squads to celebrate notable convictions. He couldn't wear them all since some celebrated convictions where he himself had been defending.

But some he could.

'This one here, then,' he said to Emily, 'crossed handcuffs, with a little figure running over a pile of logs. Can you work out what that means?'

Emily leaned forward to look at the piece of Crimplene. She couldn't imagine what it meant.

'No idea,' she said.

'Well, I'll give you a clue. That's a woodpile, and the arrest took place in Brixton. Now what do you think?'

Is this man really so crass, thought Emily, or is it an act?

Then she felt his hand on her back, and she realised it didn't matter much which it was.

She had arrived at court early, even before Scott, and the staff found it perfectly normal when she headed for the cupboard where the prosecution bags of documents were kept.

There were twelve of them, large brown paper bags each with an inner lining, designed originally to hold shredded waste. But now they were full of large plastic bags, each holding, shoved in higgledy-piggledy, assorted scraps of paper. This was 'unused material' brought to the trial for the defence to see, papers which were probably going to be of no importance in the case.

Each plastic bag had a label attached to it showing where the pieces of paper had been gathered.

Oddly enough there was no list of exactly what each contained, so one was marked 'Contents of bedroom at 16 Dalberg Road', another 'Papers found in Audi 90, A828 ASF Possession of Janwarsan'. It would have been an impossibly lengthy task to list each document separately.

Somewhere she would find a plastic bag labelled 'documents taken from Janjoa 7th November'. She hoped it had not been sealed.

Carefully she sorted through the bags, digging through them like architectural layers in an excavation, each relating to a particular era of the investigation. She felt herself coming nearer to the events of his arrest.

Here was the bag that held the unused hotel documents, she was getting warm. Then she found it: 'Correspondence in possession of Janjoa, 7th November', signed by the custody officer.

It wasn't sealed, only press-folded: she shook it out, it contained a tube ticket, a, what was it? she unfolded it – a hairdresser's advertising hand-out. And there was no list of contents.

She looked behind her, crazy really, the room she was in was not much bigger than a cupboard and if anyone else had come in she could hardly have missed it. She put the taxi card in the plastic bag just as John Howard had demanded of her.

Closing the bag, she shoved it back into the bigger bag, snatched up another pile of documents as an alibi and retreated into the courtroom.

It was stupid to feel that she looked suspicious. She was part of the prosecution team and had an absolute right to go into the exhibits cupboard, no one would have suggested otherwise, but she nearly jumped out of her skin when Tozer loomed up in front of her and said, 'Hello, Emily. Been doing a bit of work?'

'Hello, Tozer,' she said, backing away from him. She reminded herself yet again there was no reason why others should suspect her of anything. What she was doing was what she or Jeremy did every morning, and had done for the past ten days of the trial. She put the plastic bag of documents down by her papers.

'No, I've done it,' she said, then realised her mistake.

Tozer immediately took this as an invitation. 'Then let's go and have a coffee,' he said.

What's happening to me? she thought, I used to see these things coming a mile off. 'OK,' she said.

The barristers' dining-room overlooked the car park, and they sat watching people arrive. Tozer was scathing about the cars people drove. 'I know what everybody in chambers has. We've got three BMWs and two Mercedes, and Doryan has got a Land-Rover. Look, there's Jeremy Scott, what on earth is that? A Ford Orion. My God, a salesman's car, it must be at least ten years old. Has the man no self-respect?'

Emily watched Scott get out of the car. He looked up at the window as though he knew he was being watched. No, she thought, he hasn't, but not in the way Tozer thinks.

'What sort of car have you got, Tozer?' she said, he had obviously been waiting for the question.

'Over there.' He pointed. Behind the gatehouse there was a bright-red E-type Jaguar.

'Good Lord,' she said. Tozer took that as a compliment.

'Yes,' he said, 'rather nice.'

'Why on earth do you own one of those? Don't people laugh at you?'

He looked at her for a moment then discarded the second question as not relevant.

'I always promised myself one.'

'What did you do to deserve it, Tozer?'

'I became successful, didn't I?' he said.

There was nothing to say to that, and she picked up her coffee reflectively, only to be interrupted by Tozer leaning over and showing her his tie. 'Went to a CID dinner last night, they gave me this.'

All the time he had been edging slightly closer to her, and when she felt his hand on her back she looked around for some way out. At that moment Monty Bach appeared at the door. Monty hesitated and then walked over to their table.

'Hello, Monty,' said Tozer.

'I've got some more papers for you,' said Monty, pulling at his briefcase. He looked away from Tozer at Emily with a questioning motion.

'Emily, could you get Monty a coffee?' said Tozer. In Tozer's world pupils fetched coffee. She got up to get it, grateful for the break.

'I've been in touch with a witness, he rang me this morning to confirm he will give evidence. His name is Bill Green. He says that he remembers taking an Indian as a fare from Heathrow to the Argyle Hotel last 7th November. He's a mini-cab driver. And listen to this, even better, he will say he suggested the hotel – he always does when passengers ask him. Sometimes he can get a commission from them.'

'This is fantastic, Monty.' Tozer took the witness statement that Monty was handing him. 'How do you do it? You always come up with the goods.'

'Look, it goes further.' Monty leaned forward confidentially. He glanced over to where Emily was organising him a coffee from a big brown machine. He didn't want the prosecution to get any wind of this till the time came. 'The witness is sure that he gave Janjoa a business card. You know, a taxi number with his name on it.

'Now, that card might be somewhere. Janjoa was arrested at the Argyle only seconds after getting out of the cab. I've got all the property that Janjoa had when he was arrested, I've looked and it isn't there. But on the custody officer's record there is a reference to correspondence. Perhaps it's in the Crown bundles of unused material. If it's there then you . . .'

'OK,' said Tozer. Emily arrived back at the table carrying a brown watery liquid. 'Secrets, secrets,' he said. 'We don't want Miss Clarke to upset our plans by hearing our defence, do we?'

As he said this he raised his voice so that Scott, who was arriving in the room at that moment, could hear him.

Tozer sheltered the witness statement with his arm in an exaggerated manner from the prosecutor, and winked at Monty Bach.

'Come on, Tozer, what have you got there?' said Scott.

'You'll see, you'll see,' said Tozer, 'but Mr Bach and I feel that you will want to drop the case against Janjoa as soon as you are able to. You see, now we *know* he wasn't involved in this dreadful enterprise. And that it was all Muazzam's fault.'

Again he raised his voice, this time to greet Wesley Divall's entrance.

'Tozer's got something,' Scott said to Wesley Divall as he sat down. They all paused as Divall cleaned the chair where he was going to sit.

'Yes. It's a tape of your client discussing the world situation

231

in flawless English. Now we know all this interpreter stuff is a con,' said Tozer.

Wesley Divall had been the butt of Tozer's remarks throughout the trial. He had tried not to react to it, aware of his position – very junior, a latecomer, and only in the trial as Tozer regularly reminded him because of a stunt pulled by Khan.

He was beginning to regret the association with Khan – he didn't want to become one of his men – but on the other hand it was a good brief, and if the messages he was getting from Pakistan were anything to judge by it would get more exciting as it went on.

'Great, Tozer. Let's hear it now, then.' Wesley called Tozer's bluff by opening his briefcase to get his Walkman out. 'I shall be very surprised since my client does not speak English, and never has.'

Scott interrupted. He had the list of witnesses whom he still had to call in his hand. 'I'm going to do some tidying up witnesses today, and I'll finish the prosecution case tomorrow.

'I need to call the detailed stuff about the hotel accounts. That doesn't affect you two. I've got someone who calls himself the Appointed Plumber to the Customs and Excise to explain the lavatories to the jury and I've got the various custody officers with their documentation – only those who have been asked for.

'Emily, can you check whether the plumber and the accountant have arrived? I'll call them first.'

Emily started to get up when Tozer spoke, 'I need to see some of the unused documentation if I can.' Her heart missed a beat. 'And I need to see it before you call the custody officer who dealt with my client.'

'Well, get Mr Gregory to show it to you. He'll be there by now,' said Scott, 'tell him I said it's OK, he'll have to stay there with you while you look.'

* * *

Paul Gregory didn't like Tozer but had to put up with him. Tozer affected to be on Gregory's side when they were alone. Tozer was the last person Gregory wanted on his side.

'You'll be Divisional C, won't you?' Tozer said. 'Do you know Wally Winterspoon? He and I were on the Prendergast Gold fraud case together. That case went three months and we had a hell of a party at divisional headquarters afterwards. One of the chiefs looked in, I remember.'

They were knee-deep in documents so Gregory wasn't obliged to answer. It was lucky since he knew Wally Winterspoon only too well.

He and Tozer had unfortunately chosen the wrong bag to start and had got bogged down with all the documentation seized from the office of the hotel.

He had been through it a number of times before but seemed to find something new every time he looked. Here was a receipt from A. J. Dawson's Chemical Suppliers. Could that have been for a cutting agent or a testing agent for drugs? It ought to have been followed up.

Tozer had gone quiet, and Gregory glanced over. 'Have you got it?' he said.

'I think so. Look, I don't want to open it. You check the label and then hang on to it.'

Gregory checked the label: 'Correspondence in possession of Janjoa, 7th November', and it was signed by the custody officer. He checked the bag. It wasn't fully sealed but the press seal was not open, or at least it was closed now and Tozer hadn't opened it. Inside he could see a hairdresser's hand-out and a white board card. Nothing there of importance. 'Your client wanted a haircut, Mr Tozer?'

'Something like that. You keep it, please, Mr Gregory.' Tozer had already seen what was printed on the white card, just what Monty had forecast.

* * *

The accountancy evidence dragged on and everybody in the court began to feel drowsy. Scott had to keep awake if only to ask the questions.

'Go to the 15th August, please, Mr John. How do the receipts of that month ending compare with the expenses?'

'Well,' the Customs' accountant rubbed his hands together with pleasure as he surveyed the computer-generated figures in front of him, 'the figures demonstrate that the hotel was not making anything like the amount of money necessary to stay open and certainly not enough to spend money on plane tickets to the Caribbean.'

'Wait a moment,' said the judge, 'let's just get that down.' He continued writing, slowly and meticulously, as he had done throughout the trial.

Two men on the back row of the jury who had enjoyed the start of the trial as a change from work, but who had long ago been completely distracted by the painstaking process of taking evidence, glanced at each other and raised their eyebrows. One of them shut his eyes and seemed to go to sleep.

A jumbo jet, descending as it approached Heathrow, flooded the court with noise. The judge held his hand up, and everybody waited for the next question as it passed. The prison officer could feel his teeth rattle.

He took a sip from his glass of water and turned the page of his Sven Hassell book.

Chapter 25

Paul Gregory stepped forward and took the oath. Scott called no evidence and only tendered Gregory for cross-examination. By now the whole court was quiet, overwhelmed by the accountant's figures.

It was just the right atmosphere for Tozer to drop his bombshell.

He started slowly.

'Mr Gregory,' he said, 'I am right that Mr Janjoa is a man who has not been in any trouble before?'

Gregory said, 'Yes, as far as we know.'

'As far as you know? But you have Customs officers stationed in Pakistan and in India, Mr Gregory?'

'Yes.'

'And if Mr Janjoa were a known smuggler, then your men in Pakistan would have access to that information?'

Gregory had to answer yes. Officially this was so. In fact the British Customs officers knew they were spoon-fed only a tiny part of what information the foreign authorities acquired.

'But if Mr Janjoa had been known then he would have been noticed at Customs and followed?'

Again Gregory had to answer yes.

'He would have been followed – just like Muazzam?'

Wesley Divall wondered whether to object at the implication of what Tozer was saying, but decided not to draw it to the attention of the jury.

'Yes,' said Gregory.

'But he was not, was he? He was first seen on the steps of the Argyle Hotel.' Tozer allowed no time for a reply. 'Did anybody see him arrive there?'

'I didn't,' said Gregory.

'Did anybody?'

'I didn't,' repeated Gregory. He was fed up with Tozer.

'That's because he arrived in a taxi. He did not travel with the others,' said Tozer.

Gregory said nothing. So this was Janjoa's defence. Up till now, save that he was blaming Muazzam, his exact defence had not been clear.

'Have you the property that was taken from Mr Janjoa at his arrest?'

'Yes,' said Gregory. 'It's over there.' He indicated the desk where he had been sitting. The bag was brought over to him.

'This is the bag?'

'Yes.'

'It hasn't been opened?'

'No,' said Gregory. 'You were with me this morning when the bag was pulled out of store.'

'Can you show the jury what it contains?'

Gregory unsnapped the bag. Emily watched him.

'There is a trade card for a taxi company, a hairdressing hand-out. Nothing else.'

'Is there a name written on the taxi card? The name Bill? Is it Scala Cabs?'

'Yes.'

'That's the taxi that he came from Heathrow in,' said Tozer. He turned to the jury and smiled at them, they would realise, wouldn't they, that if Janjoa came by taxi from the airport then the whole case against him began to disappear?

'I don't know. No one saw him arrive,' said Gregory. He thought for a moment. 'But if he did go by taxi then where did he get the hairdressing hand-out from? Did the taxi-driver give it to him? Normally these things are handed out in the street.'

Tozer had his instructions and was ready for this. 'The moment he opened the door of the cab it was thrust into his hand. He is a visitor here, how would he know what it was?'

Gregory could say nothing.

Had he really not noticed that Janjoa had a taxi card in his pockets? He remembered checking whether there was anything of relevance on him at his arrest. He had had nothing. But things were about to get more complicated.

As he unfolded the hairdressing hand-out, something fell out. It fluttered to the side of the witness-box. The usher stepped forward and picked it up. It was a tube ticket. Gregory took it. From Heathrow, dated the 7th November, the same date as their arrival.

'It's a tube ticket, Mr Tozer,' he said. 'Heathrow. The date of your client's arrival.'

As Gregory looked up Tozer was already talking to Monty, taking instructions on the new development. He turned back to the witness-box.

'You'll see it is unused, Mr Gregory. My client Mr Janjoa came by taxi. And the taxi-driver is outside the court now.'

It wasn't a question but a speech. But the defence was clear now.

He sat down.

Tozer was angry. What ought to have been the complete destruction of the Crown case had been shaded off by the discovery of the damn tube ticket. Why hadn't he seen it in the bag that morning?

Gregory was thinking the same thing. He had only examined

the contents through the plastic bag and it had seemed that there was only the hand-out there. That would teach him to open packets completely in the future.

The judge asked a question.

'A tube ticket and a taxi card. Where has this package containing Mr Janjoa's property been since his arrest, Mr Gregory?'

'In the exhibits room since the trial began, and before then in the case cupboard at Customs headquarters.'

'Could anyone have access to it?'

'No, only myself, and in the court – the Customs solicitor and Mr Scott.' Then he corrected himself, 'And of course Miss Clarke.'

Scott had been listening to this evidence glumly. His case against Janjoa was almost completely destroyed.

'What a cock-up, didn't Gregory check this?' he said, turning to Emily. 'What are we going to say? That someone got to the bag and planted it?'

He saw that her face was white and rigid but thought nothing of it, it only reflected his own anger.

'Mr Scott,' the judge interrupted him, 'have you any further questions?'

'No, Your Honour.'

'Is that your last witness?'

'I only have one or two almost formal points to deal with. Mr Gregory is the last substantial witness.'

'Then we shall take a break now.'

Gregory came over to Scott. 'That card wasn't there when he was arrested. I'd swear it. He never came by taxi.'

'It's a bit late to say that now.' Scott tried to keep the anger out of his voice.

'There was no card,' said Gregory. He paused and then repeated, 'I know there was no card in his things. It would have been noticed, for one damn good reason. That taxi company "Scala Cabs" is one of Scully's.'

'Who?' said Scott.

Behind him Emily sat down.

'Scully is a drugs dealer. He's a Jamaican posse on his own almost, one of the biggest suppliers in London. He delivers by taxi.' Gregory looked round him to make sure they were not being overheard. 'He has six cab firms that work for him, maybe more. With all the taxi firms in London – there must be hundreds – the coincidence of it being this one is just too great.'

They began to move away from the row of benches where Emily was sitting. She felt sick.

Scott turned round and looked at her. 'We're going for coffee.' As his glance took her in, his expression altered. 'Are you feeling well?'

'No. No. I'm all right,' she said. She got up to follow them. She had to hear what was said, and followed them to the canteen.

'Scully sells cocaine by phone,' said Gregory.

They each got a thin coffee and settled down at a table. 'He can get twice the street price on personal delivery, and his only problem is the occasional bright young man who runs up a debt with him. It's the only operation I've ever heard of where the supplier gives credit. But he can afford to, because most of the buyers are in steady work and can't cope with trouble. The ones who get into debt become suppliers for him and work off the debt. If they don't then life can get nasty.'

The table at which they sat had, it seemed, been designed to be particularly uncomfortable. The chairs were attached to the table and could not be moved. Emily sat on the inside, next to Scott, opposite Gregory. She began to feel trapped.

'So you reckon this is an arranged defence?' said Scott.

'I'm sure of it,' said Gregory, 'that card has been put in that bag. I know he didn't have it on arrest.'

'Well, what have we got? Janjoa's going to say that he came

in a cab from Heathrow. Tozer said that the cab driver was outside. That'll prove he wasn't travelling with the others.'

'How can we deal with that?'

'The tube ticket.'

'The ticket's no use. It's unused. Tozer'll say Janjoa changed his mind and took a cab.'

Scott paused, and then answered, 'But was it unused? Did you look at it?'

Gregory pulled the exhibits bag out of his pocket and put it on the table in front of them.

Scott laughed. 'What on earth are you doing with that here? That's an exhibit.'

'No, it's not. Tozer didn't ask for it to be exhibited. I offered it to the court usher but she didn't want it. So here it is.'

Gregory spilled the pieces of paper out on to the table.

Emily stretched forward to pick up the taxi card.

'No,' said Gregory, and he pushed her hand aside. 'I'm going to have that fingerprinted, I want to know who put it there.' He looked at her face and saw what Scott had seen earlier on. 'Tozer forgot to ask for it to be exhibited. He was as upset by the tube ticket as we were by the taxi card.' He picked up the ticket by the edges. 'Has this been used?'

Scott spoke without thinking. 'Put it through the dummy and read it.'

'What do you mean?' said Gregory.

'The dummy! Of course,' said Scott, 'you can read those tickets. The ticket barriers imprint details of use in the metallic strip. You can get a print-out. There's a room somewhere – Baker Street, I think – that has got a dummy barrier sitting in the middle of it. If it was used then it will tell you exactly when.'

'I'll telephone now,' said Gregory, 'I can get down there immediately.'

Scott said, 'Look, I'm going to have to close the prosecution case this afternoon. Maybe I can keep it going till tomorrow. I need it by then or it's certainly no use, whatever it proves.'

Gregory left to find a phone and Scott turned to Emily, 'What do you reckon?'

She did not immediately understand him. He said, 'I meant what effect will all this taxi business have? Does it wreck our case? What's your opinion?'

'On its own it doesn't,' she said. The significance of the document that she had planted had nearly overwhelmed her judgement. 'Especially not with the tube ticket to make it less obvious.'

'Yes,' said Scott. 'But why the tube ticket? They wouldn't have planted that in the packet, what would be the point? Maybe it was used.'

Behind him at the coffee machine Monty Bach moved carefully holding a brown plastic tray. He had two cups of coffee and a Danish pastry. Littered on the tray there were packets of sugar and cream. A plastic stirrer slid down the surface of the tray, over the edge, bounced on his foot and skittered as far away as it could manage.

Scott watched and then said, 'It must have been a complete oversight. Janjoa travelled by tube. Gregory must have missed it. Janjoa forgot it, and whoever put in the other card didn't notice it either.'

Tozer came into the room.

Scott continued, 'They are going to call evidence now, and Tozer's already said that the taxi-driver is here. Look, that's probably him there.'

Tozer had sat down opposite Monty, who started talking to him, moving his arms and emphasising something. Then, as Scott watched, Monty indicated a man sitting at a table nearby, Tozer looked over to where he was pointing.

Scott looked over to the man, but the angle at which he sat meant that he could not easily see him.

Emily, however, could see clearly.

It was Howard. He was dressed in a track suit with a pair of old scuffed trainers. He was rolling a cigarette and looking down at a copy of the *Sun*.

She said without thinking, 'Is there no check on who witnesses are?'

'What do you mean?'

'Well. Who they are. Where they come from, who they work for.' She wished she had not spoken.

'No, not really. All you can do is ask for their date of birth when they give evidence to see if they have a criminal record. But they only have to give an incorrect month of birth and the whole thing is useless. We'll ask him who he is.'

At that moment Howard turned and looked directly at Emily. He held her eyes for a moment then with a movement of his head transferred his attention to the window behind her. There had not been a flicker of acknowledgement, but he had sent her a message.

Gregory had seen the man in the track suit and Monty's gesture towards him as he went out.

'I need to find out what car a witness owns,' he told the police inspector in charge of the court. 'It's urgent.'

He was standing outside the door of the cafeteria. 'It's the man sitting there by the side.' Gregory could see Howard through the door and pointed him out to the officer. 'I don't know his name, and I can't check on him till he gets into the witness-box. By then it will be too late to get anything save his date of birth.'

The inspector was unimpressed. In twenty-five years in the police force he had seen too many enthusiastic young officers to be rushed into anything.

'Oh, yes?' he said, solidly doing nothing, waiting to be persuaded.

Gregory explained, 'He is going to give evidence in support of a defence that has been planted in the Crown papers.'

This got the officer's attention and Gregory saw his chance. 'I think the document that matters was planted this morning in the court exhibits cupboard. Court three.'

That brought the event well within the inspector's immediate concerns.

'I think it may even have been . . .' Gregory didn't finish his sentence.

He had looked over at the other people in the canteen and he saw Emily's face again.

He had seen her in the exhibits room that morning talking to Tozer. She had access to the exhibits unsupervised. She had responded to Scully's name. He had thought nothing of it at the time but now he saw a way of getting the inspector's undivided attention.

As he spoke he realised that he may have stumbled over the truth   merely saying it out loud made it sound more possible – 'I think it may even have been counsel who planted it.'

The inspector's eyes followed his to near where Tozer was sitting.

'Is this the case Mr Tozer is in?' said the inspector.

Gregory nodded.

'A big drugs importation?'

'Yes.'

'I think I can help. I will need half an hour. Don't speak to me again, telephone my office at about twenty to one.'

Gregory left for Baker Street.

As he left, the court Tannoy interrupted the talk in the canteen.

It called for the court inspector to go to the car park. The same message was being relayed to every Tannoy in the court.

In one interview room, the size of a lavatory, next to court one, the voice became so annoying that a junior solicitor

243

climbed up and pulled the loudspeaker off the wall.

A little later the Tannoy crackled again.

There was a pause and then a request for the owner of a blue van – the registration number was read out – to go to reception, please.

The request was repeated twice, the second time with a note of impatience in the receptionist's voice.

Listeners in the canteen laughed, and so it was no surprise when two policemen began to move around with clipboards ticking off a list of number plates.

'Excuse me, sir. Did you come to court in a car today?'

The inspector looked away indifferently as he asked the question, calling to his colleague over the other side, 'Have you found it yet?' So uninterested was he that Howard thought he was not even going to wait for a reply.

'I've not got a blue van,' said Howard.

'I'm sure you haven't, sir,' said the inspector, looking bored, 'but your car's got a number, hasn't it? We may have to clear the car park of all cars not claimed.'

Howard looked out of the window. The car he had borrowed from Scully was parked by the side. It wasn't registered in Scully's name, he had made sure of that, an elementary precaution.

He gave the man with the clipboard the number and just as he did so it became unnecessary. There was a call from the other side of the room. 'It's sorted, we've got it.'

'My advice is that we do not call Mr Janjoa to give evidence.'

Tozer and Monty Bach were sitting in the cells of the Crown Court during the midday break talking to Nadim Janjoa.

'The Crown case is about to end, it's our turn and we are going to have to decide now what we do. There is only the one piece of evidence against you, Mr Janjoa, the mere fact that you arrived on the same plane as the others and ended up at the same hotel. Is that so great a coincidence? There's nothing else, no admission of guilt. No drugs anywhere near him. No money from him to anyone.' Tozer summarised the case against his client for the umpteenth time. 'And now Monty's found the taxi-driver, what's his name?'

'Green,' said Monty.

'Green, now we've got him, that's all the evidence we need to call.'

Janjoa nodded. 'Won't the jury hold it against me if I say nothing?'

'No, they're not allowed to. They'll be told that by the judge, and in my experience they don't; it will just make the lack of evidence against you the more obvious.' Tozer paused. 'But there is one problem. Muazzam will be calling evidence after you. Will he be saying anything against you? You won't be able to go into the witness-box after he has given evidence and if he says anything to hurt you it will be difficult to answer him.'

Janjoa paused – rather longer than Tozer liked.

'No, no. He can say nothing against me. I know that.'

'You're sure?'

'Yes.'

'Well, I'd like Mr Bach to put that in writing for me,' said Tozer. He smelt trouble. 'It's always better to avoid misunderstandings, don't you think?'

Chapter 26

Paul Gregory asked to use the phone, and grudgingly, they let him. It had taken Gregory an hour and a half to get across to Transport Police headquarters, longer than he had calculated, and now he was ringing the court later than promised.

As if in response to his delay the phone rang at the other end unanswered. He sat listening to the insistent tone and while it rang he surveyed the office – protected from his hosts by the receiver at his ear.

He had persuaded them, after they had checked who he was, to let him into their dummy room to run the tube ticket through their equipment. Now he was waiting for the print-out.

'If it's any good then I shall need a statement in the correct form from someone,' he had said. They had looked at him expectantly then he had had to explain what he meant. It hadn't made for an easy relationship.

Meanwhile they sat watching him and filling out his requests in triplicate. He told them his name again. He handed over his warrant card. Slowly it was all copied out.

Eventually the ringing stopped and the phone was answered. Gregory said who he was. 'I got you the number of the car,' said the court inspector and he dictated the registration number. 'It's a blue Honda.'

'That's great. Anything else?'

Gregory had judged his man correctly. The court inspector had, without being asked, done a computer check on it. 'Nothing. The last owner notified a sale but there is no new owner registered.'

'Of course,' said Gregory.

'But here is one thing, it's been circulated as being of interest to number two crime squad. There's a phone number, Gray's Inn Road, I think.'

'Right,' said Gregory. One lead kept opening after another, the thing had a nice feel to it.

The ticket machine buzzed and whirred and printed out a slip. Gregory finished his call and went to look at the screen. 'Last used: 7 November 11.34 a.m. at Earl's Court station. Exit barrier.'

So he was right. Clearly Janjoa had used the ticket and then completely forgotten he still had it, it must have become folded into the hairdresser's hand-out.

'Could you put that in a statement?'

'We can do it tomorrow,' said the machine's keeper.

'But I need it this afternoon.'

'Tomorrow.'

Gregory looked at the man and realised that he was going to get nowhere. He looked at the clock. It was nearly half-past three already. The court would have risen by the time he got back. He'd be able to manage it tomorrow.

'Can I collect it tomorrow morning?'

'Of course,' said the man, all sweet reason, 'anything to help. As long as we have it ready.'

Scott had kept the prosecution case going for as long as he could, but by half-past three there was nothing more he could decently do.

The judge was getting impatient. 'Mr Scott,' he said, 'you have been reading bits and pieces to the jury which, though very interesting, are, I am sure, not necessary. Now, is there anything of importance that has to be done or can you close your case? Before the lunchtime adjournment you said you were just finishing.'

Scott looked glum, and turned to Emily. 'No sign of Gregory? Where is he? He does realise what it means if I close the case, doesn't he?'

'No, there's nothing,' she whispered, 'reception said they would phone through if he got in touch.'

'Well, Mr Scott?' said the judge.

Scott couldn't go on stalling the court without reason. It was already beginning to look very odd. He had to decide. 'That's the case for the Crown, Your Honour.'

The judge made a mark in his book, then he turned to the jury.

'That is all the evidence you will hear from the prosecution, ladies and gentlemen. Now we shall turn to any evidence that the defence wish to call.'

'I have an argument of law to raise and it might be better if I made it in the absence of the jury,' said Tozer.

Wesley Divall watched Tozer, standing, waiting for the jury to leave the court. The jury filed out. It was clear what was going to happen, Tozer was going to argue that there wasn't even enough evidence for his client to remain in the trial.

Divall rehearsed the phrase in his mind: 'there is not sufficient evidence upon which a reasonable jury could convict'. It's a question for the judge to decide, if he said there wasn't enough evidence then Janjoa would be acquitted.

He studied Tozer. There was no doubt he was a good advocate. Every time he got to his feet the court buzzed with expectation. He stood with his hands clasped at his chest, his head cocked back, waiting to speak.

As Divall observed, Tozer suddenly looked over at him. Obviously he could feel himself being observed. Divall was struck by the man's sensitivity, an animal awareness of what was going on around him.

As it turned out, Tozer didn't need to speak to begin with. 'Well, Mr Tozer? You are going to say that there is not even enough evidence to justify the prosecution asking the jury to convict?'

'Yes, Your Honour.' Tozer stood and said nothing.

Divall recognised what he was doing, letting the judge do the talking. When a judge talks he starts to commit himself, people like the sound of their own voice.

'Your argument is that Mr Janjoa is not connected with this incident save by the coincidence of his travel arrangements. That's not enough to show he's a smuggler?'

Tozer stood quite still, and after a few moments said, 'Yes, Your Honour.'

Divall remembered the training he had had at Bar school: set out the basis of the argument, deal with each part then summarise and state the conclusion. All completely disregarded here, the whole thing was done with one question and answer. How did they get to it so quickly?

'Mr Scott?' the judge turned to the prosecutor.

Divall couldn't see how Scott could answer it, there was no evidence, was there?

'The coincidence is evidence itself, Your Honour, it's a remarkable coincidence,' said Scott. 'A man leaves Karachi, comes all the way to London and then he happens . . .'

Divall watched him, Scott paused before the word 'happens' and emphasised it, but not too much. Divall thought, I would have overdone that.

Scott was continuing, 'He happens to stay at the hotel where there is equipment for recovering the smuggled drug. Not just

250

that. The jury is entitled to say to itself that in such an operation there would be a minder, someone looking after the couriers. They can decide that Mr Janjoa was the minder.'

'That doesn't follow, Mr Scott,' said the judge. 'Because a drug smuggler might have behaved in a certain way, that does not show that someone who did behave in that way is a drug smuggler. Unless what was done is something only a drug smuggler would do. You're using a false syllogism. It's a "dark deed, dark night" argument.'

Divall's head reeled, Scott's point had seemed a good one to him until the judge replied. He started to repeat the judge's objection to himself, but was interrupted by another bomb.

Scott said, 'That's a proper objection. I discard that argument.'

What struck Divall was the decisiveness and certainty with which they were arguing.

Then Scott started again: 'But there is this also. The defendant Janjoa was found outside the hotel, without any property at all. He had just arrived from Pakistan yet he had contrived to get rid of any evidence, which in normal circumstances he would have been carrying, of his plane journey and of his identification. Where had his passport gone?

'This is conduct which the jury may regard as indicative of dishonesty. It is of course as yet unexplained. The defendant may decide it does not need any explanation, but in the absence of explanation the jury may decide that it was intentional, intended to conceal his identity. And why, they are entitled to ask, should he wish to do that?'

Scott stood silent for a moment, and then said, 'That's our argument,' and sat down.

Neither the judge nor Tozer had seen the point coming.

'What do you say to that, Mr Tozer?'

Tozer said, 'How can the prosecution prove that my client had not just put the documents down and left them somewhere?'

Immediately Divall saw that Tozer had lost the contest.

The judge's head went back sharply and from then on he listened in a different, less intense fashion.

Emily leaned forward and said to Scott, 'What did the judge mean by a "dark deed, dark night" argument?'

'Like, "This is such a foul crime we must assume it was committed at night, Inspector" . . . It was quite common in the nineteenth century to reason in that way,' Scott whispered. 'We still do, though sometimes we don't notice it. I did it with my courier/minder point.'

Scott, Divall could see, had also stopped listening at exactly the same moment as the judge, now he was chatting to his pupil.

For once Divall felt he belonged. He had been there when it happened.

He looked around the court. There were ushers, clerks, Customs solicitors, a number of people there, but it was clear that none of them save himself, Scott, Tozer and the judge had followed the argument. They thought it was still going on. It wasn't, it had finished when Tozer made that answer.

It had been too fast for them. The whole thing had taken about two minutes, maybe even less. For Janjoa, ten years or more of his life had depended on seconds.

Tozer continued to argue his point, uselessly, and Divall's attention drifted away.

'No, Mr Tozer. I find that there is a case for your client to answer, the trial must go on against him.'

The judge stopped the argument.

'Fetch the jury back,' said the judge.

If I could do whatever I want, thought Divall, I would do this. I get frightened so that I worry at night, and I wake up early in the morning still worrying. I know that I am not doing it well. I know that sometimes I look like a fool. Sometimes the people watching me think who's that silly bugger screwing that up, what's he on about? Sometimes the people on the jury look at me and say, "What's he got to tell us?" but, it's still me telling them. I'm doing the job. They can't take that away from me. I am dressed up like a booby. Tozer dislikes me intensely, even Scott dislikes me though he doesn't show it. But I'm doing the job. Wesley Divall looked around himself and his usual frown softened. This is proper belonging. Not belonging to a club, or going to the right school, or being the right colour or that stuff. No, it's being there when something is understood, and knowing you understand it.

A young woman at the back of the jury noticed the lightening of his mood and felt good for him. She didn't know why.

'Now, Mr Tozer,' said the judge, 'we can carry on, can't we?'

Immediately Tozer got to his feet. 'On my advice, Your Honour, Mr Janjoa elects to give no evidence.'

A curious hush greeted this remark as though the whole court had missed a step and was readjusting itself. 'But I have one witness.'

The judge carried on without dropping a beat, 'Well, go on then, Mr Tozer.'

'Call Bill Green,' said Tozer.

Emily sat holding her breath and John Howard came into the court.

He moved in a slouch, wiping his hand against his hip as though getting rid of the moist heat of cigarette smoke from his palm. He smiled at the usher, who handed him a card, and Emily could see gapped teeth. He looked completely different.

He began to read from the card and then stopped and leaned over to the usher, who prompted him. It was clear he had trouble with the long words of the oath and a hush of embarrassment momentarily stilled the court. Finishing, he looked up and then stepped back in the witness-box, leaning against the rail. He grinned at Tozer, who was on his feet, and said, 'Yes?'

'Are you Bill Green?' said Tozer.

'Yes,' said Howard, 'who are you?'

'Please answer,' said the judge. The jury were immediately interested.

'Well, I'm sorry, I'm sure,' said Howard. Emily caught a slight inflection in his voice, and then realised that he was speaking in a Liverpudlian accent, but one that had almost disappeared. It seemed to reassert itself only in the short syllables.

Howard pulled a newspaper out of his pocket and put it on the shelf of the witness-box in front of him. As he spoke he picked it up and folded it, and on one occasion spent some moments sliding it into his back pocket.

'Is your name Bill Green?' Tozer started with the formal question.

'Are you a taxi-driver?' Before the question was half out of Tozer's mouth, he was interrupted by counsel on all sides. 'Don't lead!'

Tozer corrected himself. 'What is your occupation?'

'I drive a mini-cab.'

The witness seemed nervous to Scott. He continually looked around the room and swallowed sometimes before he answered. Tozer timed his question about that perfectly, 'Have you ever been in a courtroom before?'

'No,' Howard answered.

Monty Bach observed the man closely. He was almost certain now that he was watching the man who had come into his office. But there was something else also, something about the way the man held himself in the witness-box. He was reminded of someone he had known a long time ago, and he knew that this man had been in a courtroom before. What was it? The memory of a schoolmaster came into his head. A Schoolman? What was it?

The memory was elusive and destroyed by Tozer's sitting down.

Tozer had only brought out the bare evidence that the witness had driven Janjoa to the hotel and had given him the taxi card which had later been found.

Monty recognised Tozer's technique, the best evidence was yet to come, and there was no doubt that it would – in cross-examination. It would be much more effective for coming that way.

Scott rose to cross-examine at about twenty to four. It was as bad a twenty minutes as he had ever had in a court.

'I suggest this. What you have told us is not true.'

'Oh?' said Howard.

'Mini-cabs are not even allowed at the airport to pick up passengers.'

'I know,' said Howard, 'I was touting, I could have been nicked.' He paused and then added devastatingly, 'That's why I got him at the tube station, just after he had bought the ticket. That's not normal, is it? I even offered to knock the cost of the ticket off the fare.'

The witness had accounted for the tube ticket in Janjoa's pocket, answering one line of Scott's possible attack.

Scott changed tack and again immediately ran into trouble. 'Why did you take him to the Argyle Hotel?'

'Well, he didn't ask me to.'

He paused. The whole Crown case against Janjoa was tottering as he answered, 'I took him there because I knew that if I went back the next day I would get a commission. He just said he wanted a hotel, he didn't name one.'

Howard let this sink in. Then he turned to the judge. 'We call them dosser drops. They're the kind of hotels that have to buy customers. I could name a couple near the Temple if you want.'

As Howard relaxed, beginning to enjoy it, he gave himself away.

What was it? A way of standing, a movement of the arm? Suddenly Monty Bach remembered him, despite his being completely changed – Ronnie Teacher, Teacher, that was it, not Schoolman. It was Ronnie Teacher, from all those years ago, nearly twenty now, wasn't it?

This was no place to stay. Monty Bach got up and left. The less he knew about this the better.

Scott ploughed on. Sooner or later he was going to have to accuse the witness of lying, and he wasn't any too hopeful about the reaction he was going to get. He had better do it sooner.

He put it directly. 'You're lying, Mr Green.'

Howard had been waiting for just that question. 'Who says?'

'I do, Mr Green. I suggest you are lying, and that Mr Janjoa travelled by tube. You didn't take him in your cab.'

'Why do you say that?'

The judge intervened. 'You are here to answer questions, Mr Green, not ask them. Now please answer the question.'

'Well, that's just the point,' said Howard, 'he didn't ask me a question, he just said I was lying. What's he know that says I am lying? I'll bet there's nothing. He's just saying it because he wants to prove this Janjoa person guilty. If he's got any evidence to show I'm lying then let's see it.'

There was nothing Scott could say. He had no evidence, save the coincidence of Janjoa leaving Pakistan on the same plane and then ending up at the Argyle Hotel.

He changed the subject. 'I'll ask the questions, Mr Green.' He heard himself sounding weak. 'What cab firm did you work for?'

'Scala – I still do.'

'Are your journeys logged?'

'Some.'

'What car were you using?'

'This one.'

'Number?'

Howard gave it.

'Was the journey out to the airport logged?'

'Yes.'

'Where?'

'In the controller's book.'

'Where's that?'

'At the office.'

'Can we see it?'

'Go and get it, it's not my book.'

Howard had done his homework in the weeks he had worked as a cabbie. He had managed to get at the book. It wasn't impressively kept and was easily altered, but that didn't mean he wanted to be in court when it was examined.

'You say then that you were at London airport that morning in that car?'

'Yep.' Howard paused. 'And I made twenty-five quid out of it, if you want to know. And I would have got a tenner from the hotel when I went back, but when I did I discovered your people had closed it.'

'I suggest that you did not take Mr Janjoa.'

'Suggest what you want, mate.'

Scott sat down sweating, hoping it did not show.

He turned to Emily and said, 'Where the hell is Gregory?'

Tozer got up. 'I have no re-examination.'

The judge said, 'Where do you live, Mr Green, you never told us that?'

Howard paused, this was the only point he knew he might have difficulty with. He gave the address of a hotel in Ealing.

The judge then asked the question that mattered. 'Is that one of those dosser drops you told us about?'

'Yes,' said Howard.

'Then I think it better that you should not be released from the court, I don't mean you can't leave, I mean that the court may need to recall you.'

Before anyone could say anything the judge went on, 'Have you more witnesses, Mr Tozer?'

'No, Your Honour.'

'Is that your case, then?'

Tozer said, 'Yes.'

'You next, Mr Divall,' said the judge, 'but we'll do it tomorrow.'

The judge got up, walked to the door behind him and stood facing it.

It was not for him to open a door. The usher, who had been at the back of the court, did not come forward quickly enough and for a few moments the judge stood facing the door like a statue.

The absurdity of it broke the atmosphere in the court and those left got up laughing. The jury stretched and shuffled out.

Hygienic sunlight streamed in through the metal windows.

'Well, I'm off,' said Tozer. 'I've got a conference.'

He gathered up his papers and edged down the benches to the door.

As he passed Emily, Tozer said, 'Let's check the plumbing together sometime?' He grinned at Scott, and flashed his eyes at Emily. 'Hard luck, Scotty, difficult witness, eh?'

'What did he mean by that? The plumbing bit?' said Scott.

As he asked the question he realised that he was jealous. His anger and embarrassment at his failure with the witness rapidly transformed itself into dislike of Tozer. Snivelling little toad.

'I think he was referring to something you said this morning.' She smiled.

'What did I say?'

'You told me to go and see the plumber. He thought that was funny.'

'Good Lord. Was I being rude to you?'

She looked at him. He really did seem bewildered.

'Did I make you look silly?' he said.

'Not at all.'

She touched his sleeve where his hand was resting on a book, and there was a spark as she touched him. He shook his arm. 'It's these nylon carpets,' he said, but he knew it wasn't.

Scott was left with Emily in the courtroom. In the corner there was an usher clearing away exhibits.

The air-conditioning suddenly stopped and silence descended on them like dust. Time slowed. It was so quiet that the usher paused to listen, then she shut the door and left.

They were alone in the court. He looked at her. He was a little taller than she was and she had to look slightly up at him. Her mouth moved slightly and she smiled, beginning to speak.

He took no notice but took her shoulders, bent her backwards and kissed her. He felt her body shudder. He stopped and breathed out. 'That bastard Tozer,' he said.

'If it's me you want,' she said, 'you can have me, but I can't help you to dislike Tozer. Not that you seem to need it.' She turned to move away.

'No, that's not what I want you for,' he said. He stopped her and pulled her towards him. He put his hand at the back of her neck and felt the soft tracery of the muscles beneath her head. She bent her head back, almost trapping his hand against her neck, and he kissed her again.

As he did so her wig fell off.

'It's an offence against the Courts Act 1989 to kiss a barrister's wig off,' she said, and bent down to retrieve it. 'It's a contempt of court,' and they laughed.

A great weight had been lifted from each of them.

At that moment Khan appeared, he hadn't been around since the trial began. He walked over and said, 'We have a problem.'

Chapter 27

Peter Khan had woken that morning as his plane crossed the English Channel. He had stirred earlier when there had been a stop at Frankfurt, there had been some confusion as some passengers left, but he and the woman sitting next to him nursing a child had not been affected.

It was only after a difficult search that Khan had found Mrs Muazzam – he had taught himself to call her that for the immigration authorities – as she was living with her parents.

Some months after her husband had failed to return she had left the house she had shared with him, leaving no trace, until Khan discovered that her address was being concealed from him by her neighbours. They were intimidated by the arrival of another large jeep.

When he found her, Khan had to prove who he was. It wasn't easy. He had not been allowed by the British prison authorities to take any of Muazzam's personal belongings to Karachi as proof.

He had asked, naturally, back in the UK, but the Home Office had been suspicious of anything that might, as they put it, facilitate an escape attempt.

'It can't be done, sir,' said the gate officer at Brixton prison when Khan asked to be allowed to have some private item.

'Any request for property to be released must be made to an assistant governor.'

The gate officer turned to the assistant governor sitting beside him for confirmation.

'Also, it has to be made in writing.' The assistant governor nodded absently and folded his newspaper.

So, hoping it would be enough, Khan had taken copies of the court papers and left for Pakistan.

Khan showed the nervous woman the prosecution photocopies of her husband's passport. He repeated what Muazzam had told him of his life. He sat silently in front of her. Then her reserve broke and he was accepted.

At Heathrow the immigration officer checked the woman's passport. Then he looked at the baby. He looked at Mr Khan.

'You're not married, then?'

Khan was tempted to repeat everything that he had just said with the exaggerated slowness that he might have used to speak to a child, but he controlled himself.

'No. We are not married. As I said, I am a lawyer. I represent this lady's husband who is on trial here. We hope she will be a witness for him.'

The immigration officer was suspicious. The woman was clutching a baby. She was dressed in a sarong. Was it a sarong or a sari? A startling bright colour certainly, but obviously poor and uneducated.

She didn't speak a word of English. It was also clear that she could not possibly afford the ticket to this country. So someone must have bought it for her.

The officer considered. The man with her spoke English rather too well – for someone who was not English.

He shifted his attention to him. 'I am sorry, sir' – despite this being the end of a long shift he was able to be polite, it made him feel more in control. 'I am sorry, sir, I don't understand your relationship with this applicant.'

'I am her husband's solicitor.'

The officer remembered his training manual. The immigration service, it had emphasised, was an 'arm of the executive', part of the Government. It was not part of the court system. Solicitors belonged in courts.

Applicants to come into the country have not yet entered the system which gives access to the courts. That was the whole point. They were not entitled to solicitors.

'I am afraid I shall have to ask you to step aside for the moment,' he said.

Khan stood still. Behind him there was a queue of people waiting.

'You have nothing to do with this lady's application to enter. Please step aside for a moment, sir.'

'But she speaks no English.'

'We can arrange for that, sir.'

'But she is with me.'

'Her application to enter this country is her application. She is an adult.'

'I can explain on her behalf why she is here.'

'That is entirely the point, sir. It is her explanation we want not someone else's.'

'We have explained to the immigration service abroad.'

'There is no immigration service abroad, sir. We are not bound by what anyone in a consulate may have said to you. Now, I must invite you to step aside, sir. You will be dealt with there to the left, over by the EEC and UK citizens' section.'

'But . . .'

'If this lady is allowed to proceed then you can meet at Customs or outside Customs.'

'*If* she is allowed to proceed? She's a witness, she's needed to give evidence.'

'So you have said, sir. But am I right that neither you nor

she is employed by the Government?'

'No, she is a defence witness.'

The immigration officer had him there.

'I am sure you will understand that we are not here to facilitate the defence of criminals, sir.'

The immigration officer continued, and as he did so a slow smile spread across his face, 'It would be a most strange thing for Her Majesty's immigration service if that were so.

'Now. Please, sir, move along. I am sure we do not want there to be any trouble.'

He turned his head to where a police-officer stood watching the argument with interest.

Khan tried to speak to the woman.

'No, sir,' said the immigration officer. It was clear to him now that these two had not sufficiently prepared their story, and that the man wanted to prime her again. He had noted already that they chose not to speak in English in front of him.

He raised his arm. It was apparent that the man was not prepared to leave.

The police-officer had expected this to happen. He had already marked out the man in the dark suit as a troublemaker. In fact he had singled out the two of them and the child even before they had stepped forward to the desk. It was a classic example of 'nose'.

He knew he had a good nose for crime. He had even argued the point with a member of the prosecuting lawyers department once – why was it, he asked, that a forecast, a prediction of trouble, was not evidence, when the prediction came true?

In science the prediction of results was central to proof, why was it not so in the criminal courts? He had spotted this man as a troublemaker, almost . . . almost by the way he walked.

'Please move on, sir,' said the policeman.

It took Khan a moment to realise that matters had entered a new phase of misunderstanding, and not much longer to realise that this was now serious.

264

He had seen and dealt with hundreds of cases like these, where the circumstances demand only one triggering event – a look, a movement, even a tone of voice – for the policeman's anger to ignite. He immediately adopted a posture so neutral that even the notion of a threat could not be projected on to it. He sucked in the officer's anxiety.

'Hey,' he said, putting his hands up to his eyes and bowing his head before the policeman, 'do you ever get so tired?'

He spoke of tiredness, but his attitude was one of classic submission, so formal that it might have been a demonstration in acting school.

'You're entirely right, Officer,' he looked up and smiled with thanks, 'I've taken up too much time already. Is that my queue?' He spoke to the immigration officer, but included the police-officer in the question.

The immigration officer answered, and the police-officer's dominance over the situation was broken. Khan was able to walk easily away.

Muazzam's wife watched, not understanding a word, but she had seen such events before in a myriad little official confrontations and she was pleased that she could see so easily what was happening.

The two people in uniform had attempted to join up against Khan. But he had evaded them skilfully. Her understanding gave her more confidence – the world was not so strange after all, indeed bits of it seemed to be much the same wherever you were.

As Khan walked away he turned. 'Tell them everything I have told you. I shall return. Do not be alarmed.'

Again his direct look reassured her. What were these people but that they owned more property than she? They were in the same grip of desire as all humanity. She held her baby more tightly.

'Our preliminary determination is that her entry to this country is not conducive to the public good. We also have reason to believe that she is here in order to support someone who is at present the subject of an adverse preliminary determination.'

Khan was on the phone to the immigration service.

'Do you mean by that that she is here to give evidence on behalf of someone who is charged with criminal offences?'

'Yes. For the moment we must regard that as the outcome of the entry officer's preliminary decisions. Also, it must be noted that the person on whose behalf she is here is himself subject to having his entry clearance withdrawn.'

'But if he is innocent then there will be no reason to withdraw his entry leave,' said Khan.

'That may be the case, but at the moment he must be classed as a person against whom there is a preliminary determination of unlawful entry.'

'But that would mean that any attempt to prove his innocence would be an attempt to give support to someone who is under suspicion and therefore would not be conducive to the public good?'

'Precisely.'

'But that is what I am engaged in doing the whole time.'

'Exactly.'

'But I am meant to do that.'

'That we cannot stop. We only stop what we are empowered to stop.'

The conversation was becoming too bizarre, so Khan hit the button of the tape recorder. He looked at Wesley Divall.

'What do you make of that, then? I recorded the phone call. It's so astonishing I find it difficult to credit. The immigration authorities will not allow her to enter to give evidence to prove that a man is innocent because' – he began to mark the points on his fingers, bending them back – 'the purpose of her entry is to support someone who, because he is accused of importing drugs is therefore presumed to be here unlawfully, and therefore she is coming here to give support to someone who is presumed not to be here for the public good, so it follows her presence is neither conducive to the public good.'

He paused then said, 'What shall we do?'

Wesley Divall began to speak, but then realised that his opinion was not being asked, Khan was using his presence to express his anger.

' . . . some little prick of an officer who has not got the faintest clue of what a trial is about, let alone the presumption of innocence. What shall we do?'

Wesley still kept quiet.

'If we go to the trial judge we will probably have to show him the statement we've got from her, and that maybe means showing it to the prosecution. If we go to the civil courts we will have to tell the trial judge anyway which means the same thing.'

'What does she, the witness, Mrs Muazzam, that is, say?' said Divall. 'You haven't told me yet.'

'Oh, it's fantastic,' said Khan. 'She'll be a good witness. She'll turn the trial round. But we can't call her if the immigration authorities ship her back to Pakistan.'

Khan didn't trust Scott, but he and Divall had decided they had no other choice. They had to tell the prosecution of their problem.

'But what if he uses it against us?' Khan had said.

'How can he? We point out to him that if we can't call our witness we'll appeal. It's in his interest for him to help us, otherwise his conviction goes. And what's more it will help convict Janjoa.'

'We have a problem. We have a witness. She's important, but the immigration authorities are preventing her from entering the country. Can you help?'

'But how can I help?' said Scott.

He could still feel the touch of Emily's skin against his and the tension of her back under his hand. Frankly he wasn't much interested in what Khan was going on about.

Khan caught the tone of his voice. I thought this might

happen, he said to himself. He hardened his own voice. People on the look-out for an argument are more sensitive even than art critics and Scott picked it up immediately.

Khan said, 'Well, counsel advised me you might be able to. But I can understand if you're busy.'

His temper was the equal of Scott's and he could easily throw away a carefully worked out plan because he smelt an insult.

Wesley Divall had come in and he saw what was happening. He stood there sheepishly, he should have done this himself.

Scott's next reaction was anger. This was how he lost friends. He looked at Khan for a moment and thought, What a nasty piece of work. He said, 'Why do you assume the worst against me?'

'I'd be a fool if I didn't,' said Khan, 'since it's not you I'm talking to, it's what you represent.'

'What I represent is fairness,' said Scott.

At that moment Emily leaned forward and put her arm on his. Scott could feel her hand on his shoulder, her middle finger pressed on the point of his collar bone. His back turned to fire. He had not known he had been so lonely.

She laughed. Her movement and her laughter cut through the moment, stopping both men's anger in its tracks.

'No arguing,' she said. 'Just because you both do it for a living.'

They looked at her.

Scott remembered every detail of the moment he had seen her first, and realised that he was in love.

'Of course I've got the time, you silly bugger,' Scott said, turning back to Khan.

Now, suddenly, because of her intervention, they could talk like ordinary people. She had drained the atmosphere of its anger like a precipitate.

'It's not you I'm angry with, it's Tozer,' said Scott.

He was still standing next to her, and his hand went to her waist. He could feel her move under the cloth.

The moment he said what he was angry about then his own intentions became clear to him. This was no longer a trial, but an argument with Tozer. That bastard.

'Will your witness help me against Janjoa? If she does I'll get her here for you.'

Khan acted as though he too had been unblocked. 'You bet. It drops him right in it.'

'Right,' Scott said, 'she'll be here.'

They left the court and walked down the corridor towards the robing room to change out of their robes. As they did so they saw Gregory checking in through security at the other end of the long passage.

'I'll tell Gregory about it now,' Scott said to Khan, and he waited in the passage with Emily.

Gregory walked towards them and saw Emily. He thought, Now, young lady, maybe you'll tell me what you know. He kept walking. The long passage gave him plenty of time to think how he was going to manage it.

'Well, young lady,' he said as he reached them, 'in here.' She turned and looked at him. Had he said what she thought he had? Scott had not noticed.

They sat down.

Gregory said, 'You should have been here earlier this morning before court sat, Mr Scott. We went to the exhibits room. The taxi-driver is a fake. So is the taxi card. It's a . . .' he coughed. 'This morning. There it was. We were all in there.' He looked at Emily.

He knows, thought Emily, how could he?

Gregory was watching her. She looked at him, he could tell she wasn't puzzled at what he was saying, only apprehensive. She did it, he thought.

'What did you say?' said Scott, completely unaware of what was going on. Gregory wasn't making sense.

'I think the taxi card is a fake. Or at least I think it was planted in the papers. We can prove Janjoa actually used the tube ticket. So the taxi-driver must be a liar.'

'Did the machine read it?'

'Yes. Janjoa went into the tube station at Heathrow a minute after Muazzam went in and he came out at Earl's Court in the same minute that Muazzam came out. He was probably three steps behind me.'

Scott was about to speak, but Gregory carried on, 'The jury will see the point.'

'I'm afraid it's too late,' said Scott, 'I had to close my case. I told you before you left I might have to. The defence have started and already called the taxi-driver. Janjoa didn't even give evidence.'

Gregory was suddenly angry; he had put up with this all day, the bloody Transport Police, the delay, rushing around London; he snapped, 'You what?'

'I told you.'

'No, you didn't, you said you'd be able to keep our side going until tomorrow. Anyway, we can call this evidence any time, we've only just found out about it.'

'No, we can't. We can only reopen the prosecution case for evidence we couldn't have known about before we closed it. We had the ticket all the time.'

'We didn't know.'

'We should have done.'

'It's OK for you to say that.'

'It's not me who is saying it, it's the law. If we don't notice it because we don't look that's our fault. We can't call it.'

'But the exhibit has been interfered with.'

Scott was bored with this. 'Prove it,' he said.

He should not have said that. Things would have been better without it.

'I will,' said Gregory, and turning in anger he left the building.

Chapter 28

Gregory went straight to Gray's Inn Road. He got there at about seven p.m., not sure that the people he wanted would still be there.

The door to the counter of the police station was locked and he had to ring for attention. A police constable looked up at him through the glass, half obscured by a notice telling Gregory that it was for his safety and comfort that he was being kept outside. The officer clearly decided there was no immediate need to move and he returned to the document which he was filing, at one stage he reached out for a great loose-leaf file which he opened. As he moved it from the counter in front of him he looked up again at Gregory, but instead of acknowledging his presence his eyes moved on past him and then back to the file.

The policeman wanted it known precisely who was in charge here.

Gregory rang the bell again and this time kept his finger on it. Just what the police-officer wanted. He operated the door switch. 'Is there some sort of problem, sir?' he said. The question was an invitation to argument.

Gregory recognised the opening move, designed to put the

271

policeman in the role of amused and tolerant authority figure, able to dispense help as he wished, not as it was demanded.

'I want the duty inspector,' he said, ignoring the challenge. He laid his warrant card on the table, and turned his back on the policeman ostensibly to open his briefcase. 'I need to see him now, constable,' he said, still not looking at him.

The police-officer held his position for a moment, but then realised that he had been passed by. He picked up the phone.

'I shall have to tell him what it is about,' the officer said.

'I need to see him now. On behalf of the Commissioners of Customs and Excise. Please fetch him, or get him on the phone.' Still Gregory did not look up.

The phone was answered. 'There's a Mr . . .' the policeman picked up the warrant card, ' . . . Mr Gregory here to see you. He's a Customs officer.'

He paused and looked up at Gregory. 'Yes,' he said, and then 'Yes' again. He put down the phone and pointed to the door. 'Through there, sir, up and turn right at the top.' Gregory was able to look at him at last and he mopped up the tension with a smile.

He took the stairs quickly, pushing the papers back into his bag. At the top stood a plain-clothes police-officer.

He was tall. He was so tall that as Gregory took the last step he felt he ought to take yet another. The man was a head taller than he. Gregory hardly came up to his chin. He had a huge face, and as he put out a hand towards Gregory a memory stirred at the back of the Customs officer's mind. Arlot, wasn't it? Moses Arlot?

Gregory had heard of him – who hadn't in the area they worked? It was Moses Arlot who had driven his car off a bridge while Wally Dread held a gun to his head. Wally Dread had drowned.

That huge face, acromegaly? That was it. The man suffered from an illness characterised by hugeness. His hugeness was an illness. Gregory's hand disappeared into his.

'Who are you?' said the man. 'I'm Moses Arlot.'

'Gregory. I'm from Customs Investigation. Drugs investigations.'

They turned and walked away from the staircase. Arlot's arms hung down by his sides and his legs moved as though being worked by strings, and, there was no other word for it, his feet flapped.

'I'm told you have —'

'I know what you've come for and I'm not sure you can have it,' said Arlot.

Gregory stopped. Moses Arlot carried on walking.

After a moment Gregory found himself scuttling after him.

Arlot turned into a room. Along one long wall there was a bank of videos. Opposite them was a row of benches. On the benches there sat a group of tramps, and as figures appeared on the video screens the tramps called out names.

A heavy, round black woman appeared, the camera picking her up as she came down the pavement, her thighs shook as she walked. 'Fat Jenny,' the tramps shouted.

A man behind them was writing the names down.

'Identification by acclamation, we call it,' said Arlot. He plodded on. Gregory followed. 'But I'm not allowed to show you anything.'

Gregory said nothing. They went into a room opening off the big room. Again there was a bank of television sets.

'Here's the log, you'll find the car you're looking for in there,' said Arlot. He handed Gregory a pile of notebooks, pointed to a desk and Gregory sat down.

The notebooks were all entitled 'Operation Cabby – surveillance record'. Each of them was ruled in columns with the date and time on the left, and initials or names in the right margin. In the central margin the observations were set out.

As Gregory was leafing through the books, Arlot was setting

273

up a video. He produced a cardboard box of videotapes and plonked them down.

'Here's the tapes. And here's the cross-reference record. We keep this on a computer, so I am not allowed to show it to you. Data Protection Act.'

The cross-reference record showed a list of names, dates and times.

'We've got most of the Shower Posse coming in and out of here.' Arlot turned around and spoke to him, dropping his head down as he spoke. 'Do you know what I'm talking about?'

He selected a video and pushed it into the machine. The screen flickered and then settled to a steady view of the back door and garden of a terraced house.

A man appeared. 'That's Lester Coke. He's not been known in this country before, normally works in Miami. He's a friend of Skagman.' The man walked up to the door of the house, waited and then was admitted. 'We can't touch him.'

'You can't touch him?' Gregory turned, but Arlot merely looked straight ahead.

'We can't touch him. You can't watch these either,' he said. 'Here's the list of cars' – he turned the pages of the file – 'here's the one you're interested in, and here's the cross-reference to the log, check about 20.47. The videos are arranged in order by day in that box.' He indicated a large box in the corner.

Gregory found the correct log and ran his finger down the margin looking for the time – 20.47.

20.47 Blonde IC 1, girl ?25, 5'7" entered garden. Knocked. Man IC3, 6'0", 30s' into garden, knocked. Nothing. Away.
Blonde girl above knocks again. Door opened by Target 2, girl enters.
Cat leaves.

Then there was a break, nothing happened, the observers filling the log timed it as six minutes. Then a car arrived. The log had the number plate noted down in the margin. It was the same number, the same as the car in the car park at the court. Gregory thought, I've got him.

The observation continued. 'Man gets out. Target 1. Enters house.' This was the last entry, and was finished off with five or six signatures, some feathery, some precise.

He checked the reference to the videotape and searched for the one that showed what happened. He turned and looked behind him, he had been left alone.

He put the video on and one of the screens flickered into life. It was the same view. It was wet and darkness was falling. There was no sound and the picture of the still house became mesmerising. Nothing happened.

Gregory flicked the tape off, took it from the machine and checked the times written on it. It started at five in the afternoon and was marked as running at triple speed. He checked the U-matic equipment, he found he could slow it down or speed it up, or stop it, if he wished, on any one frame.

He pressed his finger down and things began to happen. He watched people call at the back of the house, moving jerkily as they scurried about in response to the fast button. Each of them paused, handed something in through the window, took something in exchange and then moved away. As they did so Gregory noticed a movement that recurred – their hands went up to their mouths.

Gregory scrolled through, the minutes and seconds flashing past in the top corner of the screen. The back of the house became as busy as a tramcar in a Keystone Cops movie. As he approached 20.45 he slowed the tape down to ordinary pace.

Night had fallen in the miserable back street, it was still wet, there was rain on the ground with puddles on the street.

From the right there appeared a figure, he could see it was a girl. He couldn't make out the detail and she did not turn her face to the camera.

As the girl went to the back door the camera closed up on her. Clearly the cameraman had some limited control. She stood at the door and knocked. There was movement at the window. The figure bent down, clearly speaking to the person behind the window, then straightened up. Another person, a man, walked up to the door.

Suddenly Gregory's attention was distracted from the screen by a shout in the room next to him. He leaned back and looked out of the door.

Two or three of the tramps were on their feet shouting, 'It's Joseph', they were pointing at the screen. Gregory checked the log, he had six minutes before the car came, the girl was of no interest, so he stood up and walked in to the other room. The group there were gathered round two or three of the screens, and other people attracted by the noise were joining them. At the back stood Arlot, able to see easily over the heads of the people in front of him. They seemed like schoolchildren playing in front of a teacher.

'What is it?' said Gregory.

'Joseph's arrived. He's the major dealer in the area.'

'What? Is this live?' Gregory had assumed that the televisions were showing a video recording like the one he was watching. The camera was closely focused on a large bearded man standing beside a traffic sign.

'Yes, it's live. It's at the Cross, just up the road, outside King's Cross station.'

'Shall I go?' One of the men crowding round the television turned towards Arlot. 'I've bought from him twice.'

Arlot stepped forward. 'What about him?' He pointed at a figure on the screen leaning against the window of the betting shop. 'OK, Tony,' Arlot spoke to the man who had asked to go, 'see if you can get him involved, he's been standing there too long. I don't like that.'

Tony disappeared. Arlot, Gregory and the rest remained watching the screen.

Moments later Tony appeared crossing the road. He had his hands deep in his pockets and seemed not sure whether he wanted to go backwards or forwards.

'That's where Russian pushed Steinhof Harry under the lorry,' said Arlot, 'he'd better be careful or he'll end up like Harry's head.' As if to prove his point a lorry swept past blocking the camera's view.

Gregory looked at Arlot. 'What's happening?' he said.

'My man will make a buy from Joseph. But we can't touch Joseph, so we'll organise it so that our man is directed towards the drug dealer by the guy at the window. Him we can arrest.'

'What's this "can't touch"?' said Gregory, but by then everyone's attention was on the events on the screen.

Tony went up to the man leaning against the window and spoke to him, at first from a distance of about six feet, but then closer. Tony pointed behind him in the direction from which he had come, then to his left.

The man against the window shook his head. Tony gesticulated again. The man pushed himself away from the window and then took Tony's arm. He half-turned him and pointed to one side. The camera panned back giving the wider view which included Joseph. The man leaning against the window seemed to be pointing directly towards him.

Tony detached himself and made his way towards Joseph. He went up to him. The cameras closed up on them and caught him handing over money. It was almost possible to see the amounts. In return he was given a little ball of silver paper. He slipped it into his mouth. Gregory, watching, suddenly understood the gesture that he'd seen the people on the video make.

Then the policeman turned and walked back the way he had come.

The watching group relaxed and awaited his return. After a few moments he came in, he was laughing. 'What did it look like?' he said. He held up the piece of silver paper.

'OK,' said Arlot. 'What did you ask him?'

'Would you believe it? The man would simply not accept that the railway station was over there' – Tony pointed behind him, repeating the gesture Gregory had just seen on the screen – 'in the end he was saying, it's over there, you wanker. And he pointed straight towards Joseph. Did it come out all right?'

'Let's replay it,' said Arlot. He took out one of the tapes and went to a new screen. The same picture came up. The lorry rushed past. 'We thought you were a goner then,' a voice said.

The figure made its way up to the man at the window and Tony watching said, 'How about this? This is where I say . . . here's a script . . . "I thought I could get some wizz over there, but there's nothing," ' he was pacing his words to the movements on the screen like an actor dubbing a film. ' "Do you know where I can get a hit?" ' The man on the screen took his arm and pointed to Joseph in answer to the question.

'That'll do,' said Arlot. 'That's assisting in the supply of drugs if I ever saw it, and I just saw it, didn't I? Arrest him this evening.'

He turned to another officer. 'Jock, you follow him. Don't tell him when it was he did what he's being arrested for, and try and avoid telling him what he did. Though I don't suppose it matters, he won't know what you're talking about, anyway.' He laughed. 'Do the paperwork, Tony.'

Gregory stepped back into the other room. He thought, What jury would believe that what they had seen was a man being asked the way to the railway station? He was staggered.

The video that he had been watching of the house before

278

the interruption had dissolved into white noise and he started to run it back towards the 20.47 mark.

Arlot came in.

For a moment Gregory thought he was going to have to react to what he had just witnessed in the other room and he found himself hunching his shoulders, not wanting to commit himself, closed in against the subject. But Arlot said nothing.

They watched the video screen in silence.

Gregory ran it fast forward and the girl entered the house. He ran it on during the few minutes of inactivity and a car appeared. He stopped the tape, took it back and made the car appear again. He could see the number plate. The same number.

'Who's in it?' he said. 'Can one see?' He inched the tape forward again until the screen was filled with the back of a man getting out of the car and heading towards the house.

'It's Scully himself,' said Arlot. 'We think he was taking something there . . .' He leaned forward and moved the tape through. The man went into the house, he speeded the tape up again until the door opened once more to let someone out.

'He was taking a package there, when we went in we found nothing,' repeated Arlot, 'but while he was there he picked up a girl.'

The door opened, Scully walked out, and there behind him, framed in the door and lit by the street-light, stood Emily.

'So he did,' said Gregory.

Chapter 29

What was different was now they were sharing the car.

Scott had driven Emily to and from court many times, but now, sitting in the passenger seat, she was free to touch things, pick them up and examine them as though they were her own. Everything lay inside the barrier which had previously kept them apart, they were intimate now.

'Why do you keep it so dirty?' she said, kicking at a piece of orange peel.

'I don't,' he said. 'It gets dirty.'

'Rubbish,' she said.

'Yes,' he said, 'that's the problem.'

'What's this?' She pulled out a book from under the seat. It had oil mixed with dust and fluff on the cover. 'Heidegger. Poo!'

'I know a café,' he said, 'they give you proper coffee and magazines to read. We can go there.'

'You don't need magazines now,' she said. 'You've got me.'

He put his hand under her leg, sliding it under her thigh and resting it palm upwards, feeling her weight shifting as she moved. She did not look at him, nor he at her. 'You've got me now,' she said.

The car approached the wide right-hand turn into Earl's Court Road. At the last moment he had to change gear and take his hand away.

A large van over to his right tried to push in, forcing him left towards the Sega building. A bicycle insisted on the direction, squeezing him back towards the van, a lorry attached itself to his back bumper, and a girl in jeans stepped out in front of them all.

He saw Emily's eyes flash towards him as they waited for the long slim legs to cross the road. She was beginning to be possessive. It was a good feeling.

The road cleared, his hand was free and he moved it under her again. She relaxed her muscles, allowing his hand to slide into place. It was as though it belonged there.

All the way to Chelsea, down to the Embankment, left at Cheyne Walk, past the Royal Hospital, he kept the car in fourth gear. He didn't need to move his hand. The lights were miraculously in their favour.

He could feel her tighten the muscles in her leg, he could feel the slight depression where her leg joined her bottom, and with his thumb he could feel the roundness and the hardness of her pelvis as it curved away towards the inside of her thigh.

All the way she looked straight ahead.

'You said you knew a café? You said we were going to a café,' she said as they drew up at his block of flats.

'I forgot I had you,' he said. Just exchanging words was a pleasure.

Bill was leaning on the porter's desk, 'Hello, Mr Scott. Hello, miss,' he said. He stepped forward and pulled the lift door back with a crash.

The lift lurched upwards, clicking and humming its way past the lower floors. They stood watching the inside walls slide past them.

Scott pushed the door of the flat open, crushing the morning post against the wall. The flat smelt of wine. There was half a bottle on the floor by the sofa.

He shut the door and turned towards her. She stood facing him.

'What are you going to do now?' she said.

He took her jacket off and slipped the zip on her skirt down. It fell to the floor. Then, as she stood in her shirt and tights, he slipped his hands down and she was naked save for her shirt.

Scott put his arms around her waist and lifted her up, her arms went up to the lintel of the door. For a moment she hung there, then she slid down, and he was completely inside her. She lifted her legs till they clutched his waist.

The movement caused her to shudder so that for a moment her grip was loosened and she nearly fell backwards.

Scott followed the movement and lowered her on to the low table by the sofa. She was looking up at his face as he began to move, lifting her whole body with every motion, then she closed her eyes and they came together.

Bill the porter heard Emily cry out as he stooped over a plastic bag of rubbish in the passageway and he remembered a girl that he and a friend had taken out to sea in a longboat in 1952 for a long afternoon. He shook his head and scratched himself.

They lay together and slept. When she awoke they were lying in exactly the same position, abandoned to each other.

He was still asleep. She was lying, protected by his shoulder, his left arm holding her, resting on her back. Her leg lay between his and under his other ankle. Her left arm was bent up under her towards her face and her other arm lay on his breast. He possessed her in his sleep.

She looked at her hand and moved it. She could feel the hardness of his rib. She turned her thumb slightly and ran the nail gently down his skin, no more than an inch. He moaned softly.

If she lifted her head she could see his face. He was relaxed there was no strain. No nervous look either, the look he had so often had when he was with her was gone.

Then she lowered her head and her head was under his shoulder. She tested the warmth of it, and the sweetness of the scent of his sweat and moved her head slightly. He didn't wake but turned a little and held her nearer him. In his sleep he held her near him.

Emily had chosen a pair of his boxer shorts to wear. She found them in a drawer in which she rummaged while Scott took a shower. They hung on her like a pair of bloomers. She stood with her back to the stove, her arms crossed covering her breasts. She held a glass of red wine.

Scott was pulling some ice out of the fridge, and she spoke while his back was turned to her, 'I think I'm in trouble.'

As she spoke he dropped the gin bottle, it didn't break as it hit the floor but it did when it bounced. Glass shattered over her feet, and the smell of alcohol filled the room.

'Oh bugger,' he said, 'hang on.'

He found her a pair of his shoes to protect her bare feet and they mopped up the liquid and the glass with a thick cloth. Then they threw it all away.

He opened a bottle of wine instead and retreated with her from the kitchen to the sofa.

'What did you say?' he said.

'Doesn't matter.'

The moment had passed. The day's events began to gather around her, and she knew that she could not tell Scott about what had happened.

Telling him would give him no choice but to go to the police. And, anyway, how could she tell him given what had just happened? The whole thing would seem as though it had been calculated.

But that wasn't the reason for not telling him. She didn't want to now. What she wanted was to see Howard. She still wasn't free, the idea that she could get free by finding a man to hold her tight was a joke.

'Go on, what did you say?'

'I'm in trouble,' she said. Then she added, 'I'm late already. I have to go – to meet someone.'

'Don't go,' he said. 'Who is it?'

'Oh, it's nothing. I said I would meet someone for a drink.'

'Where?'

'El Vino's,' she improvised. 'Look. It's a kind of interview. Someone said they might be able to help.'

'Oh,' said Scott. 'Help what?'

'Just chambers and things.'

'I'll take you,' he said. She had not expected that, and was not able to deal with it.

'No, don't bother,' she said, 'I can manage OK.'

It was then she felt alone and wished that she'd gone straight, and for a moment the shadow of future events fell across her.

She shivered. Then she realised that what she was doing now was not important, but what she wanted to do was important. No, important was not the word. It was just that what was happening made everything else unimportant. What was happening was she had to see Howard.

She got up and went to the bedroom and dressed. He came and stood by the door. 'I'll take you,' he said, 'I've got to go to collect papers from the Temple anyway.'

There was no way of avoiding that. Scott caught her indecision.

'What is it? Am I pestering you already?'

She said nothing, luckily she had her back to him and did not immediately have to show her face. Then she took a breath, turned and said, 'Look, I'm sorry. I was just getting back to reality.' She moved forward so he had to take hold of her. 'It's OK,' she said, 'I want you so bad. "Honey, I want you so bad." ' She laughed. 'At least that's what the song says,' and the tension seemed to be gone.

For a moment she believed it. But what she wanted was Howard. What Howard had.

The back room of El Vino's was crowded, they stood looking round to see who was there.

'He must have gone,' said Emily, 'after all, I'm very late for him.' And she began to turn away from the entrance, but a familiar voice stopped them. 'Emily, Jeremy!' It was Tozer.

There was nothing for it but to sit down. They manoeuvred themselves around the clumsy table, squeezing in between the backs of the chairs from the other tables.

'Where've you been?' said Tozer. His voice had an edge. Scott knew it could not be true but he was willing to believe Tozer could smell sex on their breath.

Tozer had. Their momentary hesitation had showed. 'Where've you been then? I bet Scott needed consolation after what my witness did to him.' He laughed and turned to the morose man sitting next to him. 'I was telling Ned here about it.' Ned attempted a grin, but he was not very successful.

Tozer said, 'Come on, sit down,' and he waved for glasses. 'Tell you a joke.' He stopped and puffed himself up. 'What do you call a black man in a suit?' He paused. 'The defendant.'

Ned let out a loud laugh and lurched forward. He was drunk.

Tozer grinned triumphantly. 'Not funny, eh, Scott?' Giving Scott the choice, no choice at all, of sniggering at a racist joke or being a prig.

But Tozer didn't press it, he turned instead to Emily, taking her arm.

'What will you have to drink? I am glad you arrived.'

Scott watched. So this was the appointment?

He looked at Emily. She was detaching herself from Tozer's hand, which was just as clammy as it had been on her back that morning. That morning? It seemed a different world away. She lifted his hand and said, 'That'll be enough, Tozer,' dropping it on the table like a piece of steak.

The glasses arrived and Tozer poured out the wine looking pleased – even being refused by a woman was a start, at least he was noticed. He didn't doubt that it would not be long before he would take this girl to bed, especially if he offered her something.

The conversation returned to the trial. 'Well, my guy's out of it, isn't he?' said Tozer. 'It's clear that Muazzam isn't what he says he is. Not that he's ever said what he is, has he?' He laughed, and went on, 'Monty heard him chattering away in English in the cells, and yet he claims not to speak English. Obviously he's the guy in charge.'

Scott said, 'We can prove he used the tube ticket.'

Tozer was not surprised, and he was ready. 'Not any more you can't. You should have proved it before you closed your case. You've had that ticket for months. And my chap's already decided to give no evidence, you can't change the case against him now. He wouldn't be able to answer it. Even Stebbing wouldn't allow that.'

Scott knew he was right. He could twist and turn but he wouldn't be able to get the evidence in. It looked as though Tozer was right, Janjoa would walk out of it.

Another bottle of red wine arrived. The wine served here was, or seemed to be, much stronger than elsewhere, and Scott began to feel detached.

Tozer was going on. 'And the plumbing,' he said. He turned to Emily and repeated the joke he had made that morning, 'Emily and I are going to examine the plumbing.'

Ned looked at Scott and at Emily and sniggered. Scott

watched him. He knew Ned, he had a desk in a room with him for some time, he was a man so consumed with ambition that everything else seemed to have been burned away, leaving a series of stock reactions learned in university common rooms and pubs – reactions that could be provoked by calling out silly names or speaking in funny voices.

Emily got up to leave. She said, 'I have to go,' and did.

Scott found then that he had reached the stage of drunkenness when events occur apparently disconnected with each other.

'Can't you leave her alone for just a minute, Tozer?' he said. He was angry, and he started to disentangle himself from the chair behind his which was preventing him getting up.

Tozer took this as a compliment and grinned with pleasure.

Ned caught the echo of a saloon bar back-slapping session and gurgled with laughter. ' "Touch 'em up Tozer" – that's what they call you,' he said. 'More like "touch 'em all over Tozer".'

'I wasn't thinking of touching her,' said Tozer, 'more plumbing her.'

They both coughed with laughter again; Scott got up and left. Scott made it to the door but there was no sign of Emily, only a taxi taking off into the distance.

In novels the cool night air is meant to clear your head, but it didn't for Scott. He was drunk because the wine was very strong and he hadn't eaten anything all day. The cool night air made him feel worse.

He felt worse because he realised just how bad he felt.

He set off down the long slope towards the Inner Temple car park, more because it was easier to walk downhill than for any other reason.

As he came out of the archway at the side of El Vino's he realised it was raining. It was cold, it was very wet, he felt sick. Tozer and Ned were still sitting at the table he had left.

The impulse to go back and tell them what he thought of their stupid faces went away as quickly as it came.

At the Cloisters Arch he turned right and began to cross the great flagstones. After a few moments he became fascinated by the pattern that they formed. The pattern had been carefully worked out, very carefully, that was clear. But why? It didn't go anywhere. That sort of symmetry was worse than chaos – at least chaos had dignity.

The pattern, as he followed it, slipping away to smaller stones all the time, moved him over to his right until he found himself beached outside the entrance to the Temple Church.

Inside in the dark a complex intertwining of sound was echoing. The door was slightly ajar and he could hear the organ-master's stick, he supposed it was a stick, being tapped on the rostrum.

The singing stopped, and then began again, twisting and turning on itself, hardly moving forward until the music must have bumped up against one of those double lines with dots on, and it went back to the beginning again.

He was standing at the door, his hands deep in his overcoat pockets, when it opened.

Judge Stebbing stepped out.

'Oh, hello, Scott,' he said, 'just been listening to my nephew singing.' He cleared his throat loudly. 'Very good.'

Scott watched him. He said nothing.

'Look,' said the judge, 'I shouldn't talk to you like this, but I got a call from the immigration service. Home Office, actually, from the top. Apparently your chaps the Customs are raising Cain about some witness. Saying that you say she has to be got to court or the trial will be aborted? Is that right?'

Scott hadn't expected his angry words to come back to him so quickly. He immediately wished that he had been a bit more temperate on the phone after Gregory had left the court.

'Well, yes,' he said.

He couldn't trust himself to say any more, his tongue was thick enough with drink to make him slur even that.

'Well, I said to them, "If Scott says so, that's good enough for me".' Stebbing grinned and turned to move away. 'Don't say I asked, but shall I just sit still and enjoy myself tomorrow?'

'Yes,' said Scott.

'And will Tozer enjoy it?'

'No,' said Scott, wondering what the judge had guessed was happening.

'Good news,' said the judge, and headed off into the darkness. 'Don't drink any more or you may spoil it for yourself.'

Chapter 30

The next morning the phone woke Scott early. It was Emily.
'Can you pick me up this morning?'

'What happened last night?' said Scott.

'Answer the question,' said Emily, mimicking what she had
learned from him in court.

'The question has changed,' he said, 'now it's, "What
happened last night?" '

'Look, we'll talk about it later. If you can pick me up, I'll
see you in the café in Kensington. Half an hour.'

'OK,' said Scott.

He heaved himself out of bed. One of the pleasures of living
on his own was being able to slop about without any fear of
annoying others by leaving a mess. Was that going to change?

He took a shower and got dressed. There was no point in
having a coffee since Bernardo at the café would make him
one.

He went downstairs; Bill was leaning on the porter's desk.
'Hello, Mr Scott,' he said, 'that your car?'

Scott turned. He remembered now he had had to leave his
car on the pavement. 'No room,' he mumbled.

'Well, no harm done,' said Bill, 'the police were enquiring

last night, but Simms told them you weren't here.'

'My God! Bill. What did you say?'

A broad smile spread over Bill's face and he rubbed his nose. His face seemed to be made of rubber and his nose spread sideways. 'Some policemen came to the door a little while after you came in last night enquiring whose car it was . . .'

'Yes?' said Scott.

'They were talking about drink —'

'What!' Scott interrupted him.

Bill was enjoying the consternation he was causing. 'Simms said you weren't in.'

'Good Lord!' Scott was staggered. 'Bill, you're not kidding me?'

'No,' said Bill. 'Look outside.' Scott turned and looked at his car and then beyond it. At the corner there was a police car with two officers looking over towards the flats.

'They haven't been there five hours, have they?' Five hours. He looked at his watch. Yes, it was gone two when he finally got back.

'No,' said Bill, 'they come round every half-hour or so and stay about ten minutes.'

'What shall I do?' said Scott.

'You're the lawyer, Mr Scott. But I think they think we're taking the piss. They don't like it if you take the piss.'

Bill nodded, and started fishing in the pocket of his jacket. He pulled out an old tin and started rolling himself a cigarette.

The police car started up and pulled away.

'There you are, Mr Scott. You'll be all right now.'

Bill popped the cigarette in his mouth and lit it. He grinned at Scott and stepped forward to open the door.

They both went outside and looked around. Nothing. Scott got into his car. After a moment he got it going and went off in the opposite direction from the police car.

* * *

At about the same time in his flat in Barnes, Wesley Divall woke up with a knot in his stomach.

All night he had dreamt that he was in court, but in a case he couldn't understand and with a set of papers he hadn't read. He was standing before an expectant judge unable to say anything. The scene replayed itself in his mind again and again.

As he woke he relaxed and the anxiety of the dream drained away. For a moment he lay there. Then he remembered Muazzam. The knot in his stomach returned immediately. He knew it wouldn't go away until the court sat that morning and he would carry it with him till then.

He washed and dressed. He stood in front of the mirror and tried to breathe deeply, short breath in then a long breath out, dropping his shoulders and letting his arms hang beside him, fluttering his fingers.

The pressure of the case was affecting him. Every day it became a little more difficult to lift himself to the challenge. The doors, the keys, the cell gates, the unspoken hostility of the prison officers on top of Muazzam's despair, all were beginning to wear him down. This was a more difficult case than he was used to.

Muazzam faced eight, ten, perhaps even more, years' imprisonment if convicted – and the evidence was piling up against him.

And that bastard Tozer isn't helping, he said to himself in the mirror. Let's hope to God we get the witness.

Scott driving along Lower Sloane Street realised a police car was following him.

For a moment his stomach turned over then he calculated that it didn't matter. His last drink had been hours ago, he was certainly under the limit and they had no grounds to test his breath. He was insured and miraculously he had remembered to tax the car.

293

He watched the police car as it hung on to his tail, left into the King's Road at Sloane Square and then right towards Kensington. The car stayed with him until he pulled up outside the café near South Kensington tube.

It was still half an hour before parking restrictions began and he was able to leave the car right outside. He went in.

'Hello, Bernardo,' he said to the man behind the counter. He was handed a coffee and he went to sit in the window.

The police car was still there but the people in it did not seem to be interested any more. Scott remembered Bill's remark 'just pissed off'. They had probably been following to see if he gave them an excuse to hassle him.

There was a movement and he looked up. It was Emily. She was dressed in a plain black waisted suit, with a long skirt. Her blonde hair shone in the light from the window.

He caught his breath. She leaned forward and holding his cheek bent down and kissed him full on the lips.

'I'm here.'

'Yes.'

She put her bag on the table and turned to the café owner. 'Café – espresso,' she said. As she turned he caught the glimpse of her jaw from the side and saw the purity of the line.

He hadn't yet had the opportunity of just looking at her – just looking and looking at her – at her waist and her legs as she stretched them out beside the table. He marvelled at how she could be so perfect. Across the road in the police car Moses Arlot said, 'We can go now. That's the girl in the video, no question.'

'Well, Mr Divall?' The judge sat down and turned to Wesley Divall, 'Have you a witness?'

The knot in Divall's stomach which had grown to resemble a stone now miraculously disappeared. 'I do, Your Honour,' he said, quite calm now. 'Call Shaheena Muazzam.'

The court sat expectantly. Two women in the back row of the jury turned and whispered to each other, then they looked at Muazzam.

He was leaning forward, rubbing his mouth with one hand.

It occurred to one of the women that Muazzam had probably not seen his wife since he had come here and she turned and said so to her friend.

Over the weeks the jury had built up a personality for each of the defendants but Muazzam was still a puzzle. He didn't seem to them to be like a drug smuggler – 'Whatever a drug smuggler is like,' they said, which, of course, they agreed 'we don't know'. Except they did know they wouldn't trust Janjoa an inch.

Shaheena Muazzam? Tozer heard the name and turned round to Monty Bach and started talking urgently to him. Then he got up and went to the back of the court where Janjoa was sitting. They whispered to each other and then both looked at the door.

Silence descended on the court, nothing happened.

The clerk of the court glanced at the clock on the wall behind the defendants and then opened a thick file. He pulled out a green form and selected a ball-point pen. Slowly he began to tick the boxes. He made a slight rustling. Everyone became conscious of the noise.

Outside, Shaheena Muazzam was escorted down the long passage by two immigration officers. Each of the officers held an elbow. For them the whole thing was extraordinary.

They had read the file in the taxi on the way over. This woman had been refused entry because she was trying to help a drug smuggler, and now she was being allowed to do just that. But – they had to do what they were told. It was another example of the stupidity of the system.

They reached the door of the court, which was being held open by the usher.

'You can't take the child in there.' The usher pointed as they stepped into the area between the double sets of doors.

Shaheena Muazzam turned to her, clearly not understanding what was being said, but she gripped her small baby tightly.

'She can't take the child in,' the usher repeated to the immigration officers. 'No, she can't, not in there.'

The female immigration officer sighed as if to demonstrate that however distasteful her duty was, she was prepared to do it – making it clear that holding some woman's child was just that. She reached forward to take the bundle that Shaheena was clasping.

Suddenly she found herself crashing back against the wall as the woman, with surprising strength, pushed her away. The woman said something.

'Now, that'll be enough of that,' said the other immigration officer and he stepped forward to take hold of the tiny bundle, 'we'll just look after it for a while.'

Shaheena Muazzam had not let go of her child since the plane landed. She wasn't going to let go now – for all she knew she would never see him again. She hit the man in the chest with the side of her fist. 'No!' she shouted.

Both the officers came back at her. They were used to dealing with recalcitrant prisoners, and were not going to allow this . . . this . . . Pakistani . . . to behave like that towards them.

But she was wiry and strong, she buried the child in her clothes and the officers were not able to get their hands around the bundle.

During the struggle the usher was pushed back against the door and it swung open.

Everyone in the court was watching. As the door opened the entrance framed the immigration officers desperately trying to drag the child from its mother. The usher turned and faced the court, her face was torn in distress.

'What is happening, Usher?' said the judge. The door swung shut again and the sounds of the struggle continued.

'She won't let go of the baby.'

'Let her in,' said the judge.

The usher disappeared and the sound of struggling became muffled, then stopped.

The two women at the back of the jury gripped their handkerchiefs tightly. One of them bit her lip.

In the dock, unnoticed in the tension, Muazzam slowly got to his feet. The door opened and Shaheena Muazzam entered.

She was dressed in a scarlet and blue sari. Her black, black hair was tied tightly back and her eyes shone with tears. She moved slowly into the large court holding her child tight, looking around her, searching for a face.

Then she saw her husband. By now he was standing, his hands stretched out. He called out. She unfolded the cloth wrapped into her dress and gently lifted the new-born child from the folds.

Puzzled, the baby blinked in the light.

She held it up and spoke to him.

The woman at the back of the jury held her handkerchief tighter. The tears began to pour down her face.

The judge said, 'What does he say?'

No one responded.

The baby cried. Muazzam called out again.

The judge repeated angrily, 'What does he say?'

The interpreters could not move.

Khan stood up. 'He says, "My son, I see my son." '

'The court will rise,' said the judge.

'I thought she couldn't say anything against you!' Tozer was angry.

He was walking up and down the small room in the cell block talking to Janjoa. Shaheena Muazzam had given her evidence and Tozer had asked the court for time before he responded on behalf of Janjoa.

'She identified you. She has a photograph of you at the wedding she attended and she gave the exact dates she saw you in the village.'

Tozer didn't like losing cases and Janjoa's case had just been blown out of the water by the woman's evidence.

Janjoa said nothing, he sat hanging his head.

'The woman even knew where you bought the tickets for the flights – or at least her bloody solicitor did.'

There was nothing to be said.

Monty broke in, 'Look, we have to ask you about this. She said that you and another man, a white man, recruited her husband. She said the other man told her that her husband was coming here as a tailor. You told her that he would fly overnight to London and that he had to swallow medicine to help him fly.'

Tozer said, 'And after that bloody display with her baby this morning, who's going to disbelieve her?' He snorted. 'How can I cross-examine a woman while she's carrying her baby in her arms? She'll probably pull out a tit and start feeding it in the witness-box. Disgusting.' His skin crawled at the thought.

Janjoa looked up at him, he was being deserted. He shook his head, he could see what was happening.

Monty Bach persisted, 'But we have to ask you what you say. She says that you and the other man came to see her and told her that everything was proper and that her husband would be quite safe. Is that true?'

'No,' said Janjoa, but his heart wasn't in it.

'Well, what about the photograph?' said Tozer. 'That was you, wasn't it? And who was the man with you in the photograph?'

'Please, Mr Tozer,' said Monty, trying to calm him down. 'Well, what about the ticket payments, did you make them?'

'No,' said Janjoa.

'But the same Toyota jeep as was in the photograph was outside the ticket agency.'

Janjoa shrugged. The evidence had come too suddenly.

The shock of seeing the woman at the door of the court – he recognised her immediately – and the evidence that had been coaxed out of her by Wesley Divall had been too much for him. And now the obvious distress of his barrister was finishing it off.

'What can I do?'

'Do? Do? What do you want *me* to do? Have you no sympathy for me? You want me to stand up and look a fool trying to cross-examine this woman?' Tozer was dying for a cigarette, but he had none.

Monty looked at Tozer. Who was this guy? He wasn't the fighter he had thought he was.

He tried to slow the whole thing down. 'Mr Tozer has got to tell the witness whether we accept her evidence or not in, well . . .' he looked at his watch, 'about an hour and a half.'

'What can I do?'

The question annoyed Tozer again, and he was about to speak when he saw Monty's face.

Monty said, 'You must tell us what you want us to do. You can get Mr Tozer here to attack this woman. If you tell us it's all lies then Mr Tozer will say that for you. You tell us whether it's true or not.'

Monty wasn't particularly confident now that Tozer would do it but he had to act as though he would.

Janjoa paused and looked at Tozer, who watched him waiting.

'Well . . .'

Monty said quickly, 'What you tell us is what we act on. If you say she is right, that you did this, then we are stuck with that. We can't change back again.'

'The judge will knock time off the sentence if you plead guilty – even if it's at the last moment,' Tozer said.

Once Tozer had said it he started to relax, he didn't think he was going to have to cross-examine the wife.

'You get even more time off if you help them.' Tozer began to think about a couple of days' holiday if the case ended early. He might even be able to get down to the practice race-track.

'I think I can help them. I can tell them some things,' said Janjoa helplessly.

Tozer wondered whether he might even get that girl Emily down with him. Women like powerful engines.

Then Monty spoiled it. 'Look,' he said to Tozer, 'this is just one witness, she's the wife of a co-defendant. She's got her own purpose to serve, why should the jury believe her? We need time to sort this out. We don't just give in. I'll get a message to the judge.'

Scott was sitting with Emily in the court canteen.

'I've got to cross-examine her,' he said, 'but remember, I do it after Tozer's done it. Defence go first then prosecution. Tozer has to say it's all lies, so I won't have to do much.'

Emily nodded.

'Though I don't fancy calling a woman standing with her new-born baby in her arms a liar. She might drop it on its head if I'm nasty to her. No wonder Tozer's asked for time.'

They sat opposite each other, trapped by the plastic seats.

'Anyway, you still haven't answered me, where did you go last night?'

'Home,' said Emily.

'You weren't there when I phoned,' said Scott.

'You don't own me.'

'That's not what you were saying yesterday.'

'I didn't say that. I said you could have me. I remember that happening.'

'But why did you leave?'

'Because I couldn't stand the sight of Tozer and his slob friend for one more minute.'

'That didn't mean you had to walk out on me.'

'You were fairly drunk too,' she said, 'and I didn't notice you standing up for right and justice against anybody.'

'Well,' he paused, 'I assumed it was Tozer that you'd gone to El Vino's to meet.'

'Do me a favour, for God's sake.'

'Well, where did you go?'

'I told you. I went home.'

Wesley Divall appeared at the door and started threading his way towards them.

'Well, when you take off like that next time tell me what's happening,' said Scott.

Scott looked up at Divall and said, 'Hello.' The change from private to public conversation only emphasised the pleasure of being with her.

Divall sat down. He felt more comfortable with Scott than he had before.

'Thanks for making it possible for our witness to be here.'

Scott grinned and put his hands up. 'No problem, all part of the service.'

'Probably lost you your case, though,' said Divall.

'Why?' said Scott. 'Who says the jury will believe her?'

'After that display this morning?' said Emily. 'The two old biddies in the back row were practically sobbing.'

'But it's drugs,' said Scott, 'everybody feels sympathy for the poor courier but they're not about to let him off. You wait. Specially after Tozer's finished with her. He'll drink her blood.'

Divall looked at him surprised. 'But haven't you heard? Tozer's asked for more time. He's told the judge the jury won't be needed for some time. He's asked that we don't sit till half-past two.'

'Good God,' said Scott, 'that can only mean one thing. I'd better get going.'

He got up and squeezed out from the table. His robes caught on the back of the chair and another tear was added to the already shredded cloth.

'Where are you going?' said Emily, who was getting her leg out from the plastic table supports. 'What does it mean?'

'I think Tozer's going to throw his hand in. He's going to plead. We need to see Gregory and the Customs solicitors. Come on.'

As they reached the door, Emily said, 'I'll follow you down. I have to make a call.'

Scott disappeared down the passage, and she went to the phone and rang Howard.

'Is that you?'

'Yes.'

'It looks as though Janjoa is pleading guilty.'

'Yes?'

'She gave her evidence this morning and described Janjoa in detail.'

'And?'

'She had a photograph of him. The others think that Tozer's giving in.'

'I'll be over there as soon as I can. Come when I call you.'

As she spoke she realised what their relationship was and she knew there was nothing she could do about it.

Chapter 31

Gregory was delayed by the officers in Baker Street, though he noticed that they treated him differently now Moses Arlot was there.

Eventually they produced the witness statement.

'Here you are, one ticket – return from Heathrow, still valid if you want to use it. One statement – so it shows it was used at exit three Earl's Court, and one computer statement saying the computer was working OK.'

Gregory countersigned the signature as valid.

'And three copies. Now don't say we're not helpful.'

Gregory said nothing, he was depressed. He could see Janjoa slipping away already. How can this evidence be of no use? he thought.

But Arlot was in expansive mood as they walked to the car. 'I was on the dip squad for a time, way, way back – before they tripled the sentences – and we used to wait for Nick the Hook at Earl's Court, same ticket barrier as that ticket, pick him up on his way to work, follow him and arrest him.

'The Hook used to work office hours, he was a *Daily Telegraph* reader, he approved of private enterprise.' They crossed over the road to where the police car was parked outside Lloyds Bank.

'Talking about Americans – that's where the Bank of America job was planned,' Arlot said. 'You don't get that sort of thing now, those smash 'em and bash 'em robberies. Now it's all electronic money. That and Nigerians doing frauds.

'You know the Gulf War? Well, the Americans arranged a deal with Nigeria for back-up oil, and part of the price was giving them a hundred thousand, fifty thousand – who cares how many? – a lot of green cards. So you had a flood of Nigerians into America. And they went into the banking system like a virus. They love it. Someone ought to do a study. Do you know I think they do it for the joy of it? Of course we didn't mind that sort of thing when it was Raffles being a gentleman burglar for the joy of it, but then he wasn't black.'

'Who's Raffles?' said Gregory.

'Never mind,' said Arlot.

Arlot looked out of the car window. 'Do get on,' he said to the driver, who instantly pulled out of the inner lane, turned on his blue light and took off down Westway at ninety.

'See that?' said Arlot as they flashed past the elevated roundabout. 'That's where Scoffie McTurk jumped on to a lorry full of ping-pong balls after robbing Friends House of the Easter takings. It's a fifty-foot drop. I never held with Quakers myself. Too argumentative.'

Gregory allowed Arlot to ramble on.

They turned on to the M4 elevated section and shot past the Fuller's Brewery, up to the Kew Bridge roundabout, down the slip road and straight through the lights outside the bank.

'That's where MacMillan was killed,' said Arlot, looking to his left.

Moments later the car shuddered to a halt outside the court.

'That's the target car, Guv,' said the driver, pointing to Scott's black Ford.

Arlot walked over to it and peered in at the messy interior. 'Could do with a clean,' he said, 'who is this guy?'

'He's a good lawyer, actually,' said Gregory.

'Why doesn't he clean his car then? Anyway, I never heard of him. You don't think he's involved in the planting of the evidence?'

'Why should he be? If he wanted to sabotage the case he could do it just by not trying. Why should he want to plant evidence?'

'I've never found that a convincing explanation,' said Arlot, 'the thing about crime is that it's as varied as any other human activity. Perhaps he did it because he's bored – or bitter – or in love, who knows?'

He waved his driver away and they went into the court.

Howard watched Gregory from where he was sitting in his car down the road under the cherry trees. Gregory was with a very tall man who had walked across the road to Scott's car and checked it. Why had he done that?

Then the man, he must be a police-officer, signalled the police car away.

Why should they be interested in Scott's car? It wasn't as though it were anything special. In fact, quite the opposite, it couldn't be more ordinary.

He got out of his car. He moved down the road, buttoning his overcoat and setting the felt hat on his head. Today he was a man from the country a little lost in a London court, there was no trace left of the taxi-driver.

Gregory and Arlot found Scott in the Customs' solicitor's office.

'Well, here's your proof,' Gregory said. He had looked round to see if the pupil girl was there and she wasn't. 'This is a statement showing the print-out from the ticket, properly proved.'

Scott took the documents and looked at them.

'But you say we can't use them,' said Gregory.

'Probably not,' said Scott. 'But we can try.' He was being conciliatory to make up for the argument at court the day before.

'Try?'

'Well, I'll serve the statements on Janjoa's solicitor. We'll see.'

'And the taxi,' said Gregory. 'I can't show that the taxi card is a plant, but I've done the next best thing. This is Detective Inspector Arlot.'

Scott looked at the man with Gregory, he was huge and towered over him. Most of all he noticed his bushy eyebrows.

Scott didn't like being pressured, and he stepped back.

'He's from Criminal Intelligence, interested in drugs. The car the taxi-driver was driving is associated with drugs,' said Gregory.

'Oh,' said Scott. 'How do we prove that?'

'We can't use it, though,' said Arlot.

'Can't we?' said Scott.

'No, it's all sensitive material. We can't give it away.'

'Well, hang on,' said Scott. 'What are you doing? You can't give me this information and then tell me I never heard it. I've got a duty to the court. I may have to tell Muazzam's lawyers this, or get the judge's permission not to.'

'Who's Muazzam?' said Arlot.

'You tell him,' said Scott to Gregory, turning his back on them.

He started to check the written evidence that Gregory had produced. Then he looked up and interrupted Gregory, who was going over the people in the case again for Arlot.

'If you tell me that you can prove that the taxi-driver is a liar, that he's not a taxi-driver, then I will have to tell the defence. Muazzam has a right to know since it affects the credibility of Janjoa's evidence. I'll have little choice, or almost none.'

'We can only prove that the car was once used by a known drug dealer,' said Gregory.

'Well, that's not enough to show the witness was a liar.' Scott was aware of Arlot watching him. He turned towards him. 'Well, is it?' he said aggressively. 'To us it's a pretty odd coincidence, but that's about it. We can't say that just because the car is associated with drugs that every subsequent driver is a perjurer. And, anyway, you say we can't use it.'

Arlot shrugged, lifting his hands. 'It's not my case. I'm sure you're right.' He backed off.

Scott could see the same argument as the night before starting up again. 'Look, it may not be necessary, anyway. The shape of the trial has changed a bit. Muazzam's wife gave evidence today —'

'Sorry, Mr Scott, Customs head office are on the phone now,' he was interrupted.

He turned away, took the phone, put his hand over the mouthpiece and said to Gregory, 'Hang on, I'll just tell the solicitor at head office what's happening. Yes,' he said into the phone, 'she's given evidence that Janjoa was involved and evidence that Muazzam was told to swallow the stuff as a kind of medicine against travel sickness.'

He paused and listened. 'No,' he said, 'but let's suppose you told a peasant in this country – if there were peasants in this country – about a barium meal, he'd think you were joking, except that if you were driving a big Rolls-Royce he'd probably believe you.'

He listened to the phone for a moment. 'Yes, I'll let you know what happens. But we may be asked whether we want to continue the trial against Muazzam if Janjoa pleads guilty. It will be either that or a new trial, I don't see how the case can go on if the jury have heard all that stuff from Janjoa's lawyers, and then they are not involved any more.'

'What?' Gregory interrupted. 'You mean have Janjoa plead guilty and let Muazzam go?'

Scott put the phone down. He was going to have to explain the problem to Gregory as well.

'Look. Think what's happened. Muazzam's wife has given evidence and it's completely destroyed Janjoa. So Janjoa's lawyers have asked the judge for time to think before the trial continues. He must at least be thinking of changing his plea to guilty.'

It was always difficult explaining the twists and turns of a trial to someone who wasn't involved in trials all the time – but he pressed on.

'If that happens then think of the case against Muazzam. What do we do about him? Do we accept the wife's evidence – in which case he's not guilty. Or do we say what she says is all lies, and then how do we account for Janjoa pleading guilty? – if he does, that is.'

Scott laughed. He put on a funny voice, 'Bit of a poser, what?' Then seriously, 'I know who I want convicted if I have a choice.'

Emily walked into the room just at the moment of silence that followed Scott's remarks.

She said, 'Yes, Janjoa has asked for more time. Tozer's in the cells with him now.'

She looked at Gregory and half-smiled.

He ignored her. 'Well, what do we do?'

Scott said, 'We sit and wait. But first we deliver this. How many copies have we got?' Holding up the statement from the Transport Police.

'Three.'

'Well, the sooner we get it to Tozer the sooner he'll tell his client the bad news. You take it in, Emily.'

'Where?'

'To the cells.'

'But how do I get in?'

'You just walk in. Say you want to see Janjoa. They'll let you in immediately. You're wearing a wig and gown. It's like carrying a bucket of water at a racecourse, no one would dream

308

of asking you what you were doing.'

He didn't know that he had just arranged the catastrophe.

Emily went to the cells. She found that the door opened into a passage at the end of which there was another door. On it there were handwritten messages:

> We do not take clothes/food/cigarettes. Legal visits only. No visits between 1.00 and 1.30. Ring *once* only. Be patient.

She was clearly entering the land of rules. Someone else had added underneath: 'On the other hand, you could just piss off.'

She rang once as ordered. The little window opened and shut and a key rattled.

'Who to see?' the officer said. 'Janjoa? He's seeing two people already.'

'I'll go in, I have to take these papers to him.'

The officer opened the door, which led further into the cells, and they came to a barred gate. It wasn't locked. Sure enough, as Scott had said, she wasn't asked for identification.

'On your left, miss.' She was pointed to a door.

In the room, Tozer, Monty Bach and Janjoa were talking.

'Excuse me,' Emily said, a little nervous at interrupting the other side, 'I've got these for you.' She handed the papers to Tozer and left.

Tozer read the statement, handing the pages as he did so to Monty. 'Well, that does it,' he said.

He turned to Janjoa and said, 'They can prove that the tube, the underground ticket that you had, was used and that the holder came out of Earl's Court station nine, was it nine?' He checked his other papers. 'No, seven minutes before you were arrested.'

He looked at Janjoa. 'It's all electronically printed on the little metal strip on the back of the ticket.'

Monty Bach said, 'But can they call this evidence? They've known about the ticket all along. It's a bit late now. They should have called it to begin with.'

Tozer shrugged that off.

Janjoa looked at them and said, 'What can I do?'

'You can start bargaining,' said Tozer. He tried not to sound pleased, but this bit of evidence had done the business, he was going to get a long weekend. 'What have you got to tell them that would be of use?'

'I can tell them the identity of the Englishman in the photograph and where I saw him last,' said Janjoa.

Monty Bach listened with horror.

Tozer went looking for Scott and found him in the robing room with Emily.

'Well, there you are. He wants to plead. I think he's going to. He's got no answer to Muazzam's witness and that bit of evidence you just served finished him. Shame. I still think I had a run. But' – he looked around the coat racks and dropped into a conspiratorial whisper – 'he's prepared to give evidence for the Crown.'

'What's the point? It's too late,' said Scott.

'No, not on this. But a different angle. He can tell you who the man in the photo was.' He stopped.

'Well, who?' said Scott. 'Who was it?'

'Bill Green, the taxi-driver.'

'We thought so,' said Scott. He was rather pleased that he didn't have to gratify Tozer by showing surprise at this revelation. Tozer was pleased to notice that Emily was visibly shocked by the news.

Scott said, 'And he's prepared to say that in court? So where is this man Bill Green now? I presume that's not his real name.'

'He doesn't know, but he knows how to find him.'

'Well, we'd better tell Gregory so he can find out. And no doubt you'll want us to tell the judge that Janjoa will help the prosecution investigations so he can get a reduction in his sentence.'

'That would be nice,' said Tozer, poking Emily in the ribs, 'but we better wait until it's absolutely definite.'

Things were beginning to move fast. 'What happens?' said Emily. 'What's he saying? How can he talk to the prosecution about pleading guilty right in the middle of the trial? Why don't you just tell the jury?'

'This is all off the record,' said Scott, 'just discussions; it's all "What if?". Tozer will have told him that he'll get a lesser sentence if he pleads guilty now and helps the Crown rather than wait for the inevitable conviction by the jury.'

They were heading to see Gregory and as they went down the passage Emily saw Howard in front of her. He was standing looking at a noticeboard outside the court.

'And if he really can tell us about the man who gave evidence for him then he may get even less,' said Scott.

'Look. I'll see you in a moment,' said Emily, 'you go on, I'll catch you up.' And she turned and went back the way they'd come.

Just past the court there was a little room used for conferences, she turned in to it and there, waiting for her, was Howard.

'Janjoa's going to the police, he's going to tell them who you are.'

'Shut the door,' he said.

Chapter 32

The judge wouldn't wait for them any longer. The court Tannoy called the case and slowly everybody reassembled.

Emily found herself sitting behind Scott, just in front of Gregory and the tall policeman who had appeared that morning.

No one knew what was happening, since Janjoa's lawyers seemed not to have made a decision – or at least if they had they weren't telling anyone.

'Do we need the jury to be called back?' asked the clerk of the court.

'Not for me to say,' replied Scott, 'Mr Tozer must tell us.'

Tozer was still not saying what they had decided. He and Monty Bach were deep in conversation at the side of the court.

'Mr Tozer,' said the clerk lifting his voice, 'do we need to send for the jury?'

'I don't know yet,' Tozer said impatiently.

'Well, make up your mind, the judge is coming back,' said the clerk. The court usher was standing expectantly at the judge's entrance holding a small hammer, waiting to knock for silence at the judge's entrance.

'Bring the witness back to the witness-box,' the clerk said.
The door to the waiting-room was opened and Shaheena

Muazzam walked in. She still carried the baby and her fluid walk across the scuffed nylon carpet silenced the courtroom.

Just then there was a sharp rap and the judge appeared. He made his way to his seat with the metronomic movement that had become familiar over the weeks.

Tozer found himself stranded at the back of the court talking to Monty.

'Well, what is happening?' barked the judge. 'We have been waiting well over two hours now.'

As he spoke, Howard slipped into the public gallery and the judge looked up fiercely at the momentary interruption.

'I received a message from you, Mr Tozer, asking for time. I have heard nothing since. What is happening?'

The direct question from the judge forced Tozer to make up his mind, he paused, adjusted himself and moved straight into overdrive.

The familiar sing-song tone began.

'Your Honour is entirely right. I must apologise. The delay is entirely my fault.'

Tozer used the word 'entirely' as though he were sucking pleasure from it. Scott shifted uneasily.

He went on, 'I knew when I asked Your Honour that there was a possibility that the time of the court would be saved by the delay, otherwise I would not have dreamt of holding the court up.'

So now Janjoa's plea of guilty was going to be turned into a tribute to Tozer's saving time. Scott's anger began to work its way up his back in prickly itches.

He was getting fed up with the smugness that seemed to go with being a barrister. The trial was going to end in an orgy of self-congratulation; Tozer would be thanking the ushers next.

Scott glanced back at the dock to see if all this was being translated and he was pleased to see that the comatose interpreters hadn't realised anything unusual was going on.

One actually had her eyes closed.

'My application is,' Tozer went on, 'that when the jury returns the indictment should be put again to Janjoa.'

Already Tozer's client had lost the dignity of being 'Mister'.

As Tozer made this request there was a release of tension in the court. There was only one reason to 'put the indictment again'. Janjoa was going to plead guilty.

Immediately Wesley Divall started to go through his calculations again. Should he ask for the trial to start again? He would certainly be entitled to do so. Obviously not, he answered himself, this jury has seen Janjoa collapse. Janjoa was the man who had been attacking his client. The jury had seen his witness nearly having her child dragged from her. They must be on his side.

And yet they had also heard Tozer saying over and over again that Muazzam spoke English, that people had heard him talking English. It all supported the police-officer who was saying the same.

In a trial without Tozer none of that would be mentioned. He'd have a clear shot at contradicting the police-officer, and he could still call his client's wife.

He had to decide and he had about two minutes to do so.

His client wouldn't help, he couldn't understand the implications, or even begin to follow the arguments for and against the decision. He had to decide how to gamble with the man's liberty, where he was going to put his bet.

Wesley had begun to realise what this job was like and he wasn't sure he liked it much.

The jury returned.

They were instantly aware of a different atmosphere in the court. It was as easy to pick up as if they had entered a room where there had just been a violent argument. On everyone's face there was a look of expectation and uncertainty.

They organised themselves and Tozer stood up. 'My

application is that the indictment be put again to the defendant Janjoa.' The jury immediately began looking around them as though they could find the explanation to what was going on written up somewhere.

The clerk stood up and read the allegation again to Janjoa and the jury immediately got their answer. 'Guilty,' he said.

The judge turned to the jury. 'You have heard the defendant. He admits this offence. But nevertheless you must still decide. Please stand up.' The woman at the front on the right stood up since the judge was looking directly at her.

'Do you find this defendant Nadim Janjoa, by his own admission, guilty of the offence charged?' said the clerk.

'We do,' said the woman, subsiding back into her seat. She hadn't fluffed her lines. She realised she had done it right. Her heart was beating. What a story she would have to tell tonight!

'Well,' said the judge, 'he must go down.' And Janjoa was led away to the cells.

'Now, Mr Scott,' the judge said.

As he spoke Howard stood up and moved to the door. 'Must you move around?' the judge snapped. Howard looked at him and continued regardless.

'Now, Mr Scott, the witness is in the witness-box. She is waiting for any questions that you wish to ask her.'

Scott was shocked. He had assumed that if Janjoa pleaded guilty then he would be asked whether he needed time to consider the prosecution's reaction to the change in the trial.

Was the judge not even going to ask Divall whether he wanted a retrial?

That question was immediately answered. 'Unless of course Mr Divall has anything to say?' The judge turned towards Divall.

In that moment Divall realised that he had to go on with the case. His witness was in the witness-box. Was Scott really going to stand up and suggest to Muazzam's wife that her evidence, which had just forced Janjoa to plead guilty, was all lies? It wasn't possible. Scott would have to throw his hand in.

'No,' Divall said, he paused to find the right words, 'I await Mr Scott's cross-examination of Mrs Muazzam with interest.'

'We have waited for two hours,' said the judge. 'Mr Scott has had plenty of time for thought, and you will remember, Mr Scott, that now the case has started you are in sole charge on behalf of the Crown. What happens now is entirely your decision.'

Emily saw Howard look at her through the glass panel in the door. He beckoned. She stood up and threaded her way out. Scott could hear the disturbance behind him as he stood working out what he had to do. As she left, Arlot leant across to Gregory and spoke. Their eyes went to the door and Arlot got up to follow.

'Sit down!' said the judge. He moved from relative calm to fury in a moment. 'Miss Clarke may move around, she is counsel. Everyone else in this court will please sit still. It is most distracting.'

Emily left the court.

'I will have some silence,' said the judge.

Arlot sat down and was forced to watch Emily leave.

'Now, Mr Scott,' said the judge, 'what have you to say?'

Chapter 33

Outside the court Howard took Emily's arm.

'I want to see Janjoa. Now.'

'But how?'

'We just knock and go in.'

Emily became suddenly very frightened.

Howard said, 'We had better get in to see him. For both our sakes.'

Emily's arm started to hurt. They turned left into the corridor which led to the cells. She rang the bell. There was the familiar noise of keys and a prison officer, a different one this time, let them in.

'We need to see Janjoa, Mr Janjoa,' she coughed as she spoke the words.

'He's just down from court three,' Howard finished her sentence with easy familiarity. 'He's just gone short, he pleaded.'

'What happened?' said the officer as he led them to the cells selecting a key. He fitted it into the lock, leaning forward. 'I've been watching the telly, haven't been following what's going on upstairs.'

'He changed his plea to guilty,' said Howard. They entered the cell.

Janjoa was sitting with his back to them. He didn't bother to turn round. Emily stood by the door, her heart was pounding so hard that she had difficulty catching her breath. There was a singing noise in her ears.

Howard stepped forward and put his hands on Janjoa's shoulders. He said something in a foreign language. Janjoa convulsed and began to turn, but the friendly touch on his shoulders held him still.

'Stay still and listen,' said Howard, 'what I say now will help us both.'

Janjoa relaxed.

Howard's hand went to his inner pocket. He went on, 'Of course this is not the end, there are many things to be done. I understand why you did what you did.' On that word Howard's hand came out of his coat carrying a dagger.

With a sharp lift of his right shoulder and rising on his right foot he thrust the knife upwards, twisting it into Janjoa's head above the back of his neck – through the ligament, he felt the momentary obstruction – and into the medulla.

He pulled the knife out, wiped it on the inside of the dead man's collar and then pulled the coat away from the back of his neck. 'The blood will gather for a few minutes at his waist,' he said.

Emily felt she was going to faint.

Howard pushed Janjoa forward slightly till the body was slumped over on to the table. 'Now we must go,' he said. The singing in Emily's ears had become a roaring noise and his voice sounded very distant.

'Follow me. If you start trying to make decisions we shall get nowhere.'

He took her arm, guided her from the room and they walked towards the gate, where the gate officer sat at a table watching racing on a small portable television.

'We'll have to come back in a moment,' Howard said to

the officer. 'He's going to have to make a statement. The police will probably come in with us. We'll leave him to think for a moment.' He grinned at the guard. 'Ten years – he's got a lot to think about, poor bastard.'

The prison officer chuckled.

The door was opened and they walked away.

'Keep walking,' said Howard. 'If you run, you're lost. As you walk take off your wig and gown.'

'Now, Mr Scott. What have you to say?' Scott stood for a moment silent. Where had Emily gone?

Then he said, 'Your Honour, I was not aware of the decision taken by Mr Janjoa until the court heard it, although I was aware that it might happen. I must ask for a few moments to consider the consequences.'

The judge said, 'No. I will not rise. You have had two hours to consider your reaction to what might happen.'

'I am not asking the court to adjourn. Only for a moment's pause,' said Scott.

He sat down before the judge could refuse and turned round to Gregory and Arlot, who sat stiffly behind him.

'I shall have to stop the case against Muazzam. I told you the judge might force me into an immediate decision,' he said.

'You what?' Gregory suddenly realised what was happening.

'I cannot continue the trial against Muazzam any more.'

'Why not?'

'A mixture of what we know and what Janjoa has done.'

'Well, I disagree.'

'But unfortunately it's my decision alone now. The judge is making sure of that. She' – he indicated towards the witness-box and Muazzam's wife with his elbow – 'says Janjoa persuaded Muazzam that what he was carrying was lawful and Janjoa doesn't disagree with her evidence. He's pleaded guilty.

'We know Janjoa is prepared to call perjured evidence and

to interfere with the evidence. And from the start we know, a
least I know, that he was prepared to lie over whether Muazzam
speaks English. Right from the beginning of this trial Toze
has done nothing but prejudice Muazzam's case.'

Gregory looked at him. There was nothing left to say
Whatever he had said at the beginning, Scott had shown he
was the same as all the others.

Scott stood up and committed himself.

'I offer no further evidence against the defendant Muazzam
I do not ask the jury for a conviction.'

'I expected no less,' said the judge.

The judge turned to the jury. 'Madam, you must stand
again.' The lady at the front of the jury stood up. She was not
quite sure what was happening.

The judge went on, 'You have just heard that counsel
for the prosecution now does not invite you to convict
Muazzam of this offence, he offers no further evidence against
him.'

The woman sat down. She hadn't a clue what the judge was
talking about. Was she meant to say guilty or not guilty?

The man sitting next to her and the woman behind both
leaned over and whispered urgently.

She stood up again.

'Not guilty,' she said.

'No, you must wait a moment until you are asked correctly
by the clerk of the court.'

The judge signalled to the clerk, who asked the formal
question.

'Not guilty,' said the woman.

'There you are, look how the others had to persuade her to
say "Not guilty",' said Gregory, 'she didn't agree with it at
all.'

At that moment the alarm went off.

It had been hit by a prison officer who had gone into the

room where Janjoa had died. It rocked in the prison passages and moments later was joined by a jangling series of sharp bells when the general alarm went off. The lights flickered and emergency lighting came on.

The prison officers jumped up and grabbing the remaining prisoners ran them through the door into the cells.

'Is it a fire or a bomb?' a voice said.

The judge disappeared through his door and an usher began shepherding the jury out. The lawyers and the interpreters all left the court, led away to the car park behind the buildings.

Shaheena Muazzam stood silent in the witness-box. She was so still that she seemed not to be part of the present.

Muazzam himself was left sitting in the dock. 'Not him,' one of the prison officers said. 'He's not our responsibility now, he's been found not guilty.'

After a few moments Muazzam stood up and left the dock at the back of the court. He walked slowly towards his wife.

As he passed the exhibits table he saw his airline ticket, his passport and the money which the Customs had taken from him lying in a plastic bag. He picked them up and put them in his pocket.

He went to his wife, opened the little gate to the witness-box, put out his hand and took hers, helping her down the slight step to the carpeted floor.

'I think we can go now,' he said.

The two of them left the court, went down the deserted corridor and out of the front door. There was no one there.

The wind blew slightly and the cherry blossom on the trees sparkled in the sunlight.

Some petals floated down and one fell on Shaheena's hair.

They stopped and Muazzam took the child from her, hefting its weight – how light he was! – on to his arm. The child's head fell against his shoulder undisturbed in its sleep.

They continued walking.

The suburban street also slumbered softly behind net curtains. No one paid any attention to the handsome Asian couple making their way home.

Chapter 34

'I can take you to a man who can help you.' Howard turned the car south of the river over Kew Bridge. He went up to the park and turned left into the road towards Putney.

He knew that they would not have any note of his car number, he had hired it that morning. Nor would they have any description of him. It was unlikely that they would ever get one.

The prison officer would remember the blonde – not the middle-aged man with her.

'The man who can help is a friend of Scully's. His name's Russian. He can give you some stuff to be going on with and after a couple of days you can reappear. That prison officer won't be sure it was you he saw.'

Emily could not bring herself to speak. She had chosen to help Howard and now this.

'I'll drop you off at Scully's, he'll take you to Russian. He's always willing to help. We'll phone once we're on the other side of the Common and nearer Brixton.'

Howard telephoned as they passed down Clapham Common South Side.

'I'll drop you outside Brodrick's,' he said, 'go down Railton

Road, then take a cab from outside the Atlantic. Go to Myatt's Fields. Scully will be parked opposite the old nurses' home.'

Emily got out of the car. 'Where do I go?' she said. She had heard what Howard had said but none of it had registered.

'Walk down there,' he pointed, 'go into the cab office and ask for a cab to the nurses' home in Myatt's Fields. Good luck. Don't forget these.' He handed Emily her gown and barrister's wig.

Emily stood beside the car. She wanted to say something, make some accusation, but there was no one to accuse but herself.

What she had become she had chosen to become. It had all been a choice, right from the start, from the moment she was unwilling to be like everybody else, unwilling to laugh at the awful shared jokes, unwilling to enjoy Tozer's company, unwilling to hang around with the bunch.

She turned away.

. At the cab office there were six black men leaning on the counter. They turned and looked at her. Their interest in her was her sex and they made no secret of it. She stood there for a moment waiting. These looks were in a different language, no sly apologetic glances here.

'I think there's a cab for me to Myatt's Fields? The nurses' home?'

'You a nurse?' said one of the men, while the dispatcher checked his list. 'You wanna nurse me?' The man switched his toothpick from one side of his mouth to the other triumphantly. His friend sucked his teeth and laughed.

'Yup. Mr Scully's car,' said the dispatcher.

There was silence for a moment while the audience digested this piece of information. 'You take it, Carlton. You're next.'

One of the men detached himself from the crowd and held the door for her.

'Are you meeting Scully?' he said.

Emily nodded.

Scully would get her some stuff. When she thought of the promise of some crack then what she had got herself into didn't seem so bad. Or rather it seemed round the corner, not so important, not relevant.

'Is he showing you to Russian?' said the driver. Emily remembered the name and nodded.

'I don't think that's so good a thing,' said Carlton.

'Why, do you know him?' Emily was surprised at the ease with which everybody knew everything.

'Oh, yeah. I had him in this cab before time. He's a difficult man.'

The cabbie pulled over opposite the flats.

'No, that's done. This is Scully's account,' he said as Emily fished in her bag for money. 'Hey, don't you forget these,' and he handed her the rolled-up bundle of robes. It was as though she were determined to lose them.

She stood on the pavement by the side of the grass. Opposite her a blue plaque recorded that 'Dan Leno lived here, 1861 – 1904', and she imagined the house as it must have been then. He would have had at least four servants, and the servants were the lucky ones – they weren't in the gutter.

A soft wind blew but not enough to disturb the spring warmth.

To her right there was a grinding noise and out of one of the car-park entrances a blue Honda motor car manoeuvred ponderously towards the centre of the road, and Scully started down the street.

Howard made his way down the aisle of the aeroplane. Ahead of him he could see the people he was seeking. A male head and next to him, a woman upon whose shoulder a baby rested.

The plane had completely levelled out in its flight by now and emitted only an occasional change of tone – enough to make Miss Wilson, travelling by air for the first time with her daughter to India, grip the seat rests even more tightly and wish that she had not come. She knew there would in a moment be a disaster.

Although he was not jolted by any movement of the plane, Howard held the back of Miss Wilson's seat with his free hand as he brushed past her. Miss Wilson was aware of him as much as she was aware, in her heated imagination, of the angels of death gathering around her.

'There is a training course that deals with this, this fear of aeroplanes, isn't there?' she said to her daughter. She was a great one for taking courses and she wished she was better prepared for what was happening.

The plane was high above Kent now, you could see the straight arrow of the Roman road below.

They were moving so fast that by the time Howard passed the twelve rows of seats in front of him they were far out over the Channel and by the time he reached the block of seats behind Muazzam they were well outside the reach of Heathrow air-traffic control.

The captain would not turn back now, whatever Miss Wilson's fears.

He moved on.

He would not be found now. His identity was not known. Greasy Monty Bach did not know him. And as for Emily, even if she did remember, then given where she was now, it would not make much difference.

He had left no fingerprints of any sort. He still had the knife in his coat pocket, that wouldn't be found.

Scully did not know he was involved. He had left no trace. Soon he would be able to return to the Caribbean.

He reached the row of seats behind Muazzam. It would be better not to touch him on the shoulder, he smiled to himself. After what Muazzam had been through it might upset him.

He passed them, turned around and leaned forward. He put his hand in his pocket. Muazzam and his wife were the only occupants of the row of seats and Howard's back effectively blocked off any other view of what was happening.

Howard pulled out a packet and placed it in Muazzam's lap.

'This is yours,' he said. He spoke in perfect Punjabi. 'It is what you were promised, whatever the outcome.'

Howard always treated his men well. 'You were right to fight,' he said. 'Always fight. Always be prepared to fight. I am. You did well.'

Muazzam smiled up at him. Howard carried on speaking but this time in English. 'You made one mistake though, you spoke in English to the officer who arrested you.'

'Oh no I didn't. You only gave me one rule, "Don't admit you speak any English". I didn't understand what was happening, but I never spoke one word of English,' said Muazzam.

'That policeman just threw me down the stairs. I said nothing. I never uttered a word. I was very careful. It was the police-officer who lied.'

'There's Russian now,' said Arlot. A small, heavily built man, he looked Turkish perhaps, came into the television shot. He was carrying a can of Special Brew.

'She'll probably be in sight in a moment.'

The small man leaned against the window of the betting shop and watched the street. Another man came up to him but Russian shook his head and he went away.

The girl appeared. She was pitifully thin and even in the television picture Gregory could see that she had a livid bruise on her left cheek.

She stood by Russian for a few moments until he pointed to someone passing and she turned and moved away. He noticed that when she walked she did so stiffly.

'Yes, that's her,' said Gregory. 'Why not pick her up?'

'What's the point?' said Arlot. 'We've no proof she was involved in the murder. Anyway, she's not going anywhere. Russian owns her now. She'll do anything he says for a hit. He's broken her in.'

Gregory listened to him.

This hell was only two hundred yards from where he was. He could have walked out and spoken to the people involved.

'The first week he kept her indoors,' said Arlot. 'Crack all day. He invited his friends in. The third evening there was a real party, six of them stayed all night. She was a real novelty.'

Gregory stood astonished.

'Oh yes, Russian's making good money out of her. They love her fancy dress.'

They watched in silence for a while.

'We'll be picking him up soon for pimping. We got photos of them together. It'll make a good case.'

More silence. The people on the street scurried around the television screen. Arlot watched them like specimens.

'I thought I might insist on that Scott prosecuting it. It might teach him the facts of life.'